# Broken Chords

*Carrie Elks*

Broken Chords by Carrie Elks

Copyright © 2015 Carrie Elks
Published by Carrie Elks
All rights reserved
190215
ISBN: 1507563833

Cover Design: Okay Creations
Interior Image: Clipartof.com
Editor: D. Beck
Proofreader: Emma Adams

This book is a work of fiction and any resemblance to persons, living or dead, or places, events or locales is purely coincidental. The characters are fictitious products of the author's imagination.

For My Parents

To Sarah
Keep on rocky!
love
Carrie Elks
x

# 1

"Lara? You awake?"

"No." My voice is croaky and sleep-thickened. I try to unglue my lips, running my tongue across the dry skin.

"Max is crying."

Reluctantly, I open my eyes. "It's your turn."

Alex smiles, making the stud in his eyebrow rise up. He's a sexy bastard and he knows it, even at four o'clock in the morning.

"I've been up three times, but he won't settle. I don't have the right equipment." Alex is still smirking when he glances at my chest then looks down at his own. I follow his gaze to his taut, muscled skin, and the vibrant ink etched upon it. I know every line, every colour. I've kissed my way across them so many times.

Slowly, I sit up and swing my legs to the side of the bed. My head starts to swim at the suddenness of my movement, and I have to brace myself on the mattress.

"Whoa there, dizzy girl." He reaches out to steady me, his hands warm and strong, the pads of his fingers rough on my body. "You okay, babe?"

"Yeah, give me a minute." I'm not sure if I'm talking to Alex or Max now. Not that it matters since Alex lies back down and closes his eyes, while Max decides to up the ante by screaming louder. I lift him out of his cot, cradling his soft, warm body, but he won't be comforted. His face is vermillion red, his eyes squeezed shut, his mouth so wide I can see his tiny tonsils. They vibrate with the screeches he makes.

"Shh." I press my lips to his forehead. The fine hair covering his scalp tickles my face. Beneath it his skin is overheated, smelling of burning baby shampoo.

As soon as I pull him to me, Max starts to root, turning his face into my chest while his screams turn into sobs. I carry him back to the bed, climbing in and leaning against the headboard, unbuttoning my top and opening my bra.

When he latches on there's a moment of blessed silence. The ringing in my ears dulls to a faint buzz, and I let my head fall back and my eyes close. Then, he starts snuffling and grunting—sounding more of a pig than a baby—and I resign myself to another sleepless night.

I've never known exhaustion like this. It's as if I'm walking around in a constant haze; everything seems slowed down, deeper, heavier. Each movement requires an effort I'm not sure I possess. I don't own anything anymore. My time, my body—they all belong to this tiny bundle of flesh curled up in my arms. It's the side effect of childbirth they don't warn you about at prenatal class. You find the love of your life and lose yourself in the process.

Max finally falls back to sleep at six, after a nappy change followed by an hour of gurgled kicks on the mat. Moments such as these make it all worth it: his smiling eyes, his rosebud mouth, the way he looks at me as though I'm his personal angel. I lift him up to kiss his lips, and he sighs contentedly, his breath warm and milky.

One of my favourite smells.

Alex gets up at an hour later and is annoyingly chipper, considering our broken night. He showers then walks naked into our bedroom, and though I pretend to be asleep, I crack an eyelid open to watch his movements.

While childbirth has made me feel leaden and doughy, it's only made Alex more attractive. It's so annoying how that happens. All he has to do is take Max for a walk in the park and he's got a gaggle of admirers staring at him. I, on the other hand, find myself tucking my stomach into my jeans, along with whatever baby-drool decorated T-shirt I choose to wear that day.

"I can feel you staring." Alex turns round. Although this frontal isn't full, it still takes my breath away. His stomach is pale, ribbed, with a line of dark hair from his navel to waistband. The coloured edge of a tattoo peeks out; though I can't see it, I know it's the point of a star, the rest covered by his shorts.

I never found tattoos attractive until I met Alex. Back then, I tended to date clean-skinned, suited types; the sort of boys I grew up with back home. We shared the same kind of upbringing, backgrounds, cultural experiences, and the whole thing was downright boring.

Alex was a blinding light cutting through the darkest of nights. He unravelled me, thread by thread, until the old Lara was somebody I hardly recognised. Within the space of two years I was married, retrained and working in a drug clinic, counselling addicts and helping them get clean.

He pulls the covers from my body and crawls into the bed, nudging my legs apart with his knees. Putting his hands either side of my head, he hovers over me.

"Lara." He breathes my name out, lowering himself down until his body touches mine. I watch as the wiry muscles in his arms flex, then turn and kiss his forearm, tracing my name with hungry lips. His skin is warm, still damp from his shower, and I can smell the woody fragrance of his soap. When I finally turn my head to look at him, my chest clenches at his expression. He's hot and needy. I shiver as his fingers drag down my side, trailing from my chest to my waist, sinking into my hip, pulling me towards him. "Fucking beautiful."

That's how I feel when he holds me. In spite of the stretch marks that spider across my less-than-perfect stomach, and breasts that seem more milk factory than erogenous zone, Alex has this way of making me feel desirable. Wanted.

It's not only me who feels this way. A few minutes with Alex is enough to have young girls and old women eating out of his hand. Unlike other men I've known, he's totally at home with females, happy to talk, flirt, and grin his way through any situation. I guess it's a side effect of being brought up by women; his divorced mum plus two sisters. He doesn't blink twice at buying tampons, isn't squeamish about periods or leaking breasts or tears. I'd go as far to say he's at home with all bodily fluids. Positively encourages some of them.

He presses his body to mine a final time; hard planes against my soft chest. "I'm going straight to the studio after work."

Since being laid off from his printing job, he's been picking up work at building sites. Spending his days carrying bricks and wood, layering plaster and laying floorboards, while his nights are spent recording music with his band. The manual labour has honed his already tight muscles until he's taut and lean. He's a scrapper, a man ready to fight, the tattoos inked across his body only enhancing that effect. He's the sort of bad boy I'd spent my life avoiding.

The only one who knows the real me.

"Don't work too hard," I say.

"Never." One last kiss to my shoulder and he pushes himself up, hovering for a moment before jumping off the bed. Then he's fastening his tight, faded jeans. Before he can do anymore, a loud cry cuts through the morning air, piercing the little bubble we've built around us. My focus is shattered, pulled to pieces by the tiny little human who has taken over my world.

* * *

When Max wakes up from his afternoon nap, I strap him into the buggy and take him for a walk. We don't go anywhere in particular, simply meandering through the streets of Shoreditch, breathing in fresh air, inhaling the aromas wafting out of the restaurants. We pop into the local supermarket on the way back to our flat. Max has got it into his head that he doesn't enjoy his buggy and like a little dictator he groans and shuffles, his burbling turning into a full-on scream when he realises he isn't getting his own way. In the end, I lift him out of the pushchair and use it to store the carrier bags full of food. The Bugaboo is turning out to be the world's most expensive shopping trolley.

Typically he coos as soon as he's in my arms, his wet cheeks plumping when he flashes a smile at the checkout lady. She reaches out and tickles him under the chin, coaxing out a giggle that comes perilously close to a burp.

"He's gorgeous. How old is he?"

"Nearly six months." God, is it actually that long? I haven't had an unbroken night's sleep in almost half a year. Surely that must be some kind of record. Score another one for the tiny dictator.

"Bless him, he's going to break some hearts when he gets older."

I don't tell her he breaks mine every night. Just one cry and I'm torn in two.

With Max still in my arms, his tiny fists grabbing hold of my shirt, I manoeuvre the buggy out of the shop, one-handed, silently thanking the gods of sliding doors as we pass easily onto the pavement. I adjust him on my hip and we walk the two blocks to our flat, past the closed-down charity shop and boarded-up pub. Somehow, I manage to make it home without dropping anything.

There are three stone steps leading up to the front door. Another thirteen to climb up once we are inside. This is where

I long for an extra pair of arms, and start to calculate what to carry up first—the groceries, the buggy, or Max.

In the end, I attempt to lift all three. Holding Max up with one arm, I pull the buggy with the other, bumping it up each step in turn. The plastic bags slide across the seat, contents spilling out, and a jar of pasta sauce rolls off and falls to the ground. I watch in horror as it lands on the second step, the glass splintering, and red sauce flying everywhere. It covers my legs and the concrete, making it look as though there's been some kind of gore fest. For a moment, all I can do is stare, open-mouthed.

Then I hear laughter coming from behind me. I don't know whether to be annoyed or to join in, though when I turn to look at the offender all thoughts of amusement fly right out of my head.

The guy behind me is built. Tall, blonde and with freckles plastered across his skin. He has the type of face that has a smile permanently etched on it, laughter lines furrowing out from the corner of his eyes.

"You okay?" He sounds Australian. That explains the blonde hair and deep tan. "That's all sauce, right? No blood or anything?"

I look down. The sauce is now dripping onto the gravelled path. "I'm fine." Completely embarrassed, but fine. I try to hold on to the buggy while rooting through my bag for my keys, but that only causes a tin of sweetcorn to fall out, rolling through the gore until surf-boy picks it up.

"Let me help you." He bounds up the steps and steadies the buggy for me. With my free hand, I grab my key and slide it into the lock. He reaches out and touches Max on the cheek, and I pull back.

"What is he, about six months?"

I look up in surprise. "Yeah, around that," I answer, suspiciously. "How do you know?"

"I've got a one year old. Doesn't seem a minute ago she was this age."

When he catches my eye, we smile. It's stupid, because he could be lying through his teeth, but his admission somehow puts me at ease. Enough to let him help me get my stuff into the hallway.

And he seems…nice. Friendly.

"You're the first floor flat, right?" He asks.

Immediately, my hackles rise again. This time when I look at him, it's through narrowed eyes. "What makes you think that?"

He shrugs, nonplussed by my suspicious ways. "I'm on the ground floor, so I guessed you must be upstairs."

"You live here?"

He starts to laugh. "Yes. Did you think I was some weirdo breaking into your house?"

"Maybe."

"Then why did you let me in?" He's stopped laughing now. Looks more concerned than anything.

"I was being polite."

He shakes his head. "Crazy English people. You're so bloody polite you'd probably thank me for chopping your head off."

"I'm pretty sure I wouldn't be able to speak if you chopped my head off."

Smiling, he reaches out a hand. "I'm David."

I take it with my free hand. "Lara. Pleased to meet you. Thank you for your help. And... ah... not chopping my head off."

"Any time." He winks, and lifts the buggy easily, balancing the shopping before heading towards the stairs, making me wonder if I may have finally found a friend around here.

# 2

I wake up late on Sunday, a shaft of bright light invading the peacefulness of my dreams. That's when my eyes spring open and I sit right up, panic rising inside me as bubbles in a bottle of soda.

*Where's Max?*

I jump out of bed and run to his cot, half afraid to look, scared he may be lying there, lifeless and unmoving. It's every parent's worst nightmare, one that keeps me awake at night, long after I can hear him snuffling in his sleep. Even during his daytime naps, I find myself checking up on him, touching his face to make sure it's warm, and listening at the door so I can hear him breathe.

His cot is empty. The blanket is crumpled at the bottom of the mattress, the sheet askew where he's been turning in the night. For one crazy moment I actually wonder whether he climbed out himself.

The kid can't even crawl. How the hell is he going to climb?

When I rush into our living room, rubbing my frantic eyes, I spot him in his bouncy chair, and relief floods though me. He's there, having fun; his arms and legs kicking as he tries to hit the lurid plastic mobile Alex has placed above him. He spots me and smiles, a contented cooing sound rumbling from deep in his throat, and holds his arms out for me to pick him up.

Smiles in the morning. The best gift of all.

"Hey, what are you doing up?" Alex walks out of our tiny kitchen. "I was trying to give you a lie-in."

He's still wearing lounge pants, the waistband low on his hips. The rest of his body is bare.

"I woke up and he wasn't there. I panicked." Mentally, I'm kicking myself for not taking advantage of the sleep. How long have I been saying I'd kill for more than three hours at once?

"You panicked?" Alex smiles, taking a step closer. His hair is still rumpled from where he's slept on it, and I can't help but reach out to touch it.

"I thought he might've escaped."

"He's six months old, sweetheart. What did you think he was gonna do, hail a cab?" He laughs as he pulls me towards him, wrapping his arms around my shoulders. I bury my face in his chest, breathing him in, loving the sensation of skin on skin. "You're a fucking nutter, you know that?" Alex cups my cheek, the smirk still pulling at his lips. When he presses them on mine I can feel them curl.

"I'm your nutter," I whisper into his lips.

"Bloody right you are."

We spend the morning in some kind of sleep-deprived haze. Alex practices on his guitar while I make a half-hearted attempt to clean the kitchen. After Max's nap, we play with him on the floor, laughing and clapping as he rolls over and again. It seems an awkward way of travelling, but it works for him, and he has this self-satisfied expression that fills my heart with love.

Sunday afternoons are family time. As in Alex's family. We get dressed, fill a bag up with supplies for Max, and make our way down the stairs. Alex carries all our stuff while I hold on to Max. When we pass the door to the downstairs flat, I suddenly remember the new tenant.

"Did you know we had a new neighbour?" I ask. "Some guy called David. From Australia."

"What happened to Nancy?"

Nancy was the previous tenant. Though she was well into her seventies, she dressed as though she was twenty, and had a glorious array of wigs.

"No idea, I forgot to ask."

We're outside and making our way to Shoreditch High Street station. I used to have a car—a rusted, beaten-up Mini I loved—but when Max came along we had to choose between nappies or car insurance, and the former won out. Today, though, it's a pain. We have to take the Overground train to Whitechapel and change to the District Line. It would be enough of a palaver on our own, but with a baby, a buggy, and an enormous bag, it's like going on a bloody trek.

Still, at the end of it is a pot of gold. Or what I prefer to call, Sunday lunch.

On the train, Alex holds Max in his lap, and starts talking to him in gibberish, making Max laugh. A couple of teenage girls sitting on the other side of the carriage eye him up, smiling when the baby giggles and batting their eyelashes whenever Alex kisses him. He doesn't notice though—he's too busy playing with his son—and his indifference makes me grin.

Alex's mum still lives in his childhood home, on one of the nicer council housing estates in Plaistow. The three-bedroom terrace is well-maintained, mostly thanks to Alex. He keeps a toolbox here now, sick of having to carry it from Shoreditch every time a job needs doing, and I've come to terms with the fact that whenever we come here he'll disappear for a few hours with only a screwdriver and hammer for company. He's still the man of the house, even though he hasn't lived here for years.

I sometimes wonder what it must have been like for Alex growing up here. The middle of three children, he was the only boy in a sea of girls. That's probably why he finds it so easy to talk to women; it comes naturally. He's a born flirt, of course. It was the first thing I noticed about him, after the tattoos and the sculpted cheekbones. He smiles and the women come flocking.

It's a blessing and a curse.

The other side effect of growing up in a houseful of women is he's spoiled rotten. Though he does all the jobs that need doing with a screwdriver, I don't think his mum has ever let him load the dishwasher. It's all "sit down, darling, you work hard enough" and "let us girls get you a drink, you deserve a break". Every time she says it, I try to bite down a smile, knowing he'd never get away with that sort of thing at our flat.

"You're here!" Tina—his mum—opens the door, a huge smile spreading across her face. Before either of us can say a word she's whipped Max out of my arms and is cradling him close. Max nuzzles into her chest, delighted at the soft landing, while I lower my arms, unsure whether to be peeved or delighted at her love for my son.

"Come on in. Put the kettle on, will you, Lara? Alex, can you take a look at the upstairs toilet, I think there's something wrong with the flush?" Though she has her back to us as she walks into the living room, we can still hear every word.

Alex starts to laugh at my appalled expression. "Go and put the kettle on, there's a good wife."

"Piss off, plumber boy." My voice is low. His yelp when I pinch his arm isn't.

"Are you all right?" Tina seems naturally attuned to her son's cries, even though he's twenty-nine. I wonder if I'll end up that way when Max is older.

"Where're the girls?" Alex asks, opening the cupboard under the stairs and pulling out his toolbox.

"Andrea's on her way. She needed to get some petrol. And Amy's upstairs on the laptop."

Tina had the novel idea of naming all her kids with the letter 'A'. That was fine for Andrea, and even for Alex. Poor Amy drew the short straw, having spent most of her life trying to escape from her colourful name, 'Amethyst'. She hasn't let Tina forget about it.

"Is she doing coursework?" I ask. At twenty-two, Amy is the youngest of the three. The brightest, too, at least academically. Though she left school at sixteen and messed around for three years, she ended up going back to college, taking her 'A' levels a couple of years late. Now she's at the local University in Stratford, studying Business. To say the whole family is proud of her is an understatement.

"She's always doing coursework," Tina grumbles. Max makes a grab at her bleached-blonde hair, and she pulls away, tutting at him. "That kid never gets out. Her friends have given up asking."

"It isn't easy studying for a degree," I offer gently. I know how hard it is; having spent three years at York. Alex loves the fact I'm an English graduate, loves even more he's my 'bit of rough', at least in his words.

"Yes, but all work and no play makes Amy a dull girl."

"Oy, I heard that." Amy walks into the room, glaring at her mum. She smiles when she sees me, though. We've always got on well, from the first time we met when she was only seventeen. That was in her wild days, when she was spending way too much time at bars and pubs, going out with different men every night. Strange to think how different she is now.

"Good. You need to get out more."

"I'm too busy. And anyway, you used to nag me all the time for going out too much. Now I don't go out enough. I can't bloody win."

"Language." That comes from Alex. It makes me laugh because he has the dirtiest mouth I know.

"Fuck off," Amy replies.

When Alex's older sister, Andrea, arrives, muttering about road works and traffic jams and the cost of petrol, Tina hands Max back to me and the two of them disappear into the kitchen to finish cooking the roast. Alex is upstairs, elbows deep in the toilet, leaving Amy and me in the living room.

"Can I have a cuddle?" She reaches out for Max, and I place him in her arms. "God, he's getting so big. Is he talking yet?"

I laugh. Being the youngest, she has no idea about developmental milestones. Nor did I at her age. "Nah, not for a while yet."

"Or ever if you're lucky. Alex talks enough for all of you."

"True that." I smile when Max pulls at her ink-black hair, and it comes free from the perfect bun on the back of her head.

"Did you know Einstein didn't talk until he was five?" She nuzzles close to Max, making him giggle. "They say late talkers turn out to be geniuses."

"When did you start talking?"

"Dunno. Whenever it was that Andie and Alex let me get a word in edgewise."

She has a point. The Cartwrights are a family of talkers. The first time I came to visit, I was shocked by how noisy they all were. Having grown up in a quiet home in Dorset, I wasn't used to the cacophony.

"How's the course going, anyway?"

"All right. I'm applying for placements for next year. Fingers crossed I get something good."

"Where have you applied?"

"All the usual places. Banks, consultancies. I even applied for a couple of non-profits. Some of the other students are getting interviews already, but I've not heard anything yet."

"How long is it for?"

"A year. Then it's back to University for the final throes." She smiles weakly. "And please don't ask me what I'm going to do after that because I've no idea."

"Isn't that what the placement's for? To give you some ideas?"

Her eyes light up when she smiles and nods. "You get it. If only Mum understood. She can't understand why I'm spending four years studying and I don't know what I want to do with it."

"She's proud of you. They all are."

"They've got a funny way of showing it."

The door to the living room opens. "Funny way of showing what?" Alex sits on the chair next to me, slinging his arm around my shoulders.

"Nothing." Amy looks down, suddenly fascinated by Max. I try to hide my smile. Like the rest of them, she idolises Alex, can't stand for him to think badly of her. Not that he ever would; I know for a fact he adores her right back.

This is just how they are. They are loud, used to sharing their emotions, never whispering when they could shout. They're a unit, they stick together, protect each other fiercely.

Exactly how a family should be.

* * *

When people meet me now, they find it difficult to believe I used to be a hard-nosed career girl. For four years I worked in the City for GMSilver, a mid-sized investment bank dealing in securities and derivatives. It seemed the natural transition back then, for a girl with a first-class degree. When they offered me the job I didn't hesitate to say yes, my eyes full of pound signs and thoughts of glamour.

And it *was* glamorous, or at least some of it was, for a time. Along with the other interns they took on each year, I worked my arse off, arriving in the office at around seven in the morning and often staying until ten at night. We used to have a game, the other interns and I, where we'd try to be the last one to send an email in the evening. Some of them even took to hiding in the toilets so we'd think they'd gone home, waiting until everyone else had left to hit the final 'send' button. Whoever won that week didn't have to buy any drinks on Friday night.

Of course, we drank a lot on Friday nights. Hedonistic evenings full of alcohol, white powder and casual sex. It was incestuous, too; we tended to keep to our small band of interns, maybe twenty or so, hooking up with different partners each week, never mistaking sex for anything more than the basest of releases.

One Friday we were celebrating landing a major deal. One of the partners had given us his Black Amex card, and we were using it to the full. Bottles of champagne were succeeded by vintage Macallan, which I pretended to like because it was so expensive. When the bar closed for the night, we were all still too amped to go home, not ready to pair off. Instead, we headed for a seedy club west of Wapping, giggling at our bravery, smiling because we were 'slumming it'.

The club wasn't seedy as much as it was industrial. In the basement of an old, Victorian building, it was all red brick and exposed pipework. Among the crowd inside—mostly young and hipsteresque—there wasn't a business suit or a shift dress to be seen. We stood out like sore thumbs.

Yet, there was something about it that called to me. By that point I was already feeling the strain of working seventy-plus hours a week. And though I didn't realise it then, now I understand I was yearning for something deeper than ten more years of the same.

After paying the cover charge and getting our hands stamped, we joined the people clustered around the stage, entranced by the performance going on in front of them. It wasn't only that the band were good—although they were— but they had charisma leaking out of their pores, clinging onto the notes as they danced through the air.

It was impossible to do anything but watch, listen, and dance.

At some point I lost my jacket. Though it had cost me the best part of three hundred quid, I didn't care; I was too excited, too alive, too blissed-out to bother. Instead, I let myself be dragged forward by the crowd, riding the wave of their surge, trying to avoid being pulled under. When the band finished their song, the movement stopped, and I found myself a few heads away from the front of the stage.

That's when I saw *him*.

Jet black hair. A T-shirt that looked sprayed onto his muscled torso. Tattoos that seemed to cover every single part of his body. He was the complete opposite of every boyfriend I'd had. The clean-cut city types who hardly knew how to kiss.

I was entranced. Maybe it was the buzz of the alcohol, or the lingering victory of our earlier deal, but when he finally raised his head, glancing up from his guitar, I didn't look away.

Neither did he.

Though that moment only lasted for a few seconds, half a minute at the most, it was the most powerful thing that ever happened to me. I couldn't breathe, I couldn't move, I couldn't feel my heart beat. All I could do was stare at this glorious, sweaty, messed-up guy, and pray he wouldn't look away.

People say that some moments are life-changing, but seeing Alex that night was more revolutionary than that. He transformed me completely, nucleus by nucleus, until my old life was little more than a discarded snakeskin left drying in the desert sun. When he mouthed two words to me, all I could do was nod, finally sucking in a breath, still failing to do anything but look at him.

"Stay there."

That was all he said. That was all I wanted to do. So I stood, and I stayed, and I watched as Fear of Flying finished their set, all thoughts of multi-million pound deals wiped clean from my brain.

# 3

Two days after our trip to Plaistow, the sun is beating fiercely down as I emerge from the tube station and the sudden brightness is a shock after the dull gloom of the underground. I blink a couple of times to acclimatise, and the world appears before me in bleached-out colour. When I reach the street, I stand for a minute, watching the blur of people as they pass by, clasping bags, Styrofoam cups of coffee, all with a look of determination on their faces.

They have somewhere to go. So do I, but first I need to catch my breath.

I haven't been to work for nearly six months, and though I've brought Max into the clinic to show him off, this time it's different as I walk through the doors. My arms are empty, my heart is full, and my baby is being looked after by a stranger.

It's harder than I thought it would be. Everything is the same here; the harassed receptionist, the aroma of antiseptic that clings to the dull, tiled floor, the posters whose corners are peeling off the wall. They contain warnings about substance abuse and drug addiction, adverts for group therapy and various medications.

It's only been two hours and I already miss Max desperately. He cried when I left him at the nursery, his tiny fists rubbing at his red eyes, his bottom lip sticking out as he hiccoughed and sobbed. And even though the carer promised me he would stop as soon as I walked out, I could still hear his screams reverberating in my mind as I walked up the street.

I'm a bad mother and a bad employee. I can't even imagine counselling anybody when I'm hardly able to think straight.

"Hey, you're early. Want a cuppa?" Elaine is my supervisor at the clinic. When I'm back here full-time, we'll meet weekly to discuss my caseload, for me to share my worries, my fears. For now, though, our catch-up consists of a quick hello and occasional gossip while I visit the clinic for half a day. I'll only have a couple of clients assigned to me when I return and I suspect they've given me the simple cases to ease me back into the swing of things. One of them is an ex-cocaine user who has long been sober, and another is a parent of a seventeen-year-old boy who has been using crack. Though sad, their stories aren't heart wrenching. Not yet.

"I'd love a coffee, please." With the sleepless nights I've had, tea is for wimps. "How's everything?"

"Same old stuff, really. Emergency calls, relapsing patients. Poppy is doing brilliantly at arranging the outreach classes."

Poppy is my friend Beth's replacement, as Beth has moved to Brighton to start a new life. Though she seems a nice girl, somehow we don't gel as Beth and I did. Which is a shame, because I could do with some new friends.

Elaine finishes making the coffees, throwing the teaspoons in the dishwasher and wiping down the sides. I try not to laugh at her meticulousness; we both know the place is going to look like a stink hole by lunchtime. "There you go. One coffee, black, no sugar. Is that right?"

"It's what I need," I say grimly, taking the cup and letting the bitter fluid burn my lips. "If I'm going to stay awake for the next eight hours."

My office is on the first floor, at the top of a long flight of stairs. Though it's been used occasionally during my maternity leave, there's still an aroma of staleness to it when I open the door. A light covering of dust lies on top of my textbooks—

where I haven't pulled them out at all in the past six months. It feels as if I'm walking into Miss Havisham's dining room.

Even my chair seems odd. Harder than I remember, stiffer when I try to spin. I sit at my desk and drum my fingers on the table. I should check my emails, re-read some case notes, but all I really want is a hug from my best friend.

But she isn't here.

I met Beth nearly five years ago, when she started working at the clinic. I can still remember her first day, the way her eyes widened as I showed her around, the dip of her lip as I explained the range of abuse we dealt with. Back then she was still recovering from the drug-related death of her friend, a death she blamed herself for. It took her years to accept it was a tragic accident, to forgive herself for not being there when he died.

I suppose I saw something of myself in her. Two years earlier, I'd suffered my own tragedy when my mum died, and like Beth I'd found it difficult to pull myself out of my misery. If it hadn't been for Alex, I may never have succeeded. Maybe that's why we became friends. She liked my strength, and I knew she could find her own. We became so close, she even moved in with us for a while when she had nowhere else to go, and I loved the way we would all talk into the night. The way Alex liked her as much as I did.

*Likes her.* She's not dead. Just moved away.

I miss her so much. I know she's happy, living in Brighton with her lovely boyfriend and foster daughter, but I'm feeling nostalgic for the days when we used to escape from the clinic at lunch time, stuffing our faces with greasy chips and a cold glass of white wine. When responsibility was a four-letter word.

That's why I decide to call her. I pull out my iPhone and select her number, and she answers after a couple of rings.

"Hey, gorgeous."

"Hey, yourself." For the first time since I left Max at the nursery, a smile threatens at my lips. "How's life in the sticks?"

A mock sigh. "I told you, Brighton's where it's at. You need to move here immediately." I can hear a voice in the background. Her boyfriend Niall, maybe? "So what's up, buttercup?"

She's so much more playful since she started seeing Niall. I love the way he's helped her become the person she wants to be. The way she's turned into such a kind, wise mum to Allegra, her eight-year-old foster daughter.

"I'm at the clinic. I miss you." *And Max*, I add silently.

"What are you doing there? I didn't think you were going back until next month."

"It's my 'Keeping in touch' day. They're reacclimatising me, like a plant that needs to be moved. I'm hoping they might be able to give me a brain transplant, too."

"Still getting no sleep?" she asks, sympathetically.

"Max woke up three times last night. I can't even imagine how I'm going to cope when I'm working full-time."

She clucks. "You'll cope. That's what you do. And anyway, isn't Alex helping?"

"Where he can, but as he keeps reminding me, he doesn't have the right plumbing. But don't worry, I'm working on weaning Max onto a bottle, then I'll have my revenge." I let out a Dracula-style laugh. My *mwah-ha-ha* reverberates down the phone.

"Score one for the sisterhood." Her tone is the oral equivalent of a high five. "Max might sleep better when he's on the bottle."

He might... but then again, that little carrot has been dangling in front of my face for months. Maybe when he starts to roll, maybe when he starts on solids, maybe when he reaches fifteen pounds…

He's done all of those things, and still he isn't sleeping.

"Fingers crossed."

"How's Alex?" As soon as she asks, an image pops into my head; the way he cuddled Max this morning, his biceps knotted and taut as he swung him in his arms, the delighted smile on Max's face as Alex blew raspberries on his pudgy tummy.

"He's good. Their band has a new manager, reckons he can help them hit the big time."

"And that's a bad thing?" She must have caught my inflection. "Imagine if they become famous, you can give up work and be a groupie."

"Can you be a groupie if you're married to the lead singer?" I ask, not hiding the sarcasm in my voice. "Anyway, what kind of groupie drags a six month old baby around with her?"

"The best sort." Beth's voice is warm. "The baby-momma of the lead singer sort."

"Ugh, I'm pretty sure nobody wants a groupie with stretch marks."

"I'm pretty sure Alex does."

That's true. The changes to my body haven't phased him one bit. He still constantly grabs at me, running his hands down my body the same way he always has. "And how are your lot? Is Allegra looking forward to the school holidays?"

"She can't wait. I've booked her into extra dance lessons. She wants to be a ballerina."

"And Niall?"

"He's still Niall. Covered in paint and planning out his next exhibition."

Everything has finally come together for her. There's nobody who deserves happiness more than Beth. It's been a long time coming. "Maybe we'll come over and visit soon," I suggest. "I need a bit of Beth time."

"That sounds great," she agrees easily. "We could leave Niall and Alex with the kids and go out on the town. Paint the place red."

A night out? Dancing and drinking and a giggle with my best friend? It sounds like heaven. "You've sold me. I'll text you some dates."

"Perfect!" She sounds as happy as I am. "I can't wait."

\* \* \*

The first thing I notice when I open the door to our building is the smell. The usual musty aroma of damp and dust has disappeared, replaced by something I can only describe as clean. I shift Max on my hip and look around the hallway, wondering what on earth happened to the pile of envelopes that have been living in the corner for the past two years.

"Err... ooh... bwrll." Max starts to babble, pointing at the stairs.

I nod solemnly. "Yes, we're going to go upstairs now."

A click to my right alerts me. I turn to see the door to the ground floor flat open. Our new neighbour, David, pops his head around, smiling when he sees me. "Hey."

"Hi. What happened in here? Did I miss a nuclear bomb? A tornado?"

"I had a bit of time on my hands. Decided to give the place a clean-up." He shrugs, walking out of his flat and leaning on the doorjamb. "I took a look through all that stuff in the corner, I don't think any of it belonged to you. If it did, it's only out the back in the yard."

"It's okay, it's not mine. I think it belonged to the last tenant. Or the last but one, something like that." I look around, marvelling at the lack of dust motes and the way the black marks no longer line the wooden floor. "It looks great. You should have said something, I could have helped."

"Nah. I figure the ground floor is my responsibility. You guys can have the upstairs."

This time I start to laugh. "I'm glad you haven't seen it up there. It's almost as much of a pigsty. I haven't had a chance…" I look at Max as if he's an excuse. Not that he is, really. I've had a hundred opportunities to clean, every time he takes a nap.

"Ahhh, you can't do everything when you've got a nipper. Maybe when he's older."

David is way too nice for his own good.

"That gives me a bit of time to think up a better excuse. Thanks for that." I give him a cheeky grin.

"At your service." He takes a mock bow and sends me a wink. Not that he needs to, I've already decided I like him. "So, what do you guys have planned on this beautiful Friday evening?"

"I'm going to a gig."

"Isn't he a little young? Or do they have high chairs at venues nowadays?" David walks towards us and tickles Max, who starts to giggle uproariously. "Although I can see this guy being the life and soul of the party."

Max wriggles in my arms, more interested in David than staying safe. I try to pull him back. "This little fella has a date with a cot and a babysitter. It's my husband's band, they're playing at a club in Hoxton."

"He's in a band? Anybody I've heard of?"

"I'm pretty sure you haven't. They're good, though. Come along if you're free, I can introduce you."

David nods, a grin unfurling on his lips. "Sounds like a plan. Count me in."

When I get upstairs, Alex is bouncing off the walls, buzzed on adrenaline and anticipation. Before I can even close the doors he grabs Max out of my hands and starts dancing him around the room. He sings to him loudly, sweeping him up and down, and I'm grinning like a lunatic.

"What caused that smile, gorgeous?" Alex moves back towards me, pulling me into his free arm. His hand cups my hip, fingers digging in deliciously as he bends his head to my neck and presses his lips there. I breathe him in, fresh and clean from a shower, hair glistening and moulded into an almost quiff.

He's all gel and rolled-up sleeves. There's no collar on his t-shirt, so I can see the dark inked scrolls that lick up from his chest and shoulders peeking out from the material. Even though Max is in his arms, I can't help but trace them with my fingers, feeling him tense up as I flutter my hand against his skin.

"Maybe Max should have a nap." Alex's voice is thick. "He seems really tired."

Max starts babbling again; sleep is clearly the furthest thing from his mind.

"He's not due another nap until this evening." I try not to laugh at the disappointment on Alex's face. He stares at me through narrowed eyes, and I smile in response. I'm caught somewhere in the middle of turned-on and amused.

"He seems really tired," Alex repeats. "And those lips of yours look really empty."

I know where he's going with this; I feel like playing.

"They are. Really empty. Desperate to be filled."

"Then put the baby to bed," he growls.

I lean forward and press my mouth to Alex's. He kisses me back, his movements heated. Cupping my chin, he angles my head, slowly running his tongue along the seam of my lips. "Put the baby to bed, now, Lara."

As if he knows he's being talked about, Max lets out an almighty shout and then hits us both in the face. Not softly, either; there's nothing about his slap that could be classified as a 'love tap'. He's forceful, and my skin stings from the impact.

"Ow." I pull back, rubbing my chin with my palm. Either Alex is sturdier than me, or Max didn't hit him as hard, because he doesn't appear to be wincing. "I don't think the baby wants to go to sleep."

"Little cockblocker." Alex nuzzles Max affectionately. Then he whacks me on the bottom.

"Hey, that hurt."

"It was supposed to. A gentle reminder that your arse is mine. Tonight. When Max is asleep."

I flutter my eyelids at him and turn to walk into the kitchen, sending him a coquettish smile over my shoulder as I walk. "My arse is always yours, darling. And if you can manage anything after being on stage followed by God knows how many pints of lager, I'll be impressed."

"You're always impressed," he shouts. I pretend not to hear him, but he carries on, anyway. "And so you should be. I'm fucking impressive."

"I'm not impressed by your modesty," I sing out, opening the cupboard to find some rice. I bite down on my lip in my efforts not to smile. I love it when he's home. With all the nights he's been practising, and weekends at the recording studios, I've missed this.

"It's not my modesty you want to be thinking about. It's my hard, dirty…"

"Max is listening!" I peek my head around the door. "Do you want his first word to be 'cock'?"

"You said it, not me." He laughs, his eyes sparkling. "I can't believe you're teaching our son dirty words. Wait until I tell Mum."

"You do that and I'll tell her that you tried to make me suck you off while our son was wide awake. Imagine her horror."

He puts Max in his green and blue striped chair, and the baby starts to bounce and kick happily. When Alex stands up, he looks at me, still peeking around the door. His hands are on his hips, eyes narrowed.

"Are you threatening me?"

A little thrill shoots through me. I love it when Alex is playful, but his hard, strong side is what really turns me on. "What if I am?"

He walks towards me, bare feet slapping against the floorboards, the angles of his face sharp and strong. My heart starts to speed up. I know that look—intense, intent; Alex on heat.

"You want to be careful." His voice is soft, but the timbre doesn't fool me. My throat tightens as he steps into the kitchen, and I back away until I'm caught up against the work surface with nowhere to go. Even though he's only a man, he fills the room, charisma radiating from him. He's not touching me, but I can feel him all over my skin, pressing against my body. This is what he does.

Every single time.

"I'm not the careful type."

"I can see that." He puts a hand either side of me, clutching the worktop, caging me in. Lowering his head until his brow is pressed to mine, he stares at me, his thick, long eyelids fluttering as he blinks. "You're a very bad girl."

"I am," I breathe.

"And you deserve to be punished."

Yes I do. I really do.

He moves his face against mine, kissing me softly, little more than a brush of the lips. "Tonight I'm going to bend you over and fuck you so hard the snark flies right out of you, baby."

My heart flutters in my chest, and I can't think of a single, witty reply.

Then he hits my arse yet again, and saunters out of the kitchen, and I can hear the smile in his voice.

"Laters."

# 4

There's nothing I love better than London on a summer's evening. The streets are alive, thronging with people, the air thick with conversation and laughter. David and I walk past restaurants and bars, the open doors allowing the sweet fragrance of food and drink to escape into the night, wafting around us until my stomach starts to rumble.

The walk to Hoxton Square only takes us ten minutes, but it's long enough for me to grill David about his life. He tells me he comes from the Northern Territories, that he has a one-year-old daughter, and his ex refuses to allow him access after an argument that got out of control. His voice drops when he describes Mathilda, and I can hear the pain that laces it, the ache that coats every word he says.

"I'm only here for a few months," he explains. "I couldn't stand to be near her. It was driving me crazy not being able to see her. I was close to a breakdown. I've always wanted to live in London, so I thought bugger it."

"Are you planning to work while you're here?"

"I'm a website designer. I've scaled things back a bit while I'm here, but there're still a few commissions to finish. I can do that as easily here as anywhere else."

"So you'll be tapping away downstairs? God, I hope Max doesn't disturb you too much." Since our flats are part of a house conversion, the noise sometimes travels in the most embarrassing of ways. I know this, because Nancy, the previous tenant, used to wink at me after Alex and I had a dirty night.

"It's all good. I don't mind hearing a baby cry."

When we get to the club, I give our name to the bouncer and he lifts up the rope, letting us into the lobby. We get our hands stamped and walk into the main hall, which is already half-full despite the set not starting for another hour.

"What would you like to drink?" I ask, grabbing my purse and taking out a couple of notes.

"I'll get these."

"It's fine. Think of it as recompense for the noisy baby. You can get the next round."

"In that case, I'll have a beer. A proper one, not lager."

We get our drinks and find a spot to the right of the stage. As we walk I see some familiar faces, smiling and saying hello to those I know. Alex's band, *Fear of Flying*, have a pretty loyal following, but with the exposure they've been getting on some fairly popular music blogs, it has started to grow. I notice that at least half the audience is made up of younger women, drinking white wine spritzers and talking excitedly. Though I try not to listen too closely, I can't help but notice the words some of them use about Alex.

Yes, he is 'fuck hot', but he's also mine. A tiny dart of jealousy shoots through me. Not a big one; there's no green-eyed monster here. Maybe a bit of territory guarding.

"Don't you want to go and see your husband?" David asks after he takes a sip of beer. "I don't mind hanging around here."

"I try not to see him before a set. He's too amped up, we'd end up having a row." It's true; by this time Alex will be almost high on adrenaline. Electric and punchy and liable to explode. It's what he does to get through the painful anxiety that accompanies him going on stage, though once he's performing you'd never know it.

"Oh, really? I never would have guessed." David grins. I find myself blushing, mostly because he must have heard all our arguments. Alex and I love hard and we fight hard, and though that kind of relationship isn't for everyone, it works for us.

Most of the time.

A little over an hour later the chatter in the room hushes into silence, and I look up to see Alex walking onto the stage. Behind him, the rest of the group take up their spots, lifting guitars and sticks, and placing fingers on keyboards. But it's Alex everybody is staring at, the one they can't drag their eyes from. He has this incredible presence that is difficult to ignore. Stage-Alex commands the room, struts about as if he owns the place, caressing the microphone as if it's his first love.

This is the Alex I first met. Intense and serious, he stares out into the crowd, the corner of his lip curled up. I bite down on my own lip, feeling my heart start to race. I'm nervous for him, but there's something more, a need that vibrates inside me from my head to the tips of my toes.

It appears that the rest of the girls in the room feel the same way. There are cheers and screams as he strums the first chord, then Stuart hits the drums and the whole crowd erupts. I glance at David, who is staring up at the stage, and I see his foot tapping out a rhythm in time to the beat. But when Alex starts to sing my gaze swings right back to the stage, and he leans forward, singing into the mic, his voice low and sultry and full of swagger.

The boy's got game, and he knows it.

As the set continues we're pulled into the crowd, dragged along with the surge as everybody moves towards the stage. I reach out for David's sleeve, holding on tight, trying to keep him by my side.

That's when my eyes meet Alex's. I can tell the moment he spots me. His gaze stays on me for a drumbeat longer than anywhere else, and he smiles as he sings, his wink causing a hundred women to whistle and call. At the end of the song he mouths 'I fucking love you' and I mouth it right back, feeling the pounding of my heart and the aching need in my body. I'm so busy staring at him, I almost forget David's here.

He leans in to whisper in my ear. "They're bloody good."

I nod, smiling hugely. "The best."

"Your old man is the singer, right?"

"Yep." A couple of heads turn at this, and I feel the disapproval of nearby females.

"Even I think he's hot," David says.

I start to laugh, but then I see Alex's eyes narrow as he stares at me from the stage. Is he jealous? For a moment I feel indignant. What right has he got to feel anything approaching resentment when most of the women in this room want to jump him? All I'm doing is having a laugh with our new neighbour, while Alex is practically humping every female watching.

So I do the adult thing and stare right back. Then I stick my tongue out at him. He shakes his head and laughs softly, staring down at his guitar, and I feel marginally better.

\*\*\*

We go backstage after their set is finished. Alex is in what masquerades as a dressing room, though really it's a living room with a couple of mirrors. He's sitting on the black leather sofa, legs stretched out in front of him, a cold bottle of beer in his right hand. His eyes are closed, his head is back, and the sweat is pretty much dripping off him. His hair glistens with it.

"Hi." I walk over and he sits up, making a grab for me, pulling me into his lap. "Let go, you're soaking."

"I love making you wet."

"Um, this is David. From downstairs," I say, alerting him to the fact we have company. Other than the band, of course.

Those boys have known me for years. They're used to the way Alex makes me blush like a teenager.

"Downstairs where?"

"He's our new neighbour, I invited him along. David, this is Alex, Alex this is David." I stand up and let them shake hands. Though Alex seems friendly enough, I can still sense an edge to his voice. Like he's sizing David up.

"All right?"

"Nice to meet you."

"You too. You Australian?"

"Yeah, I arrived in London last month. I really enjoyed the gig, it was great." David is doing his best to be friendly, but he looks slightly uncomfortable. It could be that Alex is still hyped from the set, but he's giving out a dangerous vibe, as if he's on edge. I'm not sure I like it.

David obviously doesn't, because the next moment he's leaving. "Well, I'm gonna head off. Thanks for letting me come and watch. I'll see you around, Lara."

"Thanks for coming. We appreciate it." I put the emphasis on the 'we'. More for my benefit than Alex's. I hate appearing rude and it seems as though he's chased David off. "I'll see you soon."

I wave, and David gives me a little wave back, walking out of the door and into the hall. I count to five and turn around, staring at Alex.

"Well, that was rude."

"What?" Alex shrugs and grabs his beer, swallowing it down.

"The way you treated our neighbour."

"He wants you. It pissed me off."

"He doesn't want me." I eye roll, sighing loudly. "He's a nice, friendly neighbour who now thinks you're a bit of a twat. What's with the jealousy anyway?"

"I'm not jealous." He drains the last of his beer. "I don't like him."

"You didn't even give him a chance," I point out. "You didn't say two words to him. We've got to live with this guy; why can't you be nice?"

Alex stares at me for a moment. I can vaguely hear the chatter of the departing crowd coming from the club, but in here there's simply silence. I'm guessing the rest of the band are waiting—as I am—to hear his response.

We don't have to wait for long.

He puts his hand on my shoulder, drawing me closer. "I'll go down tomorrow and apologise to him."

"He's a nice man, give him a chance. He's new in the country and has a daughter he misses like hell. The last thing he needs is a neighbour with a grudge. Anyway, even if he did fancy me, it's not like I'm going to run downstairs for a quick shag while you're doing the washing up." I may sound flippant, but I'm not feeling that way. "You sound as if you don't trust me."

He lifts a hand to his forehead, rubbing it with his fingers. "I do trust you, babe. I'm a dick, I'm sorry."

When I look into his eyes I can see he means it. Stage Alex finally seems to have gone, taking his sharp tongue with him. I want the bad feeling gone, too.

"I happen to like your dick," I joke, trying to bring some levity back into the situation. I hear Stuart sniggering behind me. Without bothering to turn, I give him the finger.

"My dick happens to like you, too," Alex murmurs, pulling me against him, kissing the top of my head.

"Get a room, will you? You look like you need a good shagging, Al," Carl the bassist jeers. This time Alex flips him the bird, but he's laughing into my hair, and I find myself joining in, the atmosphere thankfully lighter.

"Great set, lads. Oh hi, Lara." The band's manager walks in, somehow breaking up our row and dismissing me all in the same breath. Alfie Kane has been managing the group for a few months now, and though Alex swears he is amazing, and has lots of connections in the industry, there's something about him that grates on my nerves.

"There were a couple of A&Rs out there tonight. They looked impressed. One of them asked me to give him a call on Monday." He brandishes a business card as if he's won a golden ticket.

"Which label?" Alex grabs the card and reads it. "Zephyr? Cool."

Stuart and the others join them, talking in loud voices about the gig, saying which songs went well and what notes were missed. I vaguely hear Alfie talking about some bookings; a couple of festivals and a possible tour, and I tune out their voices, retreating into my head instead. I grab a bottle of water and sit down on the sofa, chugging the liquid down, trying to ignore the fears that nag at me. I've always been a worrier; I can't seem to help it, no matter how hard I try, and since we've had Max, money—or the lack of it—has been my number one anxiety.

Even with my wage and Alex's casual earnings, we only just get by. If he stops working on sites, things are going to take a tumble pretty fast. The rent is bad enough—anybody who lives in London knows the cost of living is crazy—but it's all the baby things that are tipping us over the edge. Nappies, clothes, nursery, it's like having a second lot of rent to pay. Even though we are just about managing to tiptoe across the tightrope, financial failure looms beneath us; one little stumble and we could all plummet.

"You ready?" I look up to see Alex standing in front of me. His hair is curling at the ends, though dryer than before. "Let's go home, baby."

I take his hand and smile, swallowing down the unease. "Sounds good to me. Let's go."

# 5

I stood alone, waiting for an hour the first night we met. The band finished their set, and the crowd was dispersing, leaving behind an atmosphere soaked with the stench of sweat and beer. For a moment I considered standing in the exact same spot, alone in front of the stage, but even in my boozed-up state I was too self-conscious to stand out like that.

In the end, I went to the bar and ordered a lime and soda, trying to look surreptitious as I sipped carefully at it.

"You coming?" I looked up to see Grant Sharp. A fellow intern, he had the sort of cocky attitude only years of expensive schooling can buy. We'd paired off a few times, though his ability to do much more than kiss and fumble was always compromised by his consumption of whiskey.

"I'm going to stay here for a while." I glanced over at the stage again. Roadies were unplugging guitars and dissembling the drum kit. No sign of the band. "I'll catch up with you on Monday."

"You sure?"

"Yep. I'm all good."

The band walked over to the bar a few minutes later. I'd finished my drink and was considering leaving, second guessing myself about whether or not the singer had been talking to me. I'd managed to down more than a bottle of champagne that night, what if it had been my imagination?

But then I looked up and it was there again. That stare, the connection, the way I couldn't tear my eyes away. Unlike me, he'd changed into some fresh clothes; his red-and-black checked shirt buttoned up to his neck, revealing only the merest hint of tattoo. His jeans were tight, clinging to his legs as though they were a second skin. But his hair was still wet—damp and slick—brushed back and high.

"Hi."

I swallowed. The lime and soda had done nothing for the dryness of my mouth. I could still manage to smile, though.

"Hi."

"What's your name?" He had a thick, cockney accent that his singing voice only hinted at, and a habit of rolling on the heels of his black lace-up boots.

"Lara Stanford. What about you?" He was beautiful, but he didn't intimidate me. Chalk another one up to the champagne, liquid courage at its finest.

"Alex Cartwright." He reached out a hand and I took it, failing to stifle my laughter. There was something so formal about the way he introduced himself that was in complete contrast to the way he looked, and the way he'd stalked about on stage. "Pleased to meet you."

His eyes flickered, his gaze lowering to take in my legs, the way my short dress was almost stuck to my skin with perspiration. I didn't even want to know how bad my hair looked.

"I haven't seen you here before," he said.

"I haven't been here before. It's outside of my hunting grounds."

"You hunt?"

"Only on a Friday night." I grinned again, and he smiled back. I really liked the way his lips pulled back into his dimples. It lit up his face, made him look cheeky and dirty at the same time.

"What do you do the rest of the week?"

"I'm a good girl. I go to bed early."

"Alone?"

My heart sped at that question. It was loaded, obviously, but the way he put it out there so soon seemed genuine.

"Alone with my thoughts."

"Alone with your thoughts," he repeated, slowly nodding his head. "You use your right or your left hand for that?"

I coughed out a laugh. *Dirty boy.* "You seem very interested in my bedroom habits, Mr Cartwright. There are some things a girl likes to keep secret."

"I bet you use your left hand," he carried on, as if I hadn't spoken. His voice lowered, so I had to step forward to hear him.

The next time he spoke I felt his breath tickling at my ear. "I'd pay good money to see you alone with your thoughts."

There was silence for a moment, then the drummer joined us, giving Alex a high five. I was kind of relieved, because my mind had gone completely blank. I couldn't think of a single snarky reply.

"Who's this?" The drummer looked at me through his sandy fringe. Strands were stuck to his forehead, dark with perspiration.

"Her name's Lara," Alex said, gesturing the barman over and ordering another beer for his friend. "Can I buy you a drink, sweetheart?"

I nodded and held up my glass. "Vodka and soda please."

"Lara as in Dr Zhivago?" The drummer asked. "I'm Stuart, by the way." He reached out and offered me his hand.

"My mum was an Omar Sharif nut," I explained. "It could have been worse, if I was a boy it would have been Yuri."

"Like the astronaut? Cool." Stuart took his beer and leaned on the counter beside him. "I wish I was called Yuri."

Alex cleared his throat, giving Stuart a pointed look. Realisation slowly dawned on Stuart's face, staining his cheeks pink and turning his voice to a stutter. "Err, anyway, I'd best go and... see how the drum kit is. Nice to meet you, Lara. Beautiful name, by the way."

I felt strangely gratified at that. As if having a beautiful name was an accomplishment. "Thank you."

When I turned back to Alex, he was propped against the bar, a beer glass in his hand, head angled to the side. There was a curious expression on his face, as if he couldn't quite work out what I was. His eyes were narrow, dark.

"Where were we?" His tongue peeked out to moisten his lips.

"I think we were talking about masturbation," I whisper-replied, "and since you wanted to know, I'm left handed. And my thoughts are very, very dirty."

\* \* \*

We end up paying the babysitter with practically all the cash Alex earned from the gig. I walk into the bedroom and check on Max, who has managed to wriggle out of all his blankets and is curled in a ball right at the bottom of the cot, hands gripping the slats as if he's a prisoner desperate to escape. His eyelids flutter, and his mouth makes an 'o', moving rhythmically as if he's dreaming of food. Or breasts. Maybe both, if he's a typical male.

"Is he asleep?" I don't hear Alex approach, so when he whispers in my ear it makes me jump. His hands curl around my shoulders, fingers pushing under the straps of my black, cotton tank.

"Yeah," I reply in a whisper. "He's probably got a couple of hours until his next feed." Though we're trying to wean him onto bottles during the day, at night he still feeds from me. It beats mucking about with sterilisers and bottles in the early hours of the morning, and I love the closeness it gives us. Alex always jokes it's good to know I'll get my tits out at least once a night.

At least, I think it's a joke.

"A couple of hours." Alex presses his lips to the back of my neck. His fingers travel lower, pushing past the neckline, tips dragging along the top of my bra. "Whatever will we do?"

"Sleep?" I'm only half-kidding. These past six months of parenthood have been one long fight to get enough rest, and I've been losing spectacularly.

"I'll let you sleep afterwards, baby." His lips slide down my neck to my shoulder, teeth gently nipping where the two meet.

"After what?" I shiver as his fingers dip inside my bra.

"After I've fucked you hard like I promised." He scoops my breasts from my bra, cupping them in his hands. Thumbs graze my nipples, making them tight. "Or was it a threat?"

As I recall, it was both.

"What about the baby?" I've never been the quiet sort. If Max is in the room we'll have to be silent, like teenagers having a quickie while their parents are doing the washing up. "We'll wake him up."

Alex doesn't say a word, but I know from the slant of his lips he has something planned. So I'm not surprised when he wraps his hands around my upper arms and steers me out of the bedroom, into the bathroom on the opposite side of the hall. The only sound is the slapping of my bare feet on the floorboards, and our fast breaths.

Our bathroom is big in comparison to the rest of the flat. The Victorian fittings reflect the age of the building, the brass—elegant and delicate; the porcelain—pale and shiny. In the corner of the room is a claw-foot tub—my pride and joy.

I don't get to admire it for long, however. Alex presses into my back, his teeth grazing my earlobe and he spins me around until I'm in front of the sink.

He pushes me forward until I'm leaning on the sink, my fingers clinging to the cool, white rim. When I look up I can see us in the ornate mirror hanging above. Alex stares right back at me, his eyes hooded and dark, teeth biting into his plump bottom lip.

Blinking twice, he encircles me with his arms, and I marvel at the contrast of his vibrant tattoos on the paleness of his chest. The tendons in his forearms tense when he pushes down the straps of my vest, and the fabric bunches around my waist, leaving me only in my bra, until he pushes down the cups. The underwire pushes my breasts up, making my pale, pink-tipped skin look full and swollen. Slowly, tantalisingly, he runs his fingers in circles around my tender flesh, closer to my nipples, which tighten and peak.

"You're so fucking sexy." His voice is a growl. Thick eyelashes sweep down as he stares at my chest. "I want you so much."

His fingers pinch hard, sending a shock through my body. I clench as the pain mixes with pleasure. Then he's rubbing gently, his thumb barely grazing the peaks. I push myself to him, desperate for pressure. My back arches and I feel him against my behind, his long, thick length hard as steel. The sensation makes me moan.

I close my eyes, letting my head fall back to his shoulder. He takes the opportunity to kiss my neck, teeth pressuring my throat, lips sucking, tongue flickering, the sensual overload driving me crazy. The feeling is achingly sweet, and I turn my head to find his lips, pressing my mouth to his with a desperate kiss.

"Can you feel how hard my cock is, baby?" he whispers in my mouth. "I want to fuck you until my come drips out of you."

God, I love my dirty boy. The way he touches me, fingers demanding then soft, scraping and caressing as they move down my stomach. Then he pushes his hand inside my knickers, middle finger gliding, covered in my excitement. It slips easily inside, dragging against me, making all the muscles in my thighs contract.

"Christ, you're wet." His breath is warm on my neck. He pushes a second finger inside, moving just right until I'm begging him for more. I can never get enough of him, the way he touches me, treats me, as if I'm a cross between a princess and a whore. I hook my arm around his neck, holding on as my legs start to tremble, and he wraps his free arm around my waist to steady me. My sighs increase as the sensations layer and build, my breath shortening with every touch.

His thumb flicks me, once, then twice. It's as if my whole universe has shrunk down to the smallest dot, my only focus his fingers and thumb. When his free hand moves up to cup my breasts, pulling at my nipples, the pressure inside me explodes.

Pink, purple, bright yellow; a spectrum of colours flash across my vision. They blind me as I orgasm, and I squeeze my eyes shut tight, my body shuddering as Alex holds me up. The sensation shoots through my thighs and I hardly notice as he unclasps his belt, pulling down his jeans and his boxers. Vaguely, I register his hot, hard erection, pressing into my lower back, the tip dragging down as he lifts me and lines himself up.

There's that moment of intense anticipation, as he grazes me. I savour it, keeping still, letting him slip and slide. Then a gentle push and he opens me up, my body enveloping him as he slides deeper inside.

It takes my breath away.

"Fuck me," I breathe, leaning forward until my fingers are grasping the sink, my knuckles bleached and tight. When I look at the mirror he's staring at me, eyes clouded with need, lips set and mean. And I know him, this dirty Alex—the man who fucks strong and deep, with a passion that stings. I know him and I love him, because even at his most violent, he still holds me as if I'm china.

He's an enigma. A mixture of hard and soft, of bitter and sweet. My Dr Jekyll with a dirty Hyde mouth.

He grabs me by the hips, fingers digging into my skin, holding on, steadying me. Then he pounds me hard and fast until I see rainbows exploding behind my eyes once again, the vivid colours forming pictures in the shape of his tattoos. When the mist clears, and we are sweaty and breathless and all but collapsed on the sink, he whispers low in my ear, dirty and sweet. "I fucking love you. And I love fucking you."

If I had any breath left in my body, I'd say it right back.

# 6

Since I had Max my sense of self seems distorted, as if I'm looking at my reflection in the hall of mirrors and not recognising what I see. There was a time when I knew myself inside out; years of personality tests and self-analysis meant I was more than aware of my strengths and weaknesses. Confident, strong, occasionally reckless. Sensitive even though I tried to hide it.

But now the softness is leaching out, turning the rest of me to mush, like a cardboard box left out in the rain. I cry at sad stories in the news, at birth tales shared at massage class. At the thought of David never being able to see his daughter.

That makes me cry a lot.

He sits and watches me, at the fat tears rolling down my cheeks. Though he says nothing, his eyes are soft, and I find myself laughing at the fact it's me crying when it should be him.

"I'm so sorry, David, that's horrible, I can't believe she won't let you see her. Isn't there something you can do?" I can't ever imagine stopping a father from seeing his child. Even if I hated Alex, Max would always be his son.

"I started legal action, but Claire threatened to leave the country. If she did that I'd never see Mathilda again. It's fucking killing me, but there's nothing else I could do."

"So you came here? Was that the right decision? What if she changes her mind and you're half a world away?"

"I can get back within twenty-four hours. I'm hoping my being away will give her the chance to cool off." He looks out of the window, his eyes shadowed, brow lined. "Anyway, it was killing me being so close and not seeing her."

I can understand that.

David's quiet for a minute and his introspection allows me to take in my surroundings. Converted from the ground floor of what was once a Victorian, terraced house, his flat differs from ours. The bay window that has limited use in our upstairs bedroom is glorious here, streaming in light, the curve accentuated by a window seat that follows the edge of the glass. There are photos of Mathilda everywhere; as a new-born cradled in his muscled, tanned arms, as an almost-toddler with golden curls that cling to her head like a cap. You can tell she's his from the shape of her eyes, the way her smile makes her nose crinkle.

She's beautiful in the way only a baby can be. Skin flawless, face innocent, untouched by the world. I wonder if she misses him, if she stares at the door waiting for her daddy to swing her around. I hope one day she will realise none of this is his fault.

"So, your husband popped over last night." David changes the subject and I can't say I blame him. I go along with it, even though I've heard the story from Alex.

"He did? How did it go?"

David smiles, his teeth white and perfect. "He's all right. He said he was a dick and that he was sorry. I said it was okay and we opened a tinny."

"That'll explain why he was half-cut when he got home."

"Half-cut?"

"Drunk, pissed. Swimming in beer," I explain. David starts to smirk. "How much did you give him anyway?"

"Enough." He mimes pulling a zip along his mouth. I've known enough of Alex's friends to understand this is guy code. If a wife asks, you don't tell.

"Well, I'm glad you both cleared the air. And he *was* a dick the other night. I told him so. He's not the same when he comes off the stage, it's like he's so pumped up there's nothing left but aggression." I blush when I remember exactly how he got rid of it. By bending me over a sink with my knickers around my ankles. "He's a nice guy in real life."

"He has to be, you married him after all." David stands up, grabbing my empty mug from the table. "Another coffee?" I glance over at the buggy in the corner of the room. Max is sound asleep, sucking at his fingers, his face screwed up as if dreaming is stealing all his concentration. There's a patch of red on each of his arms where he scratches furiously at night.

"Are you sure?" I ask. "I don't want to disturb you." I'd only popped in to ask him if he was free next weekend. *Fear of Flying* are playing at a small festival in Oxfordshire. Though Alex and the band will be there all weekend, a few of us are traveling down on Saturday to watch their set. I'm nervous about taking Max to a festival—in a field in the middle of nowhere—but I figure there's safety in numbers. Maybe we can form some kind of human shield around him.

"I was getting bored with work anyway. I figure the least I can do is pay you for the ticket in caffeine." He flashes his northern-territory grin again. "I like the sound of Alex's sister."

"Amy?" My eyes widen. "Isn't she a bit young for you?" I don't mean that. What I really mean is don't go there. Amy has been on-again, off-again with the same guy since they were school kids. Their relationship is more unstable than nitroglycerine. If David gets too close it's likely to burn him.

"The librarian?" he clarifies and my eyes widen. He's talking about Andrea, Alex's other sister. Calm, reliable Andrea—the one member of the family who eschews volatility. She's the opposite of what I imagine David would like. She likes books, cooking, quiet nights in. Alex jokes she's been middle-aged since she was a teenager.

"Yeah, that one. I'm imagining her in dark glasses and a messy bun. Skirt stopping right below her arse."

I squint my eyes, trying to see her objectively. She's always been Alex's sister to me, fluttering around, looking after everybody, panicking when the roast takes too long to cook.

"She's sweet." It comes out as a warning. My tone surprises me, but with his muscled bulk and lascivious smile, David looks like he eats librarians for a mid-morning snack. Plus she's Alex's sister, and I don't care how much they managed to smooth things over last night, David shouldn't go there.

"Does she have a boyfriend?"

I shake my head. The teensiest bit of regret starts to bloom in my gut. "She's single, I think she likes it that way. Andrea is an independent woman." If she has any flings she keeps them well out of the way of her mum's house in Plaistow. I've probably only seen her with a guy twice in the last five years.

My warnings do nothing to cool David's interest. When I mention her independence his eyes light up. "She sounds perfect."

Seeing Andrea through his eyes makes my stomach hurt. I feel guilty I've dismissed her as being a sister, a daughter. Now, the thought of her is blooming in my mind like a rose, and though I'm no matchmaker, I can't help but wonder what she'd think of him. Because from the little I know of David, she may be the one thing he needs.

"She is."

"So what are the plans for the concert?"

"The festival? I haven't firmed anything up yet, but I'm hoping Andie might drive." She's the only one of us with a car—as old and temperamental as it is. Alex will be going in the van with the band, but that still means four of us plus Max need to squeeze into Andrea's car. "It should be fun, though," I say brightly. "Lots of good bands are playing there."

I'm understating it. Landing a spot at the festival has been a huge coup; Alex is so excited he's practically vibrating. The whole band are constantly talking about record deals and

YouTube discovery, and if I'm being truly honest I feel a little bit left out. Even worse, I feel as though I'm a dead weight, holding Alex down when he should be soaring.

If it wasn't for Max and me, I know he would have given up his building jobs by now. It makes sense he should be recording songs and travelling the country rather than carrying bricks and laying floorboards. Underlying it all—the black thought I keep trying to swallow away—is the awareness that I was the one who wanted a baby more than Alex. Even if he came around, I can't help but feel that one day he might resent me.

"I saw the list of bands, they're amazing." David smiles, totally unaware of the shamed thoughts flashing through my mind. "It's going to be great, thanks so much for asking me."

"You're welcome." I mean it, I really do. "As long as you know you're second in command with baby duty. Amy's never changed a nappy in her life, and I can't see Andrea being a fan of dirty ones."

"Dirty nappies I can do," he agrees easily. "A small price to pay."

\* \* \*

The day passes in a blur of naps and baby rice, set to a soundtrack of gurgles and wails. When I glance in the mirror at seven o'clock I realise I haven't even brushed my hair, let alone put on any make up. Not that it matters; apart from my jaunt downstairs to see David, the farthest I've been all day is a trip out to the local shop to pick up a pint of milk.

When Max is finally asleep, I check my phone to see if Alex has called or texted. It's their night at the recording studio, so I'm not surprised when there's no message. I busy myself with cleaning up the kitchen, putting some bottles on to sterilise as I sip at a cup of tea. Apart from his night time feed, Max is finally weaned to the bottle, and I'm hoping to drop the final one, just as soon as he sleeps through the night.

Sleep. It seems like the Promised Land, a nirvana I can never reach. Alex's mum has suggested controlled crying, but the irony is I'm too tired to listen to his grizzles. Faced with a choice between a night awake listening to him cry, versus a short feed followed by blissful sleep, I'm going to take the easy way out.

At nine, I take a welcome shower, letting the hot water soothe my skin. Steam fills the cubicle like fog in a horror movie, rising up, seeping through the cracks. I stay in there for so long that even my towel is damp when I get out, and the glass is misted and opaque. There's the outline of a heart in the mirror, with an A above and an L below, and the sight makes me roll my eyes. I'm guessing Alex did it this morning, all happy and sated from our night time shenanigans.

I'm in my pyjamas by the time Alex gets home. He climbs the stairs to the flat like a ninja, because the first time I hear him is when his key slips into the lock. The mechanism clangs as he turns it, and I hear him having to lean on the door where the wood is stuck. It opens with a bang.

"Hey, babe. How was your day?" He shrugs off his coat and walks over, kissing my cheek. I wrinkle my nose in distaste. He smells of beer and smoke. Not the cigarette kind, either. He doesn't seem to notice my grimace, instead he flings himself into a chair, running his hand through his hair. "Max okay?"

"Fine." My mood has turned on a sixpence. I've gone from mellowed out to annoyed in one breath. Alex knows how I feel about drugs. I've been working in a clinic for five years, for goodness sake; I've seen the effects they have on families, on relationships. Even the mildest of weed can destroy lives. And yes, I dabbled when I was younger—smoked pot and tried cocaine—but I haven't touched anything for years, haven't wanted to. I've seen too many people suffer as a result of them.

Alex is completely oblivious. He grabs the remote control from the coffee table and switches on the TV, flipping through the channels until he finds a football game. Crossing his legs, he puts his feet on the table, leaning back into his chair.

"How was the session?" It's an effort to keep my tone cordial.

"Yeah, it was good. We managed to lay down a couple of tracks." His eyes are on the screen as he talks to me, as if I'm the distraction. It's no good, I can feel the anger simmering. If I don't say something I'm going to explode.

"Have you been smoking?"

This time he looks at me. Surprise lifts up his brow. "We shared a joint afterward." He shrugs. No big deal, not to him.

"Who's we?" Now I feel like his mum. This is not what I want to be doing at half past ten on a Monday night.

"Me and Stu." He mutes the TV, though I notice he doesn't turn it off altogether. "What's the problem anyway? It's not like I was stuffing my nose or injecting. It was only a joint, sweetheart." He says the word with a sneer, cancelling out the endearment.

"Don't patronise me. I know people who have died from joints, or ended up with personality disorders. Why d'you think the stuff is banned?"

Alex folds his arms in front of his chest, hands sliding over his biceps. Then he deliberately turns his head away and mumbles something.

He knows that drives me crazy.

"What?" It's like talking to a kid. "Did you say something?"

He shrugs. "Doesn't matter."

I'm nothing if not persistent. "What did you say?" I demand.

A long, deep sigh. "What I said, Lara, is that you're the one with the personality disorder."

*What the hell?*

I sit there for a moment, stunned. I know he's drunk, and high, but that's not a free pass to being an asshole. I can't deny there's a part of me that is really hurt by his comment, by the tiny truth inside that stings. Yes, I have changed since having Max. I found it really bloody hard at first, and suffered from the baby blues. But who doesn't change? Babies are supposed to do that to you.

Not that Alex has got the memo. His life has gone on pretty much in the way it always has. Work, the band, drinking, smoking. I'm struggling to think of one thing he's had to give up since becoming a dad.

"Fuck you." It comes out louder than I intend it to. "I can't believe you said that."

"If the cap fits, baby."

I want to shove the cap up his behind. "Rather than criticise me, maybe you should take a good look at yourself. Twenty-nine years old yet still a big bloody kid. Your mum has a lot to answer for."

"Leave my mum out of it," he warns. "She's been nothing but nice to you."

"If she was nice she'd have taught you how to cook, or iron, or told you that a toilet doesn't magically clean itself. But no, she pampers you and makes your tea and thinks the sun shines out of your arse." Oh, I'm on a roll now. All those little things we swallow down when things are good have a tendency to rise up when the water gets murky. Tiny irritations, mini-judgements, they're all stewing in my thoughts.

"I can cook a fucking meal. Stop moaning about how hard you have it; what the fuck do you do at home all day anyway? While I'm bringing home the money so you can put your fucking feet up?" He's leaning forward, elbows on his knees. There's a mean twist to his lips that both frightens and exhilarates me.

"I'm bringing home maternity pay. And I'll be back at work in a couple of weeks, leaving our baby in a nursery for someone else to look after. Because I can't afford to do anything else." Angry tears sting at my eyes. "So don't you ever have a go at me about money; I'm bringing in more than my share." I hate the way I can feel my lip trembling. Not because I'm sad but because I'm angry. Fury has always made my eyes water.

"It's all my fucking fault is it? Poor Lara, having to get a bloody job because her husband's inadequate. Did you ever think that if weren't for you and Max I might actually be out there making something of myself? That we could really make a go of the band if I didn't have to work on some shitty building yard all day so we can afford our bloody rent?" He's actually shouting now.

"Well, I'm so fucking sorry we're holding you back." I don't swear that much, but it slips out, lubricated by ire. "Max is your baby too, you know."

"You're the one who wanted him in the first place, not me."

I'm breathless. Stunned. What a truly horrible thing to say. The tears that fall down my cheeks aren't from anger anymore. Shock, maybe, sadness for sure. I close my eyes and more tears squeeze out, hot and fat as they roll. And though I cover my dry mouth with the palm of my hand, a sob still manages to escape.

"Lara?" His voice is quieter, anxious. "Babe? I didn't mean it. You know I love Maxie. I'd kill for him. He's the love of my life, apart from you." My eyes are still squeezed shut, but I hear him approach, the thud of the floorboards as he kneels beside me. He takes the hand that isn't clutching my mouth and sandwiches it between his own. "I'm sorry, I'm such a wanker. I know how hard going back to work is for you. It's killing me to see you so upset." He cups my face, wiping away my tears. "Please don't cry, baby."

How can my mouth be so dry when my face is soaked? I take a deep breath, opening my eyes, and through the blurry haze I see his concerned expression. He leans closer, kissing the tears from my cheeks, his lips soft against my skin. "I love you, and I love Max," he murmurs against me. "You know that, right?"

Shakily, I nod my head. I do know that. I'm also grown up enough to understand we don't always mean the words we say in anger. But, I can't help feeling there's a small kernel of truth there, a festering resentment that we are a burden he has to carry. I hate the way motherhood has made me feel so vulnerable. I'm able to take it when people hurt and attack me, but not my baby. Not Max.

"I'll lay off the joints, I promise." More kisses. "I know it annoys you so I'll try not to do it."

"Thank you," I mumble, my voice croaky.

He kisses me again, this time on the mouth, his hands pressed to my cheeks. My lips are cracked, but moistened by tears, and when I kiss him back I taste their saltiness. It mingles with the flavour of beer and smoke, the mixture filling my head with memories of our argument, of the way we both hurt each other.

"I'm sorry."

"I'm so fucking sorry, baby."

We say it in tandem, lips moving as we whisper into each other's mouths. My whole body relaxes, the tension disappearing from my muscles, and I melt into him as he holds me. Though his kisses are hard and fast, that's all they are, kisses. Not a prelude to making-up sex, or an angry roll, simply soft and sweet and everything I need.

We stay like that for a long time. Alex kneeling on the floor, while I'm perched on the edge of the seat. His hands caress my face as I dig mine into the nape of his neck, my nails scraping at the part where his hairline meets his skin. We are hot breath and soft lips, sliding tongues and muted sighs. The bitter edge of our argument dissipates, leaving only the shadow of pain and warm, sugary love.

# 7

Two weeks later and the thing I've been dreading arrives; my first day back at work. Even when Max is asleep I spend most of the night tossing and turning, waking up with the sheets tangled around my legs like cotton cuffs. My body is covered with a sheen of sweat, my skin overheated by the proximity of Alex's warm, muscled chest. His right arm is flung across me, as if he's trying to hold me down. I wonder if I kept him awake, too. I have anxieties enough for both of us.

Going back to work seems like a mountain to climb. I fret about settling Max at nursery, about getting to the clinic on time. I worry about remembering where all my files are and whether I'll be able to use the computer. It's stupid because I know this stuff, I can do it with my eyes closed, and I suspect all of it is my subconscious distracting me from the biggest issue of all.

The fact I have to leave my baby.

I get up and peek into his cot, noticing Max is fast asleep. Tiptoeing, I make my way to the bathroom and take a long shower, luxuriating in the ten minutes I get to spend alone with my thoughts. Then I remember Alex's definition of those words and I start to giggle, managing to cut myself as I drag a razor down my armpit.

Alex is awake when I go back into our bedroom, watching me as I walk into the room, my wet body covered by the tiniest of towels, my damp hair hanging down my back. I flick it over my shoulder and he grins, sitting up as if to watch the show.

"Go and get ready for work," I whisper. "This isn't a strip club."

Alex laughs. "I'd have to pay in a strip club. This show's all free. A private dance for one."

"Two." I incline my head to the cot. "And minors aren't allowed to watch the show."

"Good job he's asleep then."

I make a face. "Even you should draw the line at that." The sooner we can afford a two bedroom flat, the better.

"Spoilsport." He swings his legs out of bed, stretching his arms up. His yawn is loud, exaggerated, but I'm too busy looking at his chest to complain.

Max isn't though. He grumbles and turns in his cot, so I run to the wardrobe, hoping I have five minutes before he wakes up. Long enough to get dressed, at least.

An hour later I'm yanking Max's buggy onto the bus, trying to manoeuvre it past irritated commuters who really don't want to move. There are only five stops to the nursery, but the journey seems to take forever, the bus impeded by road works and traffic lights and the sheer volume of traffic. It's amazing how different the vibe is to later in the morning. The need to get to work makes everybody angry, unwilling to converse or meet eyes or do anything but stare out the window.

It took us nearly a month to decide on which nursery to send Max to. There are a plethora of them in London, catering to every taste, and between us, we must have visited a dozen or more. Some we immediately discounted—the one where babies were left to cry until their sobs turned to tiny gasps stands out—but in the end we narrowed it down to two. The first was around the corner from our flat—convenient for drop offs, but not so easy if either of us needed to get there quickly from work. So we chose the second—a cheery converted house a couple of roads from the clinic—which has the friendliest staff and more flexible hours. The downside, of course, is I'll be the one dropping him off every morning, since Alex never knows where his next job will be. Often he'll get a last minute phone call dragging him to Shepherds Bush or Acton, and with unsteady hours, relying on him will never work. So it's me who gets to experience the joys of the drop off.

When I walk inside, having been buzzed in, I'm struck by how bright and airy the house feels. The east-facing windows are bathed in light, as children of various ages sit in the dining room, eating breakfast. Half of them will leave pretty soon, when the bus drops them off at school, leaving the under-fives to rule the roost for a few hours. And though they all look happy and unfazed, I feel my heart clench when I realise one day it will be Max being dropped off at school, a tie knotted around his neck, his hair askew from playing around. These years are going to disappear in the blink of an eyelid, and I'm going to miss half of them.

I take a deep breath, reminding myself this is the dilemma every mother faces. As much as I love Max, I love my career, too. Surely I can somehow manage to juggle the two?

Max has been allocated to the baby room, three doors down from the spacious dining area. I cart him down there, his over-stuffed bag slung across my shoulder, and push the door open with my foot. It's altogether quieter in here; a couple of the staff are holding babies, chatting away, cooing and making them laugh. In the corner are a bank of white-painted cots, lined with fresh, yellow bedding. Two of them are occupied by sleeping babies, but the rest are empty, waiting patiently for nap time.

"Mrs Cartwright, let me take Max for you." Holly is Max's carer. She greets me with a cheery smile and holds her arms out, waiting for me to place him in them.

I hesitate. It's only for a moment, but enough to see her smile start to waver, and I wonder what is going through her mind. She must be fed up with mums like me, with our resistance, our anxieties. I can't help but feel a little guilty.

"Max, Mummy has to go to work. But I'll be back to pick you up at five o'clock, and Holly is going to look after you. I promise you'll have a lovely time." My voice wobbles. I know he can't understand a word I'm saying; it's more for my benefit than his. I press my lips to his cheek and kiss him, and he makes a quick grab for my hair. His fingers close around my tightly-wound bun, loosening it until some brown locks spill out. Then as Holly goes to take him, he grabs on tighter, and it feels as though he's pulling my hair out by the roots.

On the positive side, at least I have a good excuse for my watering eyes.

"He'll probably cry the first few times, Mrs Cartwright. It's better for you both to leave quickly, less upsetting." Holly turns around so Max can no longer see me, and he starts to protest, wailing loudly. Though it almost kills me, I walk away, the sound of his screams reverberating in my ears. They are still echoing in the halls as I sign him in at reception, wiping at my face as the tears stream unbidden.

By the time I'm out of the nursery my chest is hitching with sobs, and I'm feeling furious with the world. Angry at London for having such high house prices that we can barely afford to live here, in spite of two incomes. I'm angry at Alex, too, for not being a millionaire, and at myself for not saving more money back when I had a lucrative job in a bank.

Most of all, it's life I'm railing at. The pure, bloody minded way nature pulls at our heartstrings until we're little more than slaves to her whims. *Have a baby*, she whispered, seducing me with the thought, *it will be easy, everybody does it*. But it isn't easy, it's not easy at all. In fact, it's a nightmare.

I haven't even made it to the clinic before I've pulled my phone out of my jacket pocket, and I'm pressing Beth's number, desperate for any reassurance a fellow mother can give me.

* * *

The day is long and tiring. In the afternoon, during a lull between appointments, I find myself falling asleep. When my head falls into my chest, the sudden movement makes me jump, and I sit straight up, looking around the room with wide, anxious eyes. The disorientation is swift, and for a moment I'm looking for Max, wondering where I put him. That's when I remember where I am, what I'm supposed to be doing. The fact I'm being paid to work.

Coffee, a splash of cold water on my face, and a walk around the clinic to find someone to talk to. I do all these things to wake myself up, but they don't work. Perhaps I should make a recording of Max crying and play it on a loop, since that manages to keep me up most of the night.

I call the nursery twice, which is a huge victory for self-restraint. Both times I'm reassured he's happy, thriving, and I try to ignore the mean thoughts that tell me he's much happier because I'm not there.

I once asked Alex how he felt, leaving Max every day when he went to work. He stared at me quizzically and shrugged as if it was a stupid question. He doesn't second guess himself the way I do, at least not about Max. I wonder if this guilt is gender-specific.

Or perhaps it's only me.

My last client leaves at 4:30 p.m., and I walk him to the door, showing him out. I have thirty minutes left to type up my case notes before I need to pick up Max. Way too short a time.

I'm only onto the second case when there's a knock on the door. Fingertips against the wood. Soft. Hesitant.

"Come in." I'm never going to get this write-up done. Our data protection policy means I can't do it at home either. Somehow I'm going to have to fit it in first thing in the morning. I scowl at my laptop, wanting to throw it across the room.

"Hey, stranger."

The biggest smile pulls at my lips. I'm out of my chair, running across the room. What the hell is Beth doing here?

"Oh, my God! I thought you were in Brighton. You never said anything this morning." I'm hugging her and we're both laughing like sisters who haven't seen each other in years.

"I was. But I heard your voice and I had to come and see you. Don't worry, Niall agreed to pick up Allegra."

"I can't believe you did this for me." I'm so happy I want to scream. "You're the sweetest friend."

"After everything you did for me? I was on that train faster than you can say 'Day return to London, please.' Now I'm going to sit in the corner while you finish up here and then we can go and pick up your beautiful boy."

Instead I decide to log off right away. Today's sessions were pretty standard, and I have the scribbles I made on my notepad. Silently I promise myself that tomorrow I will be more conscientious.

"How long are you here for?"

"I have to catch the last train home. Niall has a meeting tomorrow, so I need to do the school run." She notices my glum face. "Don't worry though, the last train doesn't leave Victoria Station until one."

It's like getting a gift when it isn't my birthday. I lock the laptop in my drawer and slide the key in my purse, and the two of us leave my office.

Beth slides her arm through mine when we walk down the corridor. "God, it feels weird to be back. Almost as if I've never been away. I popped in on the after school club and didn't recognize any of the kids."

Beth used to love running the club when she worked here. To say she had a close relationship with the children is an understatement.

"They're all growing up. Some of them too fast." I wince, thinking of the last time I saw Cameron Gibb. His face smashed in after some gang deal gone wrong. It's not something I want to tell Beth about, though. One of the reasons she moved to Brighton after she fostered Allegra—the orphaned child of an addict—was to get away from these tragedies.

"Do you ever miss being here?" I ask. I'm genuinely interested. Beth was as committed to the clinic as I am, before her circumstances changed.

"I'm not really sure." She laughs. "I wouldn't change a thing, because I love where I am now. Things are great with Niall, and Allegra is settling in so nicely. Plus we've had the heads up that the adoption could be going through soon. But I do feel nostalgic when I come here, as if I'd like to turn back the clock for one day and say hello to everybody again." She takes my hand and squeezes it tight. "Of course I miss the hell out of you."

We say goodbye to the rest of the staff, and make the short walk to Rainbow Nursery, both of us chatting up a storm. I marvel at how different I feel to this morning, when I made the same walk but in the opposite direction. A few hours ago I was crying down the phone to my best friend, and now here she is in person.

When we get to the nursery, she lingers on the steps. "You go in, I'll wait out here."

"Why? Max will be so pleased to see you."

She shrugs. "It'd be like intruding on a lover's reunion. I can't do it. Seriously, go in there and make his day. I'll have a cuddle with him as soon as you're outside."

I'm so excited to see him I almost run inside. The receptionist calls after me when I rush straight past her, asking me to fill in a couple of forms. Then I'm there, walking into the brightly-coloured baby room, my face one huge smile. That familiar ache tugs at my heart. The need to see him, to hold him.

"Look who's here, Max." Holly takes his arm and makes him give a little wave. "Say, 'Hello, Mummy'."

Of course, he says nothing of the sort, but he's sporting a huge grin and babbling like crazy, his arms reaching out for me as he squirms against Holly. Then I'm holding him, burying my face against his head, breathing in his warm, baby scent. I get a rush from it, feeling giddy and high. When he grabs me with his chubby hands it feels as though all is right with the world.

It's amazing how quickly things can change. In the space of a few hours I've gone from crazed and harassed to happy and blissful; thanks in no small measure to the surprise appearance of my best friend.

When we walk out into the sunshine, Max seems as happy as I am. I can see his little legs kicking as I push his buggy down the slope they've built beside the front steps. Then Beth launches herself at him, tickling his belly, and he giggles so much I'm scared he's going to be sick.

"He's so beautiful." Beth sighs.

"He is," I agree. "Though not so cute at three o'clock in the morning when he's wide awake and wanting some company."

"Well, the next time I come up I'll stay over and give you a break for the night." She tugs at his foot and he kicks in delight.

I smile and grab her hand. "Sounds like a fabulous idea to me."

# 8

David steps back onto the pavement, his face screwed up in concentration. Lifting his hand to his hair, he scratches hard. "It's not going to fit."

"No shit, Sherlock." Amy has been watching our attempts at loading the car for half an hour. She's sat down on the front wall of our tiny garden, and is polishing her toenails with a dark blue hue. David turns around and shoots her a look. She carries on painting, oblivious.

"The buggy has to go. And maybe you can only bring one bag?" Andrea sounds apologetic. "We can take turns holding Max, or we can use that papoose?" She gestures at the tangle of fabric I've stuffed on top of the buggy.

It's no good; babies and music festivals clearly don't mix. The days of slinging a short dress and a pair of Wellington boots in a bag are clearly over. Packing for today has been like a military operation.

"Let me take out some toys." I rummage through the huge bag full of everything Max could possibly need for a day trip in the country. "And if I can work out how to attach that bloody baby sling, we can use it." I've had it since Max was born, and not once have I been able to fasten it. The one time I tried to tie Max against me, he slid out. I managed to catch him by the shoulder of his sleep suit, but it was a close-run thing.

"How difficult can it be?" David asks. He has the confidence of a man who thinks he knows it all.

"I guess we'll find out." Is that a smirk on Amy's face? For a moment she looks so much like her brother it's unbelievable. Same face shape, same inky black hair. She has the same sense of mischief, too, though I sense she still has a bit of growing up to do. Which is fine, because she's almost ten years younger than me.

Eventually, we manage to tessellate Max's things, and then we have the pleasure of trying to strap his car seat in. It's a feat of engineering when we finally succeed, and we practically collapse into the car, exhausted.

"I never realised kids were so complicated," Andrea murmurs, smoothing her dress across her knees. She twists the key and the engine rumbles.

"That's not the half of it," I say. "I thought I packed light."

I lean forward to talk to her. She's sitting in the driver's seat, with David and his long legs on the passenger side. Max's car seat is behind him on the back seat, and I'm squashed in the middle between Max and Amy. "That's a pretty dress, Andrea, where's it from?" I think it's the first time I've seen her in a dress. It complements her toned, smooth legs. I've noticed David glancing at them more than once.

"I've had it for ages," she answers airily. "I can't remember where it's from."

She's so convincing I almost believe her. Then I see the corner of a white paper price tag sticking up from the neckline and smile to myself. "You should wear it more often."

I hear a low, "Yeah," coming from the passenger seat and try not to laugh. It's kind of strange that David seems into Andrea after they've only met once. They seem to be getting on pretty well—having bonded over the boot of doom—but I still can't quite see they have much in common, unless David really does have a librarian fetish.

It takes a few hours to get to the festival site. The last thirty minutes are spent crawling in a huge line of cars as each one has to be checked by security before heading towards the car park. Max begins to get restless and we all end up trying to entertain him, with David doing an amazing rendition of a Kylie Minogue song, falsetto tone and all.

During the wait I stare out of the window at the fields spread out before us, their greenery obscured by a sea of tents that stretches out towards the horizon. I find myself getting excited for Alex, as well as a little bit nervous. When he referred to this as a 'small festival', I'd imagined a few dozen tents and a hay barn. But this is Glastonbury-Lite. Even if they're playing on the smallest stage, it's still one heck of an opportunity for them.

We park up and unload the car, the process so much simpler than when we were trying to fit everything in. David shows me how to strap the baby sling to my chest so Max is snug against me, his little legs dangling down and pressing into my stomach. Max thinks it's hilarious, being so close to me, and he gets all grabby, going for my hair, my face, and occasionally my chest.

He is, after all, his father's son.

It's one of those rare Saturdays when the sun decides it has nothing better to do than blast down on us, the lack of clouds leaving the sky a deep, cerulean blue. The result is a thousand pairs of closely cropped denim shorts and tiny flowery dresses, without a Wellington boot in sight. Even though I've managed to lose most of the baby weight I put on during pregnancy— not through any concerted effort but because Max has spent the last six months literally sucking the life out of me—I can't help but feel a little bit dowdy in comparison to these young, luscious girls.

It's okay. It's not as if I've had a baby and immediately decided I must always wear a trouser suit and elasticated skirts. At the moment I'm wearing a black and pink floral mini skirt and a tight grey vest, plus my accessory du jour; a slobbery, giggling Max who keeps pulling down the neckline to flash my tits at everybody. But there are some things you give up when you have a baby: drunkenness, debauchery, and the ability to wear crop tops. I can't help but feel jealous of all these smooth, tanned stomachs.

I used to have one of those. Not anymore, though. It's disappeared into the ether, along with the chances of a good night's sleep and the ability to hold my pee in whenever I cough.

"What time is the band on?" David asks, lifting up the bag full of baby stuff and pulling it onto his shoulder. Andrea grabs my handbag and kindly carries it for me. Amy's wandered off somewhere, walking away with a cheery "See you later", so it's the three of us.

"Alex said six o'clock, which in festival language probably means seven." When I glance at my watch I note it's not quite noon. Seeing the sun so high in the sky reminds me that Max should be wearing a hat to go along with his sunscreen, and I lean across David to rummage through his baby bag.

It's really weird having Max strapped to my front, as if I'm regressing back to pregnancy, except this time all the kicks are on the outside. I keep forgetting he's there and squashing him until he starts to squeal.

With his hat on and sunscreen liberally applied, we make our way across the fields, carried along with the stream of people all heading in the same destination. Unsurprisingly, there aren't many children here, but the few I do spot seem to be having a great time, running around on the grass, kicking footballs and throwing Frisbees. In the past few years festivals have become more family friendly, as the twenty-somethings who are the main clientele have started to settle down and have kids of their own. But that doesn't stop the family field from seeming a little ghettoized, the sole escape from the sex, drugs and rock and roll spread throughout the rest of the site.

"Have you told Alex we're here?" Andrea asks, and I realise that in the rush of our arrival I completely forgot. I pull my phone from the bag she's holding and try to send him a text. It gets pinged back immediately.

"No signal." The curse of the English countryside. It may be beautiful, but the lack of coverage is a big problem. "He said they'll be near the backstage area. We should probably go and look there." I feel a bit stupid; I've dragged them all the way over here, and can't even manage to find my own husband.

It takes us half an hour to locate the backstage area. After a long detour which takes us past the food stands, we show our passes to the security team who stand aside and let us through.

The atmosphere is different in this part of the festival; charged and edgy. It may have something to do with the booze that seems to be flowing freely, or the rush of adrenaline that comes from performing live. Though there are no huge bands playing—no superstar headliners—I recognize a lot of the faces as we push our way through the crowd. There are musicians and girlfriends, kids and groupies, all mixing in the same area.

I spot Stuart first. He's about twenty feet away, a beer in one hand as he gesticulates wildly, telling some story which is making him grin. A circle of people surround him, mostly guys, all drinking and rocking on their feet in the way that men do. I've noticed before that when a group of men congregate to drink, standing still rarely seems to be an option.

"Is that Alex?" Andrea asks, pointing to the left of Stuart. I follow her gaze and I see him.

A moment later I wish I hadn't looked.

He's standing outside of the circle, not listening to Stuart. Instead he's in deep conversation with some blonde girl who has a joint between her fingers and the biggest smile on her face. And I watch, as if in slow motion, as she slowly raises it to Alex's lips. His mouth closes around the end and he shuts his eyes as he inhales, his fingers wrapping around her forearm as if to keep it steady. When he exhales, she lifts the joint to her own mouth, and takes a deep mouthful inside, before slowly, languorously, letting the smoke escape.

And she's wearing a crop top.

Suddenly, I'm furious. Not because I think he's cheating; no matter how bloody firm that girl's stomach is, I know Alex well enough to accept he isn't the cheating kind. Neither of us are; we've always sworn we would walk away first. But what's making me so angry is he promised he wouldn't take any more drugs, and he knew I was coming here today with Max. Yet still he thought it would be a good idea to share a smoke with some blonde in the middle of a field.

It's so unthoughtful, as if he's lied to me only to shut me up, while carrying on in exactly the way he wants to. It's not only me, there's Max to think about now; a little boy who will be growing up, and possibly thinking that drugs must be okay if Daddy does them.

It hits me then, that as much as I've changed since we had Max, Alex hasn't adapted in the same way. Maybe he hasn't had to. But the thought makes me sad and angry at the same time.

"Are you okay?" David asks quietly. He must have sensed my posture stiffening, my hands balling into fists next to my sides.

"I'm fine." I sound terse, but I can't say any more, I'm holding things together by a fragile hair. This isn't the time or the place for confrontations. Not only because we are surrounded by people, although a public row would be embarrassing enough, but because this is the band's big break and a huge argument will ruin it for them.

Before I can calm myself down, Alex looks up and spots us. He says something to the blonde and she gives him a quick wave, before he slowly ambles over towards us.

I'm still surrounded by angry, red mist when he arrives. As a counsellor I've gone through anger-management strategies with clients so many times. Deep breaths through the nose, silent counting. Closing eyes and picturing a happy place. But following my own advice is harder, especially when we've been through all this before.

Alex presses his mouth to my cheek first, then ruffles Max's hair, leaning down to kiss him.

I bristle. "Don't breathe on him." Okay, so maybe I'm not in control of this at all. I remind myself where we are.

His head shoots straight up. When he looks at me, there's the merest hint of redness to the whites of his eyes, as if he's suffering from mild hay fever. "What?"

"Don't breathe your druggy breath on him," I spit through gritted teeth.

"What the fuck are you talking about?" Alex grabs hold of my upper arm and the next minute is a whirlwind. Somehow, David manages to scoop Max out of the baby sling and away from the two of us, and I'm suddenly feeling light-headed and unbalanced.

"I saw you smoking over there with that blonde. And I'd rather you didn't exhale your cannabis all over my son and give him a contact high."

"*Your* son?" Alex repeats. In spite of the intoxication, his voice takes on a dangerous edge. It holds more than a hint of maliciousness.

I'm not proud of myself right now. I said it to get a rise out of him and it worked. But it's backfired spectacularly, making me feel like shit and giving him the moral high ground.

"Our son." I correct myself. "Stop giving *our son* a contact high."

He shakes his head and lets out a bitter laugh. "You're a real fucking killjoy, you know that? We're in an open field, surrounded by fresh air. The possibility of Max getting a contact high are approximately zero. I wanted to say hello to my son and my beautiful wife who I've been talking about nonstop for the past few hours. Then you walk in here and start acting like a bitch."

"You promised me you wouldn't smoke."

"Yeah, well you promised me having a kid together wouldn't change you, I guess we're both liars now."

I open my mouth to retort, then shut it again. Even though I'm so angry I could spit, I have enough self-awareness to know I can't do this. Not here, not now. But if I stay here I'm going to explode and we will end up having an almighty argument in front of all these people. We're already making enough of a spectacle of ourselves as it is. I need to be a better person, to step back, to walk away.

I glance to my left and see David holding the baby while Andrea plays with his feet. Max is completely oblivious to everything going on between Alex and me—thank goodness—but from the awkward smile David shoots at me when he catches me looking at them, I know he and Andrea are all too aware.

I feel embarrassed. The need to get out of here claws at me. "I'm going to get some food," I mumble, not able to look at Alex. "I'll take Max for a walk."

Alex squeezes my bicep gently, then in the softest voice asks, "We good?"

No, we aren't good. We're not even in the same vicinity of good. But I force myself to look up and nod, all the while trying not to cry. "It's fine, we'll talk later. Good luck with the gig."

"I'll see you before we go on, won't I?"

I don't say anything. There's about five hours before they're due on stage, and the way I'm feeling now I can't see myself calming down by then. And the closer it gets to their set, I know what an arsehole Alex becomes. It's a recipe for disaster.

Fire, meet touch paper.

"Yeah, sure." If he carries on drinking and smoking he won't even notice I'm gone. The sad fact is, out of sight out of mind works excellently for Alex. When we're together, just the three of us, he makes it feel as though we are his world. But right now, I feel like a piece of gum clinging to the sole of his shoe.

David and Andrea are angels. When I walk over to them and explain I need to go for a walk, they don't ask any questions. Instead, David unravels the empty baby sling from me and straps Max to himself, while Andrea walks over to her brother and gives him a quick hug. Though I can't hear what she whispers in his ear, I can see him smile and nod, and for some reason that makes me feel sad.

I manage to hold it together as we leave the backstage area, clasping on to Andrea's hand while David and Max walk slightly ahead of us. I think of Alex and my eyes well up again, blurring my vision so I can hardly see. By the time we've found a secluded spot and sat down on the grass, I'm sobbing loudly, while Andrea rubs my back and David holds Max, his eyes soft and kind as he watches me cry.

"I'm sorry," I whisper. "I'm being so stupid."

Andrea hushes me. "It's okay, it's okay."

"He promised me he was giving up the weed. Then when I saw him with that girl..." I start crying harder.

"You know he'd never do anything to hurt you, right? Alex adores you, he worships the ground you walk on. I remember the first time he told me and Mom about you. He had this dreamy look in his eyes when he said your name and I knew you were the one. Then when he brought you home for Sunday lunch, God, I've never seen a man look at a girl the way he looked at you."

"He doesn't look at me like that anymore," I sob. "He thinks I've changed since I had Max. He wants the old Lara back."

"Of course you've changed, silly. You're somebody's mum now. That has to change you. Different priorities, putting somebody else's needs first. Having a baby is supposed to have that effect on you."

I wipe my damp cheeks. "Alex hasn't changed. He's still exactly the same." And there lies the problem. I'm a mum first, and Lara second. Alex is just Alex.

"That's his issue, not yours." Andrea sounds firm. "He's got a bit of growing up to do but he'll get there, and so will you. I know Max has turned everything upside down, but the two of you will get through it—you need to give each other a bit of space." She says it so confidently, I believe her. She's known Alex since he was born, has enough insight into the way he works for me to respect her judgement.

Even so, I still don't stop crying for an hour.

# 9

Despite my pent-up anger, the next two days fly past. At work I'm too busy to think about things, and at home Max has decided he can't sleep without being cuddled. I've been too tired to argue, so my evenings are mostly spent holding him in my arms. By Wednesday I feel like the walking dead, so when I see I have a two hour break at lunchtime, I decide to step outside the clinic and grab some fresh air.

As soon as I leave the building, a light breeze catches my hair, lifting the strands until they tickle my face. I inhale deeply, tasting the freshness of the air, the coolness of the temperature. The sky is blotted by hazy clouds that diffuse the light, casting a peachy mellowness to the sun.

A movement to the left catches my eye. Alex pushes himself up from the wall he's been sitting on and walks towards me, shoving his phone into his jeans pocket. His steel-capped boots are covered with a thin layer of pink dust, his jeans paint-splattered and worn. A thick checked shirt covers up an old band tee, but I know without having to look that it's a Sex Pistols one.

"Hi." Everything about him seems softer. Over the past two days we've hardly spoken. It feels strange to hear his voice.

"What are you doing here?"

"I wanted to talk to you." Nervously, he rakes a hand through his hair. "If you've got the time."

"How did you know I'd be free?"

He shrugs. "I didn't, but I've been sent over to cost a job in Brick Lane, so I thought I'd pop in on the off chance. I was about to call you to see if you were free for lunch."

I raise my eyebrows. "You're not really dressed for the Dorchester." Glancing down, I notice my frayed cardigan and boyfriend jeans. "Nor am I, for that matter."

"Well, let's go to the pub instead, then."

Ten minutes later, Alex carries over two glasses of Coke, a menu tucked beneath his arm. He passes me a glass, his fingers sliding against mine as I take it, and I try not to pull away from him.

We sit in silence for a minute, letting the low murmur of conversation from other tables cut through the tension, and I try to work out exactly how to phrase what I'm feeling. Our argument still seems so raw even thinking about it hurts.

"I'm sorry." Alex looks up at me through thick lashes. "I'm a stupid, insensitive asshole. I shouldn't have smoked in front of you, and I shouldn't have said all those things."

Unexpected tears sting at my eyes and I'm not sure if they're from anger or relief, but either way I try to blink them down.

"You know how I feel about drugs."

He takes a slow breath in. "I do. And I understand it too. You've seen some really shitty things and it affects you." Leaning back in his chair, he splays his long legs in front of him. "So I think we should clear the air and say what we really think."

"That's dangerous talk."

"It is."

"Could lead to more arguments."

"Undoubtedly. But I'd rather have you shout at me than ignore me. The silent treatment is killing me."

Though I try to bite it away, I feel a small smile creep across my face. "I wasn't doing it on purpose. I don't know what to say."

This time, he reaches forward and puts his hand over mine. "Tell me what you're thinking right now."

"I'm thinking what an idiot you were. You knew I was coming yet you still smoked a joint. What does that say about your feelings for me?"

"It wasn't about you. I was so fucking worked up I couldn't think. It was the biggest gig we'd ever played and my nerves were shot to hell. I only took a couple of drags; that was it. And I wish I hadn't."

I wish he hadn't, too.

"I hate the way we keep arguing over everything, Alex. It's so bloody draining. And I know having Max around puts a strain on both of us, but I can't keep going on like this."

"Arguments don't have to be a bad thing," he points out. "They can clear the air, too. I'd rather you talk to me about how you're feeling than let it all stew inside you. I can tell when you're getting uptight about something."

I look down at my feet. There's a truth in his words, I do bottle things up. I'm like that shaken up can of cola, fizzing and ready to explode as soon as somebody pulls the key.

"But I want everything to be perfect. *I* want to be perfect. At the moment I feel like such a bloody failure at everything. You, Max, my job, all of it."

He squeezes my hand. "You're a fucking amazing mother. Seriously, I'm so proud of the way you've adapted to having Max. Come over to the site sometime and you'll hear me going on about how great you are." He smiles at me, his eyes warm. "It's sexy as hell watching you all domesticated."

"Seriously?" I wrinkle my nose. "You like it? Barefoot and pregnant and all that?"

"Maybe not the pregnant, bit, not yet. But the rest of it, yeah. I love it. Even the hormones."

I burst out laughing. "You've been living with women for too long." We've had this conversation before. He isn't one to shy away from women when they're feeling menstrual and angry.

"I love you, babe. Everything about you. And I know that you need some support. I'm trying, I really am. I've told Alfie that if he can get the band some high paying gigs, we'll take them whatever we are. That way we can look at you working less hours and spending more time with Maxie."

There's a lump in my throat that a swallow of Coke doesn't dissolve. "Thank you. And you will get more gigs because you were amazing last weekend. The crowd loved you."

His eyes brighten. "You think so?"

I grin. "Yeah, you really were. There were so many cameras out, so many people singing along."

"It was a good show. Though I hated the fact we weren't talking to each other afterwards."

"Me, too."

Alex lifts my hands up to his mouth, brushing his lips along my palm. "Are we friends again?"

"Yeah, we're friends again."

\* \* \*

Max has developed a summer cold. It clogs up his nostrils with sticky, green mucus, and turns his breath into a sort of hacking wheeze that's painful to hear. I can tell he's frightened from his constant need to be carried, and I try to cuddle him for reassurance, but it never seems enough.

As always, I'm buried beneath a barrage of well-meaning suggestions. Alex's mum tells me to squirt breast milk up his nostrils as that will loosen the snot. Holly, his nursery nurse, suggests a little sucking device with a rubber end that will pull the mucus out with a vacuum. The doctor looks at me as if I'm wasting his time, and tells me that on average babies get around four colds a year.

*Four?* The thought panics me. It's only been a week since he caught it—another thing I'm blaming the music festival for—but it's been the most drawn out seven days of my life. His sleep has been fitful and noisy, and every time I attempt to drift off, another hacking cough makes me jump up in alarm.

So when we arrive at Alex's mum's house for Sunday lunch, we are the walking dead. A couple of mornings ago I found Alex curled up on our uncomfortable leather sofa with Max laying in his baby seat beside him. Alex had a throw draped over his legs as he twisted and turned to try and find a comfortable position. Still, as soon as we walk through the door he's pointed in the direction of the lawnmower, and he lopes off, jingling his keys in his pocket, mobile phone in his other hand.

"How's your dad?" Tina walks back into the kitchen and I follow her, Max clutching desperately to my shirt as if he's frightened I'll try to put him down. His earlier cries have mellowed into a low-level grizzle. I shift him onto my hip in an effort to hold him more easily.

"He's fine. I spoke to him a few weeks ago. Said he was enjoying the weather and getting out in the garden."

"You should invite him here for lunch some time," Tina suggests. "It doesn't seem right him rattling around that big house on his own. Does he come up to London much?"

"Not really. The last time he came was for our wedding. We took Max down for a visit a few months ago, but he didn't seem that interested."

"What a shame." With her close-knit family, and her fierce love of her children, Tina finds it hard to understand the detachment I have from my father. It's not that I hate him, or even dislike him, we simply don't have much in common.

Even before my mum died we rarely spoke. In that sad, clichéd way, she was the glue that held our family together. When she died seven years ago, there didn't seem anything left.

Just the odd sense of obligation, and even that dissipated as time went on. Visits became phone calls, which eventually petered out into Christmas and birthday cards. Nowadays if he calls, I immediately assume something is wrong.

Alex pops his head around the door. "You're out of oil. I'm gonna walk over to the petrol station."

"Ooh, can you pick up a couple of pints of milk while you're there? I want to make custard," Tina replies.

It's stupid how much the thought of custard cheers me up. After a week of no sleep, and constant crying from Max, all I want is the sweet, creamy goodness.

"You're making custard?" Alex looks as excited as I am. "What are we having it with?"

"Apple pie," Tina replies, smugly. As much as we get on, she makes no secret of the fact she likes to spoil Alex rotten with her cooking. Luckily for her, this is the one thing I don't mind her being better at than me. Especially if it means I get a proper dinner every Sunday. "I can give you the recipe if you like?"

Alex bursts out laughing. "Lara couldn't make it. She cremates water."

I'm about to say something snarky back, when Tina places a cool hand on my shoulder and turns to look at her son. "Actually, I was talking to you."

"Ooh, burn." I lick my finger and put it in the air, making a sizzling noise. "Alex doesn't even know how to turn on the oven."

He laughs and flips me the bird, grabbing his jacket from the kitchen chair. "I'll leave you ladies to your bloody gossip, while I go out and do the man jobs." He kisses my cheek then ruffles Max's scant hair and heads out the back door.

I think about the way Alex and I must seem so normal to his mum. We still joke, we still wind each other up, and yes, I still think he's the most beautiful man I've ever seen.

But... and there's always a but.

There's an awkwardness there which didn't exist before. It's like having a perfect china plate, then running my finger over it and feeling an imperfection. It doesn't matter how beautiful that plate looks, or how everybody stares at it and thinks it's flawless, the problem is I know the crack is there.

So I cover it with piles of strawberries and chocolate and hope nobody notices.

Alex is quiet when he gets back from the shop. Andrea arrives a little after two, and goes upstairs to drag a protesting Amy out of bed, who then proceeds to regale us with a long explanation of why she didn't get to bed until five in the morning, and how she ended up with only one shoe.

"So why did you give the guy only one shoe?" Andrea scratches her head. I'm glad she's as lost as I am. Things that make sense in Amy's world seem absolutely crazy in mine.

"He said he'd come and find me at the end of the night," Amy explains, getting slightly impatient. "You know, like Cinderella."

"But he didn't?" Andrea clarifies. I bite my lip in an attempt not to laugh. Tina ignores them both; she's too well versed in the craziness of Amy to bother commenting.

"Well, clearly. Duh!"

For someone so intelligent, Amy doesn't have a clue when it comes to common sense. I wish I could say this was unusual, but there have been too many Sunday lunches like this for that to be true.

Alex's phone starts to ring, and he scrambles in his pocket, pressing the button to reject the call. "Sorry." He says it to Tina. She has a strict no phone at the table policy.

Before she can say anything, it rings again. I see his mouth twitch as he rejects the call for the second time.

"Who is it?" I ask.

"It's only Stuart. I'll call him back later."

When his phone buzzes with a text alert, I hear Tina sigh. "Just answer it for God's sake."

"It's a text, Mum."

"Then read it and turn the bloody thing off. I'm trying to eat my dinner here."

The next minute, Alex is standing up. "He says it's urgent. I'll go outside and call him back, okay?"

He doesn't wait for an answer, just sidles out, and I look over at his mum. "Sorry."

"Don't apologise for him, love. He's ugly enough to do that himself."

"Don't let him hear you say that," Andrea says. "You know how vain he is."

"Oh God," Amy giggles, "Do you remember the time he used that hair bleach? His hair was so orange he looked like one of the Weasleys."

I smile even though I've heard the story before. Alex claims the whole incident scarred him for any future hair dye use. He also reckons it delayed him losing his virginity by at least a year.

He can be such a liar.

Having said that, I've seen the pictures. He *did* look like one of the Weasley twins.

When he comes back, there's a huge grin spread across Alex's face. He taps the phone against his chin a couple of times, then grabs hold of me, swinging me around before planting a huge kiss on my lips. "Guess what?"

"What?" I'm breathless from his sudden change in demeanour.

"Stuart got a call from Alfie. The Freaks' manager have offered us a gig supporting them on their next tour."

I've heard of The Freaks. They're not massive, but big enough for their songs to be played on the radio. Even if I hadn't known of them, I'd realise from the look on Alex's face that this is big news.

"That's brilliant. When do you start?"

"Yeah, that's the catch. Their original support act has pulled out. The first concert is next month."

"That doesn't give you a lot of time."

"We'll have to put the work in. We can use the same set as the festival. According to Stuart, Alfie said their record company was really interested in us. They want to see how we get on in the tour."

He's so happy, I can't help but grin. Alex has been dreaming about this for ages, ever since I met him seven years ago. "You can do it, I know you can. How long is the tour for?"

"There're only twenty dates, but spread across three months."

"That's not so bad." At least he'll be home in between. Plus I can go and watch him at the local ones.

"Yeah, I was getting to that. Although there's only twenty, they're also spread across North America, so we're going to need to stay there for the whole three months."

I try not to let my smile falter, but the combination of no sleep and Alex's casually dropped bombshell doesn't make it easy. "Three months?"

"Yeah. I know it's a long time, but the pay is good, in fact it's so good we might be able to save some cash. Like Stuart said, it's our first big break, we'd be crazy to turn it down."

"That's fantastic." Tina walks over and hugs him. "I'm so proud of you." The expression on her face is one of pure delight as she says all the words that are frozen on my tongue. By some force of nature, I keep the smile plastered to my face, but it's a lie. Because that little voice who notices everything pipes up in my brain, pointing out what I already know.

He didn't even ask me what I think about him leaving.

# 10

By the time we get home that evening we've barely said two words to each other. Every time I look at Alex a cocktail of anger and fear squeezes me from the inside out.

Alex carries the buggy up while I hold a sleepy Max in my arms. His breathing is still laboured and harsh, each feeble exhale punctuated by a liquid wheeze. His nose is raw from the way I have to keep wiping it and his lips are dry from his constant attempts to breathe. Even asleep, his eyes are still red-rimmed from his tears.

It hurts to look at him. To know he's suffering. But more than anything, it's breaking my heart to know his daddy doesn't even seem to care.

How can he? If Alex loved him, he wouldn't leave him. He wouldn't leave me, either. And he *is* leaving, I know that much. The way he announced it, using his family as some kind of buffer, tells me how serious he is. If he'd mentioned it to me first, given us time to talk it over, perhaps the outcome would have been different. But he's put it out there for everybody to hear. If I try to stop him, I'm going to look like the bad wife.

A fierce sense of protectiveness takes hold of me. Because as much as I love Alex, I love this tiny, defenceless little boy, too. I carry Max into our bedroom and lay him down in his cot, leaving the covers hanging loosely around him. His mild fever makes him kick the blankets away, tiny legs scrabbling until they're a rumpled pile at the bottom of the cot. He moans, his hands curling into tight fists.

When I walk back into the living room Alex is sitting next to the window, his guitar resting on his knee. He plucks at a few chords, the sound melancholic as it echoes against the glass. He's hunched over, his head lowered over his chest so all I can see is the top of his head. His expression is completely obscured.

"It's Sunday." My voice sounds thick and congested. Maybe I'm catching Max's cold.

Alex looks up, his face blank. "What?" A moment later his brows knit together in confusion. "What do you mean?"

I take a deep breath, closing my eyes in an attempt to calm myself. "I mean it's a non-working day. Not the sort of day that a tour manager would be making calls. It seems weird that today's the first time you've heard about the tour."

Alex stops strumming. There's a faint thud of wood against plaster as he props his guitar against the wall. "What are you trying to say?" His tone is sharp; like a needle, it pierces. "What are you accusing me of this time?"

Though my eyes are still closed, I hear his approach. His bare feet pad across the polished floor boards, each one bringing him closer. Then he's so near I can feel the warmth of him, smell his aftershave. His breaths are hard and heavy, overwhelming my senses. When I open my eyes the tears stream out.

"Is today the first time you've known about the tour?" My words come out as a sob. I've lost it again. But this time it's not anger that's burning me from the inside out. It's hurt and desperation.

"Does it matter? You've made it perfectly fucking clear what you think of it." He's still bitter, still angry. "Whatever I say, you've made up your mind I'm the bad guy. And for the record, yes, I've known it's a possibility. We discussed it last weekend at the festival, but I didn't want to upset you. You were in a bad enough state already."

He takes another deep breath, this time stepping back. The distance between us grows. "Everything's about you, isn't it, babe? Most girls would be delighted for their husbands, but you have to be so fucking melodramatic about it all."

I make his point for him by sobbing louder. Lifting my hand, I angrily wipe the tears away, wishing I didn't look so bloody weak. I'm not that girl who manipulates with tears, who bends and breaks every time she comes up against an obstacle. I'm a fighter, I don't back down. If it wasn't for all these hormones taking over my emotions, holding them hostage, I'd be giving as good as I'm getting.

"You think I'm being unsupportive?" I ask, horrified. "I've done nothing except support you. I've come to all your concerts, always cheered you on. God knows how many times I've slept alone because you've been at the recording studio. And what about paying the fucking rent so you could give up a steady wage and put everything into the band?" The angrier I get, the harder it is to get the words out. I almost spit them.

"Oh, I knew you'd throw that one back in my face. We both know I was made redundant, and we both agreed I'd spend more time on music." He takes a step closer, face red, eyes narrowed. "Who do *you* think has been paying the rent so you could stay at home for six fucking months and look after Max? Do you really think I enjoyed going to a building site every day, breaking my fucking back so you could take extra maternity leave? Well, I didn't. But I did it because I love you and I want you to be happy." He laughs harshly. "Fat lot of good that did."

"I had maternity pay."

"It didn't even cover the rent. But I knew how important being with Max was to you."

I open my mouth to breathe, but my chest constricts painfully. It hurts to speak. "To us." I correct. "Max is important *to us*."

"That's what I said."

"No you didn't. You just compared your bloody band to our son. You think I should understand how important music is to you because you understand how important Max is to me. But that's bollocks, because Max should be important to you, too. And if he was, there's no way you'd want to leave him to go running off with the band for months."

The silence that follows is thick, taking on a life of its own, loaded with anger and accusation. It stretches between us, waiting for somebody to break it. I look at Alex and it's as if I don't know him anymore. A stranger with my husband's face. There's no love or desire or understanding in his expression.

He looks as though he hates me.

Even worse, I can feel my anger reflecting back at him. It's in the set of my mouth, in the furrow of my brow. We stand here, more combatants than lovers, each waiting for the other to strike the final blow. I don't even know if I have it in me anymore. There's nothing I want more than to curl up into a ball and pull a blanket over me, hiding until the storm passes. But it's too late to batten down the hatches, the rain's already flooding in.

"Sometimes I don't know you at all." His voice is calm, maybe too calm. "I'm looking at you and wondering who the hell you are. Because you sure as hell aren't the girl I married."

It hurts as much as the first time he said it; more, probably. Because now I know he really means it. The rejection slaps me right in the face, stinging me. I have to bite at my lips to stifle another sob, but my chest hitches anyway.

"Fuck you." Though I say it quietly, I'm screaming inside. "Even if I've changed it doesn't make me wrong."

"It makes you selfish, though." With these final words he slays me.

I close in on myself, trying to dry my tears with angry hands. Then I turn away, because it hurts too much to look at him anymore.

"Then piss off and leave me alone. I'm clearly holding you back and making you miserable." I turn and leave, holding onto a thin layer of sanity with my fingernails. It hurts to talk, to blink, to breathe. Every movement is excruciating. Yet somehow I walk away.

"Lara?" He sounds uncertain. I wait for him to say something else. I'm still waiting when I walk into our bedroom, and when I throw myself on the bed. Still listening as I curl myself up into a tight, anxious ball.

I wait and nothing comes. Only the sound of a guitar case being zipped, followed by loud footsteps across the living room floor. When I hear the front door slam shut, my whole body stiffens, my mouth falling open into a single, silent scream.

\* \* \*

I hardly sleep that night. As soon as I start to doze off, Max wakes himself up coughing, the hacking turning into throaty sobs as he realises how poorly he feels. So I end up bringing him into bed with me, letting him settle on my chest, his skin hot and clammy as it touches mine. Even when he falls back to sleep he cries softly, and I bend into him, sobbing too.

I don't think I've cried this much since my mum died seven years ago. That's how it feels, as if I'm mourning something. Not the death of my marriage, that's taking it too far; I'm mourning the life I thought I'd have, the slow suffocation of my dreams, as the hopeless optimism inside me takes it's final, rattling breath.

It was meant to be easy, it was Alex and me against the world. When two turned into three we were supposed to become this perfect little unit, walking hand in hand towards a peachy-orange horizon, confident in our happily ever after.

But it doesn't work that way. Instead, I'm alone with a poorly baby, the bed noticeably empty on Alex's side. He hasn't called or texted to tell me where he is. Not that I've tried calling him, either. Because as sad as I am, I'm still angry, too, and the two emotions have fused together, planting ugly thoughts in my mind. Ones where he doesn't give a shit, just disappears and pursues his dreams, leaving Max and me behind like rubbish blowing in the breeze.

The anxiety leaves a bad taste in my mouth. I've had insomnia before, I know the crippling effects of free-floating anxiety, yet I'm still unable to rationalise the fears that wrap around my chest.

No matter how angry I am, I still miss him and the reassuring cadence of his breath close to my ear as I feel the warmth spread over my skin. I wonder where he is, if he's sleeping now. Whether he is feeling the slightest bit guilty about leaving Max and me.

Simply thinking about him again makes me cry harder, so I bury my face in Max's soft, chubby neck, comforting him, taking comfort in return. That's how we pass the night, in a miserable cocoon, our faces wet, and our throats dry.

\* \* \*

"Are you okay?" Holly, Max's nursery care worker, asks as I hand him over, dropping his bag and dummy in the process. I scramble around the floor, trying not to catch her eye, coughing loudly as if to fool her.

"I think I might have caught Max's cold. My eyes have been watering all night." It's a lie, of course, but there's no way I'm going to break down and admit everything in the middle of Rainbow Nursery. Even at my lowest, I have some standards.

"Oh no, poor you." She swings Max onto her hip, and miracle of miracles he doesn't start crying. He seems so much better than last night, which is good, because I feel ten times worse. "There's definitely something going round. Make sure you drink lots of fluids."

I'm five years older than Holly, but I find myself agreeing as if she's a kindly aunt. "I'll slump in my chair and hope for the best," I tell her. Today I plan on being a listener. A really good listener. And maybe if I'm lucky, I'll be able to put my problems into perspective. Other people's tragedies tend to have that effect on me.

By the time I get to work that morning, my limbs feel achy and sore. And though I'm lightheaded, my body feels weighed down, as if I'm trying to wade through a river full of mud. On top of everything else, I'm still on the edge of tears. As much as I try not to, I can't help thinking of Alex and the way he left last night. Our argument replays in my head on a loop, making me question my perceptions and wonder why I was so antagonistic.

It isn't him. It isn't me. It's *us*. Somehow we've got into this spiral of shouting first and thinking second. The red mist descends and blinds us both.

"Lara?" I hear Elaine calling me from her office. She's standing by the door, running a hand through her frizzy grey bob, making it puff up even more than usual. When I catch her eye, her forehead creases like an accordion and I'm thinking *don't ask, don't ask, don't ask*.

"Are you okay?"

Ugh, of course she asks anyway. Of all people, Elaine should know the effect that question has. It melts away the tenuous hold I had on my emotions, allowing them to gush out, drowning me in their wake.

"I'm fi..." That's all I get out before everything collapses. The next thing I know she's gently guiding me into her office, her arm around my waist. She smells like coffee and roses, and for some reason that makes me cry harder. When she pulls out her chair, I sit down automatically, my head dropping.

She doesn't ask questions, she doesn't say anything. Instead she leaves the room, leaving me be for five minutes, coming back with a mug of steaming tea. Lifting it with a shaky hand, I let the brown liquid scald my lips. It's sweet, much more so than I'd normally like.

When I put the mug down, Elaine shoves a handful of crumpled-up tissues at me. The room is silent, save for my sniffs and heavy breathing, and it's beginning to make me feel awkward. Not to mention embarrassed.

What kind of person breaks down at work? I feel humiliated at my little display, knowing everybody must have seen it. I've always taken pride in my professionalism. In being in control. But now I've managed to blow that out of the water, and let them all know what a wreck I am.

"I'm so sorry." I blow my nose loudly. "I don't know what came over me. It's just that Max has been poorly, and neither of us got any sleep so I feel pretty rubbish." I'm not going to tell her about me and Alex. I have to draw the line somewhere.

Elaine shoots me a brief smile. "There's no need to apologise. I've seen much worse, you know."

"From clients, not staff."

"Oh, you'd be surprised at the things that go on around here. A few tears are the tip of the iceberg." She almost looks disappointed that I've stopped crying. "Anyway, I want you to take a look at this." She passes me a piece of paper. Printed on the front are ten questions. Four answers per question. I glance at the first:

*1. I have been able to laugh and see the funny side of things.*

Swallowing hard, I look up at Elaine. "This is the Edinburgh test."

She nods. "I know."

"But that's to help diagnose post natal depression. I haven't got PND." I try to give it back to her.

Patiently, she hands me a pen. "Humour me for a moment."

Neither of us say a word as I answer the questions one by one. I realise I can't remember the last time I looked forward to things, or felt comfortable and carefree. As I get to the end of the test I hand it back silently to her, knowing I've scored well over the requisite ten that's needed to indicate PND. It feels like a personal failure that she's even considering I might have something wrong. I want to cry all over again, this time because she must think me an unfit mother.

"I love Max," I tell her.

"Of course you do. We both know PND doesn't mean you don't love your baby. All it means is that you need a bit of extra help." She hands me another tissue, noticing I've managed to use the first bunch she gave me. "Anyway, this isn't a diagnosis, only an indicator. What I want you to do is go and see your doctor now, and then take the rest of the day off."

I roll my lip between my teeth, worrying, fretting. "I won't get in on short notice."

"I'll call them. You go out and ask Janine to cancel your appointments, and I'll speak with your doctor. Then maybe you can pick up Max and spend the day together."

The thought of more time with Max does perk me up. "Are you sure?"

"Absolutely. You look like the walking dead, there's no way I'm letting you near any of our clients."

For the first time today, a ghost of a smile passes over my lips. "Thank you."

# 11

It's almost lunchtime when I walk out of the doctor's surgery, clutching a leaflet about a local support group and a card for a follow up appointment next week. This one lasted for nearly half an hour—unheard of in my surgery where patients are usually shuffled through like cattle into an abattoir.

Mild depression is how the doctor described it, with the potential to become more severe if it isn't treated. I sat there as he explained the consequences of non-intervention, finding it hard to believe the person he was describing was me.

Walking to the bus stop, I'm hit by a feeling of frustration. The streets are full of workers in their lunch hour; people with determined strides, with somewhere to go, things to do. I feel adrift among the sea of them. It's hard to admit that after everything that's happened, perhaps there is a kernel of truth in Alex's accusations.

So instead of calling my husband, I pick Max up from the nursery, signing him out early. After his sleepless night exhaustion has finally taken its toll, and he naps all the way home.

We make it there a little after two. As I turn the corner into our road, a van driver presses his horn and the loud, short burst of sound wakes up Max. Even though I can't see his face, I can hear his whine, and see his legs as he kicks them, trying to pull off his socks. Though I hate to think it, I'm fed up that he's woken up so soon, spoiling my plans of us both napping all afternoon, trying to catch up on that elusive, lost sleep.

Predictably, his cries become louder, reaching a crescendo when we get to the front door. Loud, repetitive screams, followed by noisy gulps as he fights for air. Pulling him out of his buggy, I see his face is angry, nose streaming, eyes wet.

"Come on, Max." I hug him close. But I'm tired, so tired, and it's an effort to hold him. I lean on the front door, my eyes closed, while Max empties his lungs, his fists gripping at my shirt, and it isn't simply tiredness anymore, it's fatigue. Draining me of energy, it weakens my muscles, makes my bones feel loose and floppy. It takes all I've got to keep standing, let alone hold Max in my arms.

"Stop crying." I bite my lip in an effort not to join in. "Shh now, come on."

Then the door opens, and David is standing there, looking slightly perplexed. "Did you forget your keys?"

I shake my head, afraid if I say anything I'll start all over again. Sleep, I really need sleep.

David takes one look at me, then glances down at Max, whose volume seems to have increased since David opened the door. "Everything okay?"

Once again, I shake my head, squeezing my lips shut. But in spite of my efforts, the tears squeeze out anyway, and I look down, trying not to let him see.

"Come here." He leads me inside, pulling the buggy in with his right hand. Then he gently takes Max from me, hushing him softly, bouncing him up and down. "Let's go into my place. I'll make you a brew."

Tea; the British cure for everything. Even David's worked it out and he's only been here a few months. Without answering I follow him and Max, leaving the buggy at the bottom of the stairs. Of course, he manages to quieten Max almost immediately, and though I'm glad for the silence I can't help but feel useless.

"Is he sick?"

"A cold," I reply, sitting down. "He didn't sleep much last night." Then I remember the thin walls. "Oh God, he didn't keep you awake, did he?"

"Nah, nothing can do that. I heard him crying when I went to sleep and crying when I woke up this morning. I filled in the blanks." He looks at me. "You have to be exhausted after everything that's happened."

He must have heard the row between Alex and me. I add mortification to my list of emotions. "I didn't get much sleep either," I admit.

He makes us both a cup of tea, handing me an old, chipped mug with a photograph of a surfer on it. "Do you want to talk about it?"

"I have mild postnatal depression." It's the first time I've said it to anybody. "At least, that's what the doctor says." There's a part of me that still thinks he's wrong. That I'm only tired. Angry with my husband, suffering from exhaustion.

David is silent for a moment. Still holding Max, he nuzzles him gently. "Claire had that."

"Your girlfriend?" He hasn't mentioned her name before. Rarely talks about her or his daughter.

"Yeah. Right from the start it was clear something was wrong. My mum said it was probably the 'baby blues', that she'd get better as Mathilda got older, but she didn't, she got worse. Looking back, I should have done something earlier, said something to her. Maybe things might have turned out differently."

"How did she get over it?" I lean forward, desperate to know.

He gives me a sickly sweet smile. "She kicked me out."

Oh. Definitely not what I wanted to hear. In the interest of full disclosure, I tell him. "Alex is leaving for three months."

"Really? Why?"

David listens as I recount the whole sorry tale. Some of it he knows, of course. The argument at the festival, the shouting at home. He listens, his face solemn, Max cuddled into his chest, and smiles sadly when I tell him Alex didn't come home last night.

"I'm sorry, I didn't realise how bad things were."

"I'm not sure they were, not really." I crinkle my forehead, trying to sort through the haze of events in my mind. As stupid as it sounds, I can't quite work out when our bickering turned into full blown arguments. When our insults turned from cheeky into bitchy. "But then he's been offered this tour in the States and he didn't even ask me what I thought, just assumed he was going. No mention of Max or leaving me alone with him. No thoughts that he might miss all the little milestones."

"That sucks," David agrees. "But then I can hardly talk, can I? I'm half a world away from my own kid."

"If Claire called tomorrow and said you could see her, would you fly back?"

"I'd be on the next plane out."

That sort of proves my point. Where David would be flying one way, Alex is fleeing in the opposite. It's as if I don't know him anymore. I sit back, rubbing my face with my hands. "Ugh, I'm so confused. I don't know what I'm supposed to do. I wanted a baby, a family. I didn't realise how much things would change."

"Nobody does," David comments quietly, though there's a hint of humour in his voice. "You go around for thirty years thinking the world revolves around you, then suddenly you wake up realising you're pretty insignificant compared to the tiny thing screaming in your arms."

"So why doesn't Alex feel that way?"

"Men are different to women, I think. We compartmentalise a lot better. Even though I think about Mathilda every day, I still function, have a good time. There's a lot of truth in 'out of sight, out of mind', even if I hate to admit it."

Max has finally fallen asleep in David's arms. I sit there for a minute and watch them, the man who has lost his own child, and the baby whose father is leaving him.

"You know, I'm supposed to have all the answers. I help people for a living. It's killing me not to be able to solve my own problems, it's as if I've failed."

"Kind of 'physician, heal thyself?'" He grins. "There's a reason why the mechanics always have the worst cars, and why TV chefs eat TV dinners. Just because you do something as a job doesn't mean you can help yourself. Perhaps you should give yourself a break."

He's right, I know he is. It's not as if Alex has been helping, either. The breakdown in communication is both our faults, though I'm not sure he'd agree.

My mouth pulls open into a yawn, one that starts in my jaw and works downwards, tightening the muscles in my chest. "I can't help feeling it would be easier if I wasn't so tired all the time."

"Now *that* I can help with," David says. "If you bring in the buggy, I can look after this little guy while you take a nap." He inclines his head in the direction of a door, leading, I assume, to his bedroom. "It's okay, there're fresh sheets, and I've hidden the porn."

"Do men even have offline porn anymore?" I wonder aloud, remembering the dog-eared magazines boys used to smuggle into school. "I mean the pictures don't even move."

David gets to his feet, laughing. "Of course. What if there's a power cut? Or the internet gets sabotaged?"

"What's the apocalypse without a wank stash?" I solemnly get to my feet as well, even though I'm almost grinning from my question. "As long as you've hidden it from view I'll be fine. And thank you."

"You're welcome," he says. "Oh, and Lara?"

"Yes?"

"Things will get better. I promise."

Maybe he's right. But I can't help feeling they're going to get a hell of a lot worse first.

\* \* \*

I'm basking in the lull that comes right after waking, when I'm all relaxed and cosy, the soft duvet keeping me warm. I might even be drooling a bit. Shuffling down the mattress, I curl my legs beneath me, letting my mind drift, until I'm slowly floating back.

Then I hear voices. Not loud ones, though they're clear enough for me to make out the words. David's first, instantly recognisable, his vowels rounded out with an antipodean twang.

"She's sleeping, so I said I'd look after Max."

"In your bedroom?" Brasher, shorter vowels.

Alex.

"*Alone* in my bedroom, yes. She's exhausted. The baby kept her awake all night."

I like that response. It's a shame David doesn't add *"as you'd know if you'd actually been here."*

"So why's she not sleeping in our flat?"

"Because I said I'd keep an eye on Max while I work. And knowing Lara, if she slept in your place she'd feel guilty about leaving Max here and wouldn't get any rest at all."

*"Yeah,"* I want to add. *"Because unlike you, it kills me to leave him."*

"Well, I'm home now. I'll take them back upstairs with me."

"She's still asleep. How about I send her up when she wakes up?" David's suggestion sounds so sensible and non-negotiable, but I can imagine Alex's expression right now. I suppose I should get up, go and be the buffer between them. But I'm too tired to move. The mattress is so soft it's as if I'm wrapped in a cloud.

"I don't think so."

Though I squeeze my eyes shut, there's no way I'm going back to sleep. Silently I beg Alex not to make a scene. Not in front of our lovely, sweet neighbour who managed to stop me from cracking up completely. He's given me four hours of delicious, mind numbing sleep.

David's voice comes next. Lower, deeper; a throaty shout-whisper. "I don't know what your problem is with me, but your wife is in a fucking state. I heard her crying all night, then when she came home at lunchtime she looked like death warmed up."

Charming.

"Now she may be a lovely woman, but I'm not a fucking necrophile. Nor am I interested in her like that. But I am her friend, and I want to help her, and the best way to do that was to let her sleep."

"What the fuck do you know about it?"

"A lot more than you do. I know when someone's reached the end of her tether. I know when a woman's suffering from depression."

Oh. I really do need to get up. I push myself to sitting, letting my head fall back against the wall. Bracing myself on the bed, I shuffle out until I'm standing. My legs wobble, but I don't fall down.

"She's not depressed."

"Oh yes, she is. She was diagnosed today. So while you've been off playing Jimi Hendrix, your wife's been crying herself to sleep, blaming herself for everything that's gone wrong."

Then there's silence. I walk to the door, curling my fingers around the jamb, pushing it open with a creak. Standing there, leaning on the painted wood, I watch as my husband and my neighbour, alerted by the groaning hinges, both turn to stare at me. I don't need a mirror to know how bad I look right now. I can feel the tangles in my hair where it is stuck to my cheek, and the way my eyes sting from almost twenty-four hours of tears. But more than that, I can see it in Alex's expression, the way his eyes widen and his jaw drops.

"You look like shit."

"Thanks," I croak. And it's weird, because in spite of everything, I actually feel the best I have all day. Not quite human, but pretty close. It's amazing what a few hours of sleep can do. "Where's Max?"

Alex points to his buggy. "I was going to take him up." For some reason I bristle at that. I have to remind myself Max is Alex's baby, too. Even if I seem more aware of it than Alex, sometimes.

"Okay."

"You coming?"

Throughout the conversation, David remains silent. But this time he turns to look at me. "You can stay here if you want."

Maybe it's the fact I'm still half asleep, but this whole conversation seems slightly off kilter; the kind of inane, incomprehensible words you'd hear in a dream. I have to remind myself this is reality, that Alex is asking me to go upstairs with him, and that David is offering me a refuge.

I have no bloody clue what to do.

I should go back up. Explain calmly and quietly about my possible diagnosis, suggest we both take a breather from accusations and yelling. But a part of me wants to crawl back into David's bed and bury my head beneath the duvet, because I want to block it all out.

"Thank you for letting me use your bed," I tell David. "I haven't slept so well in ages."

"Anytime."

"But I'll go back upstairs with Max. I need to get my stuff ready for work tomorrow." When I reach the buggy, Max is awake, playing with a little hanging toy I've clipped to the frame. His breathing sounds better and he doesn't look as miserable as before. In fact, as soon as he sees me he smiles. It feels like a break in the clouds, a blast of warmth on a snowy day. I crouch down and nuzzle him, rubbing my cheek against his. He makes a grab for my hair and giggles.

This is what it's about. Not the arguments, or the depression or a possible tour halfway across the world. Nothing else really matters except Max being happy and healthy. "Come on, little man. Let's take you up and get you bathed. Get that disgusting crust off your nose."

He burbles something incomprehensible and pulls at my ear.

"I'll do his bath," Alex says. "You can put your feet up and watch some telly."

Um, who is this and what has he done with my husband?

"Okay?" It comes out as a question.

"See you later, David." From the tone in Alex's voice I can tell things are still frosty between them.

David doesn't reply, walking over and rubbing Max's head. "See you later, little fella." Then he pulls me up, giving me a quick hug. "If I hear any shouting I'll be up in a shot," he whispers in my ear.

"There won't be, not from me, I'm too tired."

"It's not you I'm worried about."

As he still holds me, I look over his shoulder, catching Alex's eye. His jaw is tense, his lips a bleached, pale line, and I can tell how unhappy he is about this situation. But instead of pulling back like I normally would, I squeeze David tighter, because he was here for me when I needed him, and I'm so grateful for that.

"Thank you," I whisper into his shoulder. "For everything." I step back and grab my bag, following Alex as he pushes the buggy out of David's flat.

He doesn't even bother to say goodbye.

## 12

Alex can be ruthlessly efficient when he wants to be. As soon as we walk into the flat he deposits me on the sofa, shoving a cup of tea into my unsuspecting hand, and tells me to stay there or else. Then he proceeds to bath Max, tidy the kitchen, and give him his final feed all while I stare on with something close to disbelief. Max seems similarly gobsmacked, looking curiously at Alex as he holds him in his arms.

If I'm being really honest, I don't like him taking over. I miss snuggling up with Max, watching his rosebud lips move rhythmically as he sucks at the bottle, seeing his pale grey eyelids slowly flutter closed when he finally gives in to exhaustion. I wonder if Alex feels this pang of jealousy whenever he watches the two of us. Max is a fickle little thing, willing to batter his eyelashes at whoever happens to be in control of his milk.

After putting Max to bed, Alex heads into the kitchen and grabs a beer from the fridge. "You want one?"

I'd kill for a glass of wine, but it's a mood enhancer for me. Great when I'm feeling full of the joys of spring. Right now? Not such a good idea. "No thanks."

"A glass of water?"

Now I'm confused. Since when did I become the water guzzling type? Is it something I should be doing now I'm a mum, along with shedding the final few pounds and remembering to do my kegels every day? "I'm fine."

He sits down on the battered leather easy chair across from me and takes a long gulp of beer. His Adam's apple bounces up and down as he swallows. When he puts the bottle on the scratched wooden table beside him, he looks at me. "So what did the doctor say?"

"He thinks I have mild post natal depression. I have to go back again next week. If things haven't improved he wants to talk about happy pills."

Alex's eyes widen. "Seriously? It's that bad?"

"Not at the moment. But he's worried it could get worse."

His face crumples, and he takes another swig of beer. "How bad can it get?"

For a moment I consider telling him about puerperal psychosis, about the women who are locked away to protect themselves and their babies. But he looks shocked enough as it is, and no matter how fed up I am with this whole situation, there's no point in making it worse.

"I don't know. But the big thing is identifying it. Now I know I can work on things."

"I guess that explains some stuff."

I can feel my blood pressure rising; there's no way he's going to blame all our problems on this. The PND didn't make him smoke weed when he promised not to and it didn't force him to sign up for a three month tour in another country without even consulting me. I open my mouth to let it all out and then...

I close it again. No shouting; I promised David. Anyway, I'm so tired, I don't know if I have the energy to stand my ground. Instead I sit there, staring down at my knees, wondering how the hell we got here.

A little over six months ago I was lying on an uncomfortable hospital bed in Hackney, watching Alex holding a bundled up Max in his arms, tears pouring down his cheeks. And despite all the pain and the mess and everything else that comes with a ten hour labour, I can remember thinking how completely perfect everything was for us.

We had a healthy baby, a good, strong marriage, and I honestly didn't think anything would threaten that.

How can things change so drastically in such a short time?

"I'll call Stuart," Alex says.

I look up at him questioningly. What does Stuart have to do with this? "Why?"

"To tell him I'm pulling out of the tour."

My first thought is, *hasn't he done that already?* After last night and all the painful arguments we had, why the hell hasn't he already considered this? And it comes to me, a little flash of insight. He didn't pull out of the tour this morning because he doesn't want to. The only reason he's thinking about it now is because I've got an actual medical diagnosis.

He's acting from guilt, not concern.

"No."

He frowns. "What do you mean?"

"I mean don't cancel. Not because of this. I can cope without you."

He looks shocked. I don't blame him, I'm pretty surprised myself. "I can't go, not when you're like this."

"Like what?"

"You know, all upset and sick and stuff."

I want to throw my hands up in despair, so I sit on them instead. "What's changed since yesterday?" I ask. "I was upset yesterday. I didn't see you running to call Stuart then."

"I spent the night at his place. We talked about whether we should tour or not. But now... what if you get worse? What if you're too sick to look after Max?"

"The only reason you've changed your mind is because some doctor has written something down on my record. I'm still me. The same Lara as last night." I'm frustrated because he isn't getting my point. I don't want him to change his mind because of me.

I want him to not *want* to go.

Yes, it's a petty distinction, but it's important to me.

He drains the last of his beer, and I can tell from the way his hand shakes he wants another. I'm regretting avoiding alcohol myself.

"I can't win, can I?" His voice is quiet. "I'm damned if I go and I'm buggered if I don't. There's literally no pleasing you."

My throat constricts. He's right, of course. We've got to the point where neither of us can turn around, but we can't go forward either. Somehow we've managed to tie ourselves in knots. And it hurts, because I love him, I want him to be happy. I can't see a solution where all of us get to be that way.

"You should go. If you stay, you'll blame me and I'll blame myself."

"And if I go, you'll blame me," he points out.

"Yes, but I like that option better." I deadpan it, but he smiles anyway.

"I don't know, babe." He sits back, pulling at the foil on the neck of his bottle. "I hate to say it but it's your call."

But it's one I don't want to make. I can't win either. If I say stay, it will kill him. If I tell him to go, it will kill me.

"You should go. You want to, I know you do."

"I'm sorry," he says softly, not trying to deny it.

Maybe that's the problem. We're both sorry, yet somehow we can't seem to do anything about it. He wants what he wants and I do, too. The difficulty is our wants are too far apart. The distance growing with each passing moment.

"So am I."

So that's it. He's going to America and I'm staying here and I have no idea where that leaves us.

\* \* \*

As it turns out, it takes a lot of effort to get ready for a three month tour. I was expecting the rehearsals—they've been part of my life for longer than I care to admit—but there's a hundred other things to do as well. Time-consuming things like queueing up at embassies for work visas and arranging for import licences, as well as transportation for all their instruments and equipment. There are roadies to recruit and sound mixers to talk to, not to mention packing enough clothes for the tour. I watch Alex getting more excited by the day, his hard edge becoming more apparent than ever, as Max and I try to get on with everyday life.

It couldn't be more obvious that our paths are diverging. I go to work, to the nursery, cry my heart out at the self-help group I've started to attend and Alex doesn't even notice. He's too busy choosing shirts to wear on stage and breaking in three different pairs of shoes.

He's coming together and I'm falling apart. If I had any energy left, I'd be angry about it.

The following Tuesday I go to my first PND support group meeting. I don't know what I was expecting it to be like, but I'm surprised when I hear that our group of six will be meeting at the local park. I push Max's buggy through the gates, scanning the greenery, looking for women who are crying and screaming at their babies, but see only a serene group of mums standing near the duck pond.

As I get closer, they notice me, and a dark-haired woman steps out from the group, smiling at me. "Lara?" she asks.

I nod, feeling uncertain. They all look so… normal. Surely they can't be feeling the same turmoil inside that I am?

"I'm Diane, it's lovely to meet you. Come and join us. We're going to take a walk around the park, and then grab a coffee from the café. Let me introduce you to everybody."

In the hour that follows, I learn that our depressions run the gamut from mild to severe. There's a quiet twenty-something with a two year old strapped in his buggy who has had to be hospitalized due to her illness. She was only released a few weeks ago.

Another mum, a lady called Debbie, chats to me as we walk behind the group. "How long have you been diagnosed?" she asks.

"About a week." I feel like an imposter compared to some of the others. "My doctor referred me to the group."

She smiles. "That's good, they caught you early. They had to put me on medication straight away when I finally admitted how low I was. I'd kept it bottled up, I was so scared they were going to take Maisie away from me." We both look down at her daughter, who is fast asleep in her pram. "I wish I'd gone sooner, it would have made all the difference."

We reach the edge of a copse of trees. The path snakes through them, and we twist and turn to follow it. "My husband's leaving for a few months," I tell her. "I think that's when I reached breaking point."

"How come?"

I explain the situation to her, feeling more relaxed as she nods and consoles, never once judging either me or Alex for the way we've been behaving. By the time we get to the café, the others are already ordering from the hatch that serves the outside tables. I buy myself a latte, then join the rest of them as we sit at the metal tables, circling the buggies around us.

"Anybody want to tell us how their week went?" Diane, the support-worker asks.

Debbie starts, sharing that her medication is being reduced and that the doctor is happy with her progress. I sit back and listen, occasionally rocking Max's buggy when he starts to rouse, and it feels good to know I'm not alone in this fog of depression. Though I know it's a long road, and there are no easy answers, somehow it helps to understand that I don't have to do this by myself.

By the time the hour is up, and Max and I are heading for home, it feels like I'm able to breathe again.

* * *

Two days before Alex is due to leave I'm in the kitchen, warming up some puréed vegetables for Max, who is sitting in his highchair and banging his spoon on the blue plastic tray in front of him. He looks delighted at the racket he's making, and every now and again he throws the spoon to the floor, squealing loudly until I pick it up again.

When the buzzer sounds, I frown and immediately look at my watch. It's almost six, too early for Alex who isn't due back from a meeting until half past seven, and David always knocks, living in the same building and all.

"Don't move," I say to Max, who completely ignores me. Then I ping off the microwave and make my way to the intercom, half-tripping over a box full of music sheets. Our entire flat is full of equipment for the tour. The couriers are due to pick it up in the morning, ready to fly everything out to the States. Walking across the living room has turned into some kind of physical challenge.

"Stuart?" I'm surprised when he gets to the door after I've buzzed him in. What's he doing here? Surely he should be at the same meeting as Alex. He is, after all, the drummer. "Alex isn't here..." I make a face.

"I know." He takes his cap off and runs his fingers through his hair, shifting uncomfortably. "I wondered if I could have a quick word."

I've known Stuart as long as I've known Alex, though as an acquaintance more than anything else, yet he can't bring himself to meet my eyes.

"Of course," I clear my throat, feeling as out of place as he does. "Please come in. Mind the boxes and stuff."

"Christ, I'm surprised it all fits." He walks over to the huge black cases containing his drum kit. Runs his fingers down the thick plastic. "Make sure they take care of it when they pick it up."

"I'll be at work." That's Alex's job. I may have agreed to him going but that doesn't mean I'm going to make life easy.

"How is work?" Stuart tugs at his shirt, then shoves his hands into his pockets. "You enjoying being back there?"

I shrug. "It's fine." I'm pretty sure he doesn't want to hear about my day. In fact I still can't work out why he's here at all. But being me, I'm not quite sure how to ask him. "Would you like a cuppa? I was about to feed Max."

His eyes widen in alarm and I suppress a laugh.

"Not that sort of feeding. Vegetables." I grab the bowl from the microwave and wiggle it about.

"He can eat food?"

I nod. Despite being Alex's friend and band mate, Stuart hasn't seen a lot of Max. The only time I remember him holding him was when Max was about two months old. He'd looked so uncomfortable I'd taken pity on him and scooped Max from his arms. As I recall, Stuart thanked me under his breath.

"Yeah. We'll have him on curry next." It's no joke, either. I'm determined to introduce him to a variety of foods. I don't want him to be a fussy eater.

After I've fed Max and he's on the floor, I hand Stuart a mug of tea and we manage to find a spot to perch on the sofa. I take a sip while Stuart taps out a tune with his foot, and I notice him stealing glances at me.

Finally, he clears his throat.

"I... ah... Alex said you hadn't been well."

I feel a flush creep up my chest. "Did he?"

Stuart slumps back in his chair. "Yeah. I'm sorry to hear that."

"Okay..." I still don't have the slightest hint of where this is going. All I know is it's awkward as hell.

"But you're better now, right?"

For the first time, he holds my gaze. I hadn't noticed how steel blue his eyes were before. I *have* noticed that they always seem rimmed with red.

"Not exactly," I say. "I'm having good days and bad days. The doctor says it will take a while for things to calm down."

Stuart nods rapidly while I tell him this. His fingers are tapping out a beat on his mug, now. "But you'll be okay while Alex is away?"

I soften. His question is kind of sweet, in a weird way. "I'll be fine. I've got my friends and family to take care of me. Not to mention being busy at work and with Max."

A smile pulls at his lips. "That's good, right?"

"Sure." It's been great, actually. Everybody's rallied round since I told them about my depression. The first weekend Alex is away I'm going to visit my dad. A few weekends after that, Tina's organised a big family picnic. I may be a lot of things while he is on tour, but bored isn't likely to be one of them.

"So, I wanted to ask you a favour. Actually the whole band does." He puts his empty mug on the coffee table. "Alfie, too," he adds.

"What sort of favour?" I ask, imagining taking delivery of stuff, or taking care of their girlfriends.

"It's about Alex, really. You know what he gets like before a gig? All angry and wound up? Well, I'm guessing he's going to be like that constantly while we're on tour."

I swallow nervously, saying nothing. In spite of the sugar, the tea leaves a bad taste in my mouth.

"Well, I know what you two can be like. When you..." He trails off, tugging at his hair. "When you, um, rile him up, there's no getting through to him. And that will be a real nightmare for us all."

The apples of my cheeks start to burn. We really aren't that bad. Maybe the past couple of months have been hard, but Stuart is exaggerating. "What do you want me to do?" I ask through gritted teeth.

"Maybe try not to talk to him that much. Don't say anything that will make him react. He's nervous as hell, the last thing we need is for him to be worrying about you as well as everything else."

So this isn't about me at all. Stuart's not concerned about my welfare, or whether Max and I will be okay on our own. He's scared I'm going to do something to affect the band.

"I don't plan on upsetting him."

"Do you ever plan on it? Do you know how long it took to persuade him to go on stage at the festival? He was pulling his hair out, thinking he'd upset you. If he does that on tour then that's it. We'll have blown our big chance. Everything we've been working for all these years." He leans forward, staring at me. "I know you want what's best for him," he says softly. "And keeping him calm is what's best."

Slowly I nod, even though I'm raging inside. As much as I hate to admit it, Stuart's right. At the moment, I'm volatile enough for the both of us. I know Alex will be nervous as hell, the last thing he needs is me shouting or crying down the phone.

"So you'll help?" Stuart asks. "All you have to do is reassure him everything's okay, like you know it will be. And if there's a problem you don't want to upset him with, you can call me or Alfie. We can either sort something out or work out the right way to deal with him."

My throat constricts. I've been so wrapped up in myself and Max, I've not thought about how Alex must be feeling. And of course he's excited—it's their big break, who wouldn't be—but he has to be scared, too.

What kind of wife am I? I make a vow that for the last two nights I'm going to hold him close, try and show him how much I care. "Of course I'll help."

"Really?" Stuart's eyes light up. "Shit. Thank you."

"No problem." I flash him a smile, and remind myself it's only three months. It'll be over before I know it.

Yeah, right.

"I guess I'd better get back. The guys will be wondering where I am. They can't keep time for shit without me." Stuart stands up, glancing sideways down at Max. "Thanks for being so understanding."

I give him an unconvincing smile and show him out, scooping Max up on the way. As I get him ready for bed—bathing him and reading a story—I realise I'm already feeling like a single parent and Alex hasn't even gone yet.

The thought makes my chest ache.

# 13

"I'm going to miss you." Alex is playing footsie with me beneath the table. His expression is soft, his eyes softer. We've got through nearly a bottle and a half of red wine and it's made my focus a bit hazy, like one of those 'tasteful' photo shoots where your friends dress up like hookers.

"You won't have time," I reply, scooping the last spoonful of honeycomb ice cream. "You'll be too busy strutting across stages and being awesome. Not to mention fighting off groupies with a baseball bat."

He reaches across the table and grabs my wrist, circling his fingers around my skin. He has that look on his face, the one that hooked me, reeled me in and turned my life upside down. The one that makes me feel like the only woman in the room.

"You're the only groupie I want."

I can't remember the last time we went out for dinner. Alex has chosen a tiny trattoria in Hoxton. It's surprisingly unpretentious; the wait staff, who all seem to be genuine Italians, don't blink an eyelid at his ripped jeans and tattoos.

I stare back at him, trying to memorise the contours of his face. The curve of his lips, the slight bump on his nose. There's the smallest sliver of a scar on his left cheek from an accident when he first started shaving. Being the only male in his house growing up meant he was self-taught.

In spite of the copious amount of food and drink I've forced inside it, my stomach tightens. He's been so sweet these past few days, so caring, it's breaking my heart to say goodbye. Yet, tomorrow morning at six a car will pull up outside our flat and he'll climb inside and head for the airport, leaving me and his son behind.

I swallow hard, remembering Stuart's words. *Don't make it harder than it has to be.*

"I'll be your groupie when you get back."

Slowly, he shakes his head. A smile ghosts across his lips. "Tonight."

The waiter chooses this opportunity to hand over the bill. Alex glances at the paper then hands his card over, fingers keying in his pin. All the while he presses his foot to mine, nudging me. A physical reminder of his words.

When we step outside, the cool night air doesn't sober us one bit. Instead I stumble into him, and Alex steadies me, grabbing my waist with his strong, rough hands.

A jolt of desire shoots through me, making me light headed. Alex pushes me onto the wall behind us, his body pressed to mine, head dipping to run his lips down my neck. The hair on my skin stands up and I shiver in spite of the body heat covering mine.

When his lips reach the corner of my mouth I'm so ready for him. My breath has already shortened in anticipation, making my chest move rapidly against his. A moment later he lifts his hand to my face, cupping my jaw, angling me until our lips meet.

When he kisses me it's hard and fast, enough to turn the bones in my legs to jelly. I clutch his shirt, feeling the muscles in his back ripple as he hitches one of my legs around his hip.

It's a quiet road, but I'm thirty-one, not sixteen. I pull away, laughing softly. "I know I said I'd be your groupie, but this is a little too public, even for me."

He slides his palms down my back, following the curve of my spine. Reaching my behind, he digs his fingers in, moving them in slow, teasing circles. "There's nobody here."

"Yet..."

There's a hint of cockiness to his smile. "You're not being a very good groupie."

I bark out a laugh. "They chucked me out of groupie school. I failed the blow job in an alley class."

He inclines his head to one side. "Yeah? I beg to differ."

He's remembering... oh God I really did that, didn't I? My skin heats up as I recall that night, not long after we met, when we ended up lost in Shoreditch, barely able to keep our hands off each other. Somehow we found ourselves in a dead end, kissing and sighing and groaning. Then I sank to my knees, unzipping his jeans, slowly running my finger down the hard ridge of his cock.

"I passed?" I ask softly.

"Every fucking time."

In the end we make it home with our virtues intact. I regain my composure enough to make small talk with Alex's mum before he bundles her into a taxi, shoving a wedge of notes into her hand.

By the time he gets back into the flat I've moved away from the window and am checking on Max, standing in the doorway of our bedroom, staring into the gloom. As I watch the blankets softly falling and rising, I feel Alex behind me, his breath hot on my neck. We stand there for a little while, silent, unmoving, watching our son sleep. I try not to acknowledge how bittersweet it all feels, knowing this is his last night, that tomorrow I'll be doing this on my own.

He'll be surrounded by people, by musicians and fans all out to party. And though I trust him, I still hate the thought of anybody trying to touch him, to get close to him. Maybe he senses my change in mood, because he's gentle as he pulls me away from the door, his fingers slowly sliding down the straps of my dress until they're resting on my upper arms. He's still behind me, his hot breath whispering against my spine.

"I'm going to remember you like this." He slides my zip down, a single finger tracing down my back. "Your perfect skin. The way it's so fucking soft." His lips graze my back, then he falls to his knees, pulling my dress with him until it's a pool of silk at my feet.

Taking me by the hips, he turns me around until I'm facing him, wearing only my underwear and a pair of stupidly high heels. Neither of us says a word as he runs his hands up my legs, his fingers caressing my thighs, following the same path with his soft lips. I try not to cry out as his narrowed gaze catches mine.

My legs start to tremble as his lips reach the top of my thigh, and he brushes them against the sensitive inner skin. I steady myself on his shoulders, seeing the contrast between my pale hands and his tattoos, feeling his muscles flex beneath his flesh. Then he nudges my knickers to the side, simply breathing on me, and it's all I can do to keep upright.

"I've got you," he says, hands cupping my bottom, pulling me towards him. A moment later he trails his tongue against me, making my inner muscles contract, and I start to fall. Alex lifts me onto the sofa, pulling my knees apart and burying his face in me until my breaths become moans.

And he's right, he's got me.

* * *

Things always look darker in the middle of the night, and my thoughts are no exception. I wake up, blinking, disoriented for a moment until I realise I'm lying in my own bed. Alex must have carried me back here at some point; the last thing I remember is drifting off on the sofa, naked in his arms. Our bodies were all but stuck together, a soft sheen of sweat covering us both.

Now, he's behind me, his arm draped across my stomach, the metallic strap of his watch making patterns on my skin. Squinting, I turn my head to the alarm clock. It's nearly four, only two hours until he's due to leave.

It's only a few months. People are apart for longer. Business trips, holidays, wars. And if it was only me I think I could cope, gear myself up enough to make it through the weeks, maybe even enjoy a bit of independence.

But with Max as well? I don't know.

I think of all the milestones he could miss in three months. Max is changing every day, taking on an identity of his own. Two months ago he could hardly move, and now he's rolling like a ninja. It makes me sad to think Alex is going to miss so much.

Sad for Max who needs his daddy.

Sad for me who needs him, too.

But most of all, I'm sad for Alex.

In an attempt to get comfortable, I shuffle down the bed. Alex's arm falls away, and I miss it already. So I turn and nestle into him, breathing in the smell of soap and cologne that clings faintly to his skin, listening to his heartbeat. Tomorrow night there will be an empty space, and I wonder where he will be sleeping; in some scummy motel, sharing a bed with Stuart, maybe smelling of weed more than soap.

My stomach clenches at the thought, and I'm already regretting the things I haven't said. I'm half inclined to wake him up simply to remind him to take care. To look after his body and not abuse it. Maybe I can text him every now and then, remind him to eat his vegetables and brush his teeth.

*You're not his mum, Lara.*

I know that, but I'm his wife and no matter how up and down we've been I love the hell out of him. What's wrong with asking him to look after himself?

*When you can look after your own health, maybe then you can worry about him.*

Ugh. I roll my eyes at my own inner musings and squeeze my eyes shut, trying to block it out. Drifting back to sleep, I snuggle closer to Alex, not ready to let him go.

When I wake up in the morning, he's already left.

# 14

The following Saturday Max and I are sitting on a train, heading for Woolstone, the Dorset town where I grew up. Though it's been years since I lived here, the journey is familiar and strangely comforting. The old, derelict buildings lining the track as we pull out of London give way to the open fields of the English countryside. The criss-cross patchwork of farmlands are ripe with crops; all verdant greens and golden yellows, only weeks away from harvest.

It's easy to forget about the countryside when you're living in the city, but the grey concrete and silver-glass buildings are no match for nature's magnificence. For the first time I find myself wondering if London is the right place to be bringing up a baby.

Not that my own childhood was completely idyllic. Sure, for the first few years all I can remember are picnics in wooded glens and afternoon teas in the garden, but I suspect that's more a product of rose-tinted glasses than reality. By the time I was a teenager, living in the middle of nowhere was more of a drag than anything. I can remember grumbling to my mum that the last bus home left town at ten o'clock, just when the evening was getting started.

By the time the train pulls in to Woolstone station, I've already strapped Max into his buggy and am standing next to the door, ready to get off. A nice woman helps carry the buggy onto the platform for me, and then I'm pushing him towards the exit.

My dad is waiting in the car park, leaning on his Ford Focus, which I note is sparkling clean. He used to wash it every Sunday without fail when I was a child; I'm guessing that's a habit he hasn't grown out of.

"Hi." I push Max over to him and Dad leans forward to give me a kiss on the cheek. Though he's cleanly shaved, his skin still feels rough, his face ruddy from being out in the sun.

He looks old, even more so than the last time I saw him, almost six months ago. But what makes me feel really bad is how his face lights up when he sees us. I'm such a neglectful daughter.

"Hello, beauty." He hugs me tight, then crouches down to look at Max. "And look at you, little man. You're growing up."

Max stares at him. His lips wobble a bit, and I wonder if he's going to cry.

"I've borrowed a car seat, I hope that's okay. A friend of mine has one for her grandson."

I'm touched. This is the man who has never changed a nappy in his life, the one who spent most of my childhood working, rarely coming home before I was in bed. "That's great, thank you."

After we go through the rigmarole of strapping Max in, I climb in the front next to Dad. Like the outside, the interior of the car is sparkling. Despite being five years old, it still smells new.

"How's the garden?" I ask. Since his retirement and Mum's death, he's become a gardening addict. The last time we visited he spent hours describing all the plants he was growing. I came away knowing more Latin than I knew what to do with.

"It's good. I picked some salad for our lunch. And I've got some peas you can take back with you, if you like."

"Sounds lovely. How are the potatoes doing?"

"I'm nearly out of the first batch. I've planted some late growing ones, though."

When we pull up to the house I feel a twinge dragging at my chest. Apart from the garden—which is indeed looking gorgeous—it seems as though nothing has changed. I could be eighteen, coming back from my first term at University, and my mum could be waiting inside in the kitchen with a cup of tea.

Of course, she isn't. It doesn't lessen the lump I feel in my throat, though.

Ever the gentleman, Dad opens my door and helps me to get Max out. The baby twists and turns his head, looking at the trees, the flowers, and the vegetable garden Dad has planted at the back. When he spots some birds perched in the old oak tree, he points excitedly, his face lighting up.

"Birdies," I tell him.

Max nods, his expression serious.

"How's Alex?" Dad asks when we are sitting at the kitchen table. Max is on my lap, sucking at a Farley's rusk. We wait for the tea to brew in the familiar green and grey teapot that Mum loved so much. Leaf tea, of course. My dad has never been one for tea bags.

"He's fine. The band has their first gig tonight." The lump in my throat is back. Of course, I haven't told my dad about our arguments or my depression. Maybe if Mum was here I'd be spilling my guts, but I suspect my dad would run screaming. "His mobile phone contract is all mucked up, though, so he's having to call me on his friend's one." I make a face. Typical Alex not to have realised he needed to set up a roaming contract. And when I tried to sort it out his provider told me he had to call himself. Which he can't, because his bloody phone isn't working.

"You have it easy nowadays. I remember going on business trips and having to search out a phone box to call your mother. That's when we had a phone, of course. We didn't in our first flat."

I've heard this story before. How they used to have to borrow their neighbour's phone in an emergency, and that Dad arrived late to the hospital after my brother was born, having been blissfully ignorant at a football match.

"Have you heard from Graham?" I ask. My brother is fifteen years older than me. He emigrated to New Zealand when I was eight. Though Mum never admitted it, I'm pretty sure I was a mid-life mistake. She was forty-three when I was born.

"They sent a card and a letter on my birthday. Daniel's graduated from University." He's my nephew, who I've never met. I'm ashamed to say I'm not even friends with them on Facebook. When I think about how close Alex's family are, it makes me sad.

"What did he study?"

"Oh, I don't know, some new-fangled thing to do with computers." Dad pours milk into a cup, then places the strainer over it before tipping the tea pot up. He still has the same teacups from when I was little, too. Delicate bone china with a Chinese pattern. Mum once told me they were a wedding present.

"Sounds lucrative."

Dad scratches his head. "I suppose so."

We spend the afternoon in the garden, Dad pulling up weeds and cutting the grass as Max entertains himself playing with the mud. When he falls asleep, I put him in his buggy under the shade of the big oak tree, and I lie on the blanket, drifting off with him. I'm dreaming about bluebirds and crows when my phone rings, the piercing trill merging with my dream, morphing into a birdsong for a moment, until the persistence rouses me.

"Hello?"

"Hey, can you hear me?" Alex's voice sounds distant and tinny.

Immediately I sit up, covering my ear with my hand so I can concentrate on the phone. "Just about. How are you?"

"Good, yeah. Tired though. We ended up in some dodgy bar last night and Stu got a bit drunk. Turns out the locals really don't like being called rednecks. How are you and Max?"

I glance over at the baby, reclined in his buggy, and a smile creeps across my lips. He looks so peaceful here, it's as though the fresh air is some kind of panacea. I can't imagine letting him sleep in our rotten backyard at home.

"We're good. We miss you, though. How are you feeling about tonight?" From the position of the sun in the sky, I'm guessing it's mid-afternoon here, which makes it early morning in Seattle, where the tour is starting.

"Sick with nerves. We've got a sound check in a while so I'm trying not to think about it 'til then. Listen, I've got to go. We're heading out for breakfast. Give Maxie a kiss from me, okay?"

My stomach drops. I know he's trying not to abuse Stuart's friendship by using his phone too much, but we've been talking for less than a minute. "Oh, okay. Can you call me after the gig, let me know how you get on?"

"It'll be the middle of the night, babe."

"I'll be awake, I expect," I say dryly. "But you could text me otherwise."

"Yeah, sure. I'll try to call. Put your phone on silent in case you're asleep, I'll leave a message."

That's all it takes to cheer me up. "Sounds good. I love you."

"Love you too, sweetheart. Give Max a kiss from me."

"I will."

\* \* \*

Max is so worn out from all the fresh air that he only wakes up once. I tiptoe across my childhood bedroom to pick him up, and amazingly he goes back to sleep before I even have time to think about feeding him. Suspecting some kind of ruse, I lay awake for a while, listening to him breathing, waiting for the crescendo of cries I'm convinced are coming.

But he remains silent.

This is where I should fall back to sleep myself, make up for all the hours and minutes I've lost since Max was born. Sadly, I'm wide awake. So I toss and turn in my bed for a while, occasionally checking my phone for messages, trying to swallow down the disappointment when there isn't any flashing light.

At three o'clock I remind myself that even if they're the opening act they could still be on stage. At four I make the excuse that he's probably watching the gig. By the time six arrives, my wakefulness is only enhanced by the tuneful cacophony of the dawn chorus, as the birds wake up to another beautiful morning.

There's still no message.

Okay, so there could be a hundred reasons for his lack of communication. Most likely Stuart's phone has run out of charge. Or maybe they're celebrating a little too much, and he's too busy drinking and smoking to remember his promise.

I shake my head at my foolishness and quickly tap out a text, asking Stuart how it went. They'll call me when they get a chance.

It's still early when I creep downstairs to make a cup of tea. Though the days have been hot, the early mornings still retain an edge of chill, and I pull my cardigan around me to stave off the shivers. In my efforts to pack light, I have no slippers, and the flagstone floor is cold on my bare feet.

When I pull open the kitchen door, light floods through the entrance, casting a pool of yellow on the creamy-grey floor. My dad sits at the table, a cup of half-drunk tea in front of him. The paper is open on the cryptic crossword as he fills the squares in with meticulous script. Eventually he looks at me over the rims of the reading glasses he's had to wear for the last few years.

"Would you like a cup?"

Even when it's only him, he brews the tea in the pot. I wonder if it's simply an old habit, or whether he really prefers it that way. For a moment, I consider buying him a pot for one, but that seems so sad. So final.

"Yes, please." I pull a chair up and crane my neck to look at the crossword. "How are you getting on?"

"I've only just started. It seems fairly simple this week."

"Do you do the crossword every Sunday?"

"Every day," he says. "The crossword and Radio Two in the mornings. The garden in the afternoon."

I can remember when he was a real career man. Always talking about his projects at work. That seems a lifetime ago, now.

"Have you thought about doing some online?" I ask. "There's loads of good quiz sites, I bet there's hundreds of crosswords."

He looks at me as if I'm crazy. "Why would I need hundreds? I only need one."

While he pours my tea I pull my phone out of my pocket. No message.

"Expecting a call?" he asks.

Shrugging, I take a sip. "Alex should be off stage by now. I thought he might phone me."

Dad clears his throat, and pushes the crossword away. "Is everything okay? With you and Alex?"

"Yes." Immediately defensive, I try to deflect. "Why wouldn't they be?"

Looking as awkward as I feel, Dad continues regardless. "I don't know, maybe a few things you said. When you called last week to ask if I was free this weekend you sounded very... sad. If your mother was alive she'd be able to ask you, but she's not... so..." He trails off and shrugs, unable to catch my eye. I realise how hard it must be for him to ask me the question. He's never been an emotional man, has always been traditional. Mum did all the caring in our house, he was simply the provider.

If he can put himself out there, why can't I?

"Things aren't great," I admit. "The doctor says I have postnatal depression, and I didn't want Alex to leave. We've been having lots of arguments." I take another mouthful of tea to stop my voice from wobbling. I feel so uncomfortable it isn't even funny,

Dad's silent for a while; long enough for me to think he's gone back to his crossword. But when I look up, he's still staring at me. He hasn't shaved yet, and grey stubble has formed into a grizzly half-beard on his jaw. His eyes are pale and watery.

"You know, being a parent isn't easy. It's bound to shake up your relationship. I can remember your mother and I having all sorts of arguments."

My interest is immediately piqued. Ignoring the incongruity of getting relationship advice from my very-stoic father, I press on. "Really? I don't remember that."

"We even split up for a few days when your brother was a baby. I ended up sleeping on the floor at a friend's house."

"Why did you split up?" My eyes are wide and I'm more shocked than I can say. In spite of their traditional roles they always seemed so happy. It's strange having to look back over my family history with a revisionist eye.

"We argued about cake." He looks down, shamefaced.

I can't help but laugh. "Cake? Seriously?" I angle my head to one side. "Victoria sponge or chocolate?"

"Laugh all you want, it was deadly serious at the time. Graham had been poorly for a little while. Measles or chickenpox, I can't remember. I was doing all this stupid overtime at work to save up a deposit for a house. Back in those days you needed a hefty one to get a mortgage, it wasn't as easy as it is now."

I think of our poky rented flat, and the cost of buying somewhere in London, but choose not to say anything. Besides, I'm more interested in the cake.

Not to mention the news that my mum and dad split up.

"So I come home for tea, and there's a couple of stale sandwiches and some abomination from Mr Kipling. I turned to your mother and asked her why she hadn't made a nice lemon cake instead, and that was it. Armageddon, Mr Kipling style."

"Oh..." I say. "I bet she was angry." A sick child, an absent husband and then unwarranted criticism. It all sounds strangely familiar.

"She was furious. I couldn't understand why. How long does it take to bake a cake anyway? And I've never liked the ones you can buy from the shop."

"But still, Graham was sick. She must have been exhausted."

"I realise that now. But back then I took it for granted that she could cope. There weren't all these self-help books or people telling fathers what they should do. I assumed I'd be like my own dad. He didn't take an interest in any of us. Just came home to eat his dinner before buggering off to the pub."

"So she chucked you out?"

"That she did. I managed three days before I came crawling back with my tail between my legs. Even then she made me wash my own shirts for a month."

I laugh out loud. At this moment I miss her so much. From the look on my dad's face, he does too. No more lemon cakes, no more pithy words. Nobody to tell me I'm doing okay as a mum.

"I wish she could see Max." I give him a watery smile. "She would have loved him."

"Yes, she would," Dad agrees. "One of her greatest regrets was that she only got to see Daniel once. If she was alive now, she'd be dragging me up to London every week."

"You should come up more often," I say. "Even if you don't want to stay at ours, you could come up for the day. I'll even bake you a cake."

He catches my eye. "I've tasted your cakes, remember? Your home economics teacher said she'd never seen anybody cremate a Madeira cake before."

"You remember that?"

"Remember it? I dined out on it for days. I was so proud of how clever you were at maths. I couldn't give a damn about the cooking, I thought it was funny."

The lump in my throat grows into the size of a rock. It's strange how you have an image of your parents as you're growing up that's so different to the one they project when you're an adult. As much as we've grown apart since Mum died, I can feel this connection between us. It's peaceful, makes me feel content.

"Maybe I should bake Alex a cake," I muse.

"You're wanting a divorce then?"

We both start laughing. It feels so good, letting the giggles out as I hear my father's husky chuckles, both of us unable to stop. We stay that way for a few minutes, until I hear Max's cries from my bedroom at the top of the stairs. Though I'm not sure how, it feels as though I've reconnected with my father for the first time.

Later, when we are on the train home, I'm still thinking about his words. About how hard the first year or two are for any new family. That trying to work out how to be a good dad, in a world where everything is aimed at mothers, can be confusing and difficult. I realise that even if he was consumed by his career while we were growing up, it didn't mean he didn't love us. He was still a proud, if distant father.

Maybe Alex is still learning to be a dad, too. He had no role model to speak of—his own father ran off after he was born, and he only ever saw him on Christmas and birthdays. Amy's dad was little more than a flash in the pan, too. So he grew up with a strong mother and no father, and has never known anything different. Maybe he feels as though he isn't needed in our family.

I want to talk to him, to hear his voice, to let him know that he is needed. That I can't do this without him. But when I crawl into bed that night, exhausted from our weekend trip, he still hasn't messaged or called.

# 15

The first night we met, Alex and I ended up in an all-night café off the Thames Embankment. The interior was filled with an eclectic mix of party-goers stretching out their Friday night celebrations, and workers readying themselves for an early start. Street cleaners mingled with bankers in a way that wouldn't happen anywhere else.

We sat outside at a rusty metal table, our bitter coffees placed on the chipped surface. Every time we picked them up, it wobbled precariously.

Alex leaned back on his seat, long legs splayed out in front of him. An unlit cigarette dangled from his lips.

"You want one?" he asked, cupping his hand to shade his match from the slight breeze.

"I don't smoke. It's a disgusting habit." I smiled, letting him know I was flirting more than anything. Trying to wind him up.

He stared at me, throwing the burnt-out match into the ashtray. Already, I'd noticed Alex had this intense way of making me feel as if nothing else mattered. That I was the only interesting thing in the room—or in this case, the street.

"You're one of those, then," he said.

"One of what?"

"A crusader." He inhaled deeply, then let the smoke drift out of his lips. Even I had to admit he looked sexy.

His words made me grin. I was anything but; smoking rarely bothered me at all. "I don't kiss boys who smoke," I said.

The corner of his lip twitched up. He leaned forward, still staring intently. "That's good. I don't want you kissing them."

"You're a boy who smokes," I pointed out.

This time a full-on smirk broke out on his face. "I'm the exception that proves the rule, sweetheart."

The way he said it made my heart hammer against my chest. There was something about Alex Cartwright that made me feel breathless. I wasn't used to boys like him, ones who oozed sexuality out of every pore. Until then my boyfriends had been more friend than boy. Low key, almost feminine.

Alex didn't have a feminine bone in his body.

"What makes you think I want to kiss you, anyway?"

"You're the one who brought up kissing, not me." Another cocky response. "Not to mention the fact you keep looking at my mouth and licking your lips. I can tell you want to eat me for breakfast."

The image his words conjured up made me choke on my coffee. I spluttered the hot liquid out. Alex started to laugh.

"Kissing. I was still talking about kissing."

He may have been, but I couldn't get the thought of more out of my mind. Everything he did seemed sexual, from the way he caressed the microphone on stage, to his slow, sensual motions as he smoked his cigarette. It affected me too much.

"Now you're the one obsessed by kissing," I pointed out.

Another heated gaze. "Maybe we're both a bit obsessed." He stubbed out his cigarette in the glass ashtray, the butt floating in the ashy water collecting there. "I know I am."

Staring at my lips he leaned closer still. Enough for me to see the tall black edges of his tattoos as they emerged from the neck of his shirt. How many did he have? Was his body covered with them? Maybe his chest was one colourful canvas, spread with eagles and flowers and dirty little words. Closing my eyes, I imagined running my hands over the hard planes of his abdomen, tracing the ink down to where his stomach met his waistband.

"Hey." His voice was soft, low. "I lost you for a minute."

Embarrassed, I looked up at him. I was sure he must have been able to read my mind. That he could tell from the expression on my face exactly what I was thinking. Unfortunately, at times like those, I tended to bluster.

"I was thinking how late it is," I said. "Or how early, I guess."

The sun hadn't yet risen enough to be visible over the tall buildings of the City, but the pale orange glow that cast a halo around them told me it wouldn't be long. Glancing at my watch, I saw it was nearly 6:00 a.m. I'd officially been awake for over twenty-four hours.

I was so going to pay for that later.

"You're tired?" he asked. "I can take you home."

My shoulders slumped. "Home?"

No smirk this time. Only that hot, intense, stare. "Your place, my place. Doesn't matter. The result's going to be the same."

"You sound very sure of yourself."

He stood up, scraping the metal chair legs across the concrete slabs. I did the same, grabbing my jacket and pulling it on. A barrier against the early morning chill.

"I'm not sure of anything." Alex said it so quietly it was hard to make out the words. For a second, as he stood there in the pale gloom of the early morning, he looked so wistful I wanted to throw my arms around him. But the moment passed and we headed for the tube station, ready to catch the first train of the morning.

I hadn't really noticed how tall he was until then. On stage, among the instruments and equipment, his stature hadn't seemed so intimidating. But now, walking down the street alongside me, he towered above, making me feel tiny even in my two-inch heels.

Grabbing my hand, his knuckles skimmed my hip as he wrapped my fingers in his. The double sensation sent a shiver right through me. My skin tingled from him being so close.

"Which line?" he asked.

"District will do. I can get out at Bromley."

"Not that far from me."

"Where do you live?" I couldn't picture him in a bland, executive flat. He was too full of life, too colourful for that.

"Shoreditch. I share a place with some mates."

That wasn't too far. But though the development I lived in was nominally in the East End of London, it was full of executives more than anything else. No salt-of-the-earth types there; socially, it was a million miles away from Shoreditch. The old versus the new. Slowly but surely even the last bastions of the East End working class were being pushed out by City money.

"It's a bit of a journey from Docklands to Shoreditch," I pointed out. "You'd be better off going to Liverpool Street."

"I'm not letting you go home alone in the middle of the night." Alex looked aghast at my suggestion.

"It's the morning."

"Still not letting you," he muttered. Tightening his hand around mine, he pulled me towards the barriers, and we both flashed our Oyster cards against the sensors. I felt that delicious shiver again, warming me from the inside out. And for the umpteenth time that night, I wondered when he was going to kiss me.

If he was going to kiss me.

*Dear God, please let him kiss me.*

Stepping off the escalator and onto the deserted platform, we leaned against the tiled wall and waited for the first train. I could hear my heart thumping in my chest.

I stared at him. Waiting.

The way he stared back made me feel light-headed.

Slowly, maddeningly, he leaned towards me, never once pulling his eyes away from mine. When his lips were only a few millimetres away from my mouth, I felt his breath, warm and soft on my skin.

"Am I your exception, Lara?"

It took me a moment to recall our earlier conversation.

"Yes." Closing my eyes, I breathed him in. A hint of smoke, a smattering of coffee, but more than anything there was Alex. "Yes, you're my exception."

The next moment he pressed his lips to mine, pulling me into his arms. His hands pushed into the small of my back. Insistent, firm, fingers grazing my behind. I kissed him back as if I was drowning, a dying girl searching for her final breath.

Yes, he was my exception.

He still is.

\* \* \*

Tina's fiftieth birthday falls on a Saturday, a month into Alex's tour. She phones me early in the morning, gushing about the flowers he's sent her, and I hold my tongue, unwilling to divulge that it was me who arranged their delivery.

He called me on Thursday night from a dingy motel in Oregon, panicking, and even though I tried, I couldn't hide the smugness in my tone when I told him I'd already ordered the flowers and bought a silver bracelet to give her on the day.

"Thanks, babe." His voice sounded hoarse. It was no surprise after all the gigs they'd been doing. But there was something else, as well. An underlying exhaustion that coated his words. My smugness disappeared then, replaced by concern.

"Are you okay?"

"Shouldn't I be asking you that?"

"I'm fine." My voice was gentle. "We've got into a bit of a routine. Max slept until four last night."

"I miss you. Both of you."

*Then come home*, I wanted to say. *Get on a plane and come back to us.*

"We miss you, too. Did I tell you Max is trying to crawl? When we went to the park with David last week, he almost dragged himself across the picnic rug."

Silence. All I could hear was Alex's regular breaths.

"You went out with David?"

My stomach dropped. "It's not that way. You know it isn't."

David's one of the few people keeping me sane. Him and Beth. I don't know what I'd do without them.

Alex sighed. "Whatever. I've got to go, the bus leaves in ten minutes and Stu wants to call his girl. Give Max a kiss from me, okay?"

The bitter taste in my mouth seemed to spread throughout my body. Churning up everything. "Yeah. Speak to you soon."

"Love you, babe."

"Love you, too."

Each time he calls it feels more of a reflex response, a tap of the knee, a leg kicking out. The words spill out of my mouth like a well-rehearsed speech. We blink, we breathe, and we love. But when reflex replaces emotion, where does that leave us?

I'm still thinking about it as I push Max's buggy up a grassy hill in King Edward's Park, where Tina has decided to hold her birthday picnic. Although her friends are taking her out on the town tonight, she's decided she wants to spend the day with her family. Especially her baby grandson.

Max, of course, is oblivious to everything. Wearing a cute little pair of short dungarees, his bare legs kick out as he spots birds flying in the sky. He's already learned to point, which apparently is advanced for his age, and his finger follows the contrails of an airplane as it crosses the horizon.

I love the way small things delight him so much. He sees the beauty in everything, helping me see it, too. A car horn is remarkable, a police siren something to laugh about. He's learning so much every day.

And Alex is missing it all.

The Cartwrights have set up camp beneath an old oak tree. Tina has spread out a motley collection of rugs and is laying food out on plastic plates when we arrive. She abandons her task readily, scooping Max in her arms, holding him to her ample bosom.

"Oh, my goodness he's grown, I can't believe it. He looks so much like his daddy." She's always said he's the spitting image of Alex, but I've never really seen it until now. In the last few weeks his downy baby hair has been replaced by, thicker, darker strands. Add that to the way his face is starting to take shape and I'm beginning to see what Tina means.

"He's losing some baby fat. I miss his chubby cheeks." I give a mock pout.

"He's beautiful. Aren't you, gorgeous?"

While Tina occupies Max, I glance over at the other blanket. Amy is here, accompanied by Luke, her on-again, off-again boyfriend. Those two have had more breakups than I've had hot dinners. They first started going out at school, when Amy was fifteen, and their relationship has been volatile, to say the least. Luke is a typical wide boy, swaggering about, flashing the cash he earns from his electrician business, treating Amy as if she's some kind of doormat.

Needless to say, Alex can't stand him. I'm guessing the only reason Luke's even here is because Alex isn't. He rarely shows his face when his girlfriend's big brother is around.

"Hi Amy, Luke." I join them on the lilac checked blanket. "Is Andrea coming?"

"She's gone to pick up some booze," Amy replies. "Luke forgot to bring the champagne."

Her pointed look is totally wasted on him. He has his head bent over his phone, his fingers tapping furiously. He doesn't even look up to say hello.

Yeah. I don't like him much either.

"How are the applications going?" I ask, remembering our last conversation. "Have you found an internship yet?"

Her face lights up. "Yeah, actually. I've been offered a position at Richards and Morgan."

"That's amazing. Congratulations." I lean across and hug her. Everybody who's worked in the city have heard of Richards and Morgan. They're one of the top management consultants in London. All shiny buildings, tailored suits and massive expense accounts. Landing an internship there is a huge coup. "Isn't that great, Luke?"

"Uh?" Finally, he looks up from his iPhone.

"Amy's job. It's good news, isn't it?"

He holds my gaze for less than a second. "Whatever." Shrugging, he starts tapping away again. I flash a sympathetic smile at Amy.

Seriously, she's a beautiful girl. Long, black hair that glistens in the midday sun. Warm chocolate eyes as big as dish plates. She could do so much better than Mr Charisma.

"When do you start?" I decide to ignore him, turning my attention back on Amy. She glances at Luke and her lip trembles.

"September. My induction day's on the fourth."

"You'll do really well with your brains. They'll be lucky to have you."

I want to hug her again. In all my time with Alex, not once has he made me feel worthless. Angry, maybe. Definitely frustrated. But never has he treated me the way Luke treats

Amy. I want to shake some sense into her, can't she see what he's like?

She must sense my mood, because she hurriedly changes the subject. "Have you heard from Alex?"

From the corner of my eye I see Tina put Max onto the picnic rug. He immediately turns over onto his belly, putting his hands out to push himself up. "Yeah, every now and again. He forgot to set up data roaming so he has to call me on a borrowed phone. Half the time I can't work out what city they're in."

"I've been following them on Facebook," Amy says. "Did you see the pictures from Seattle?"

"On Facebook?"

"Yeah, their band has a page." She looks surprised that I don't know this. But Alex has never used Facebook, reckons it's a huge time waster. I'm guessing Stuart or Alfie has decided to bring the band kicking and screaming into the twenty-first century.

To be honest, I'm a little embarrassed Alex never told me. All this time I've been wondering what they're up to, and all I had to do was log on. It seems like their fans know more about my husband than I do.

"I'll have to take a look when I get home."

A gurgle comes from behind me. Max has managed to manoeuvre himself onto all fours. Though he looks a bit wobbly, there's a big grin on his face, as if he can't believe his luck.

"Look at him," Tina calls out, as delighted as her grandson. "He's going to start crawling on my birthday."

We watch with baited breath as Max moves his right hand forward, his face screwed up with concentration. Amy leans across and grabs onto my arm tightly, as excited as I am.

"Come on, Max," Tina encourages. "Do it for Nanny."

Slowly, tentatively, he shuffles his left knee forward, making the top half of his body lunge ahead.

Silently, we wait for him to do it again. And he does, managing three shuffles before he collapses in a heap on the rug, clearly exhausted from all the effort. We break out in loud cheers, clapping loudly, Amy whooping as she captures a picture of him on her phone. I lift him up, grinning, kissing his sticky face.

"You did it!"

"He did! The best birthday present ever."

Max gurgles and makes a grab for me, then he starts laughing wildly. Amy snaps away, while Tina squeals, and Luke ignores us all, muttering at his phone.

Every once in a while there are moments like these. I hold my son close as he slobbers on my shoulder, and ignore the one dark thought that tries to make itself heard.

Max crawled for the first time and Alex missed it.

# 16

On Tuesdays at the clinic I run a group session for parents of addicts. Dragging our chairs into a makeshift circle, the eight of us sit down, and I take a moment to look at each one of them. The longest-serving member is Jackie Clack. She's been coming to these meetings for five years, ever since she found her son injecting himself in their downstairs bathroom. Though Seth's fallen on and off the wagon more times than a drunken cowboy, Jackie has remained consistent throughout that time.

She's like everybody's grandma. When a new member joins, she takes them under her wings, coddling them, telling them that though things may not ever get better, they will definitely become more bearable.

Next to Jackie is Peter Stanhope. He's only been with us a few weeks. His daughter, Kate, is a meth addict and her two children have been taken into foster care. Every time Pete comes to a meeting he shows us their photos, holding them with a shaking hand, telling us that this week he hopes he'll get to see them.

The saddest member of all is Carla Dean. She's not that much older than me, though the furrowed lines that have made a home across her brow make her look at least a decade more advanced than she is. She had her only son—Connor—at the age of seventeen. He's now fifteen and addicted to smack. She hasn't seen him for three months; the last she heard, he was seen in a drug den in Wandsworth. Since then, she's been walking the streets every night, questioning the homeless, searching for a sign of him.

It's as if the streets have swallowed him whole. It never fails to amaze me how a fifteen-year-old can disappear into thin air. In this day and age, it's still possible to lose a child.

"I thought I saw him last week," Carla tells us. She won't catch any of our eyes, and simply stares down at the floor. From my position opposite her, I can see the grey roots of her hair have grown in, giving her a pale white stripe across her parting line. "But it wasn't him. It was some kid with bleached blond hair. I tried to get him to come home with me for a decent meal but he told me to fuck off." She wrings her hands nervously together. "I told him that his mum must be worried sick, as I am. But he told me his mum chucked him out." Finally, she looks up. "I mean, who would do that? Throw their kid out?"

"I threw Kate out when I found out about her drugs," Pete says, with a thin smile. "Fat lot of good that did. She shacked up with her deadbeat boyfriend instead. The one who got her hooked in the first place."

"You did what you thought was right." Jackie pats his hand. "None of this is your fault."

There's silence for a minute, and I turn my attention on our newest member. Laurence Baines is fifty-something and a headmaster of an up-and-coming school in East London. In the past two weeks that he's attended the group he's been nothing but perfectly turned out. Suit jacket still on, not a single hair out of place; he looks like the ultimate professional.

"How's your week been, Laurence?" I ask.

"I visited Tom yesterday. He cried for an hour." Laurence catches my eye. "I cried, too. For the first time since my mother died twenty years ago."

Tom was convicted for dealing while studying at Oxford University. Unlike many others, he had everything going for him from the start. Wealthy parents, a middle-class upbringing, an education people would kill to get, and yet now he's serving time in a prison surrounded by thieves and murderers. A different type of education altogether.

"How are you feeling today?" I ask him.

"Exhausted. Depleted. I spent most of the night holding Julie while she cried herself to sleep." Julie is Laurence's wife. She's taken her son's incarceration badly. Understandably so. "All she kept asking me was 'why'? I couldn't tell her I want to know that, too. That I don't have the answers."

"Do you find not having the answers difficult?" Jackie asks that question.

Laurence turns to look at her. "I've never felt this helpless before. I'm always the one with the answers. At home I've looked after the money and the house. Julie relies on me to keep things straight. It's the same at school. I'm the one who gets to make all the decisions. The one people look up to. But now I've no idea what to do. I hate feeling so bloody useless."

"Sometimes there isn't an answer," I point out, gently. "Life throws a curveball and we either duck or get hit."

These sessions are always tough. It's hard enough when it's one on one. But in a group setting there are so many desperately sad stories, they never fail to touch me. The worst thing about them is the inevitability of it all. Even when one of their children has finally kicked the habit, we all know that around 90% of them will return to drugs within the next twelve months. That's why so few of them stop coming even during a sober period.

I think of Max and the way he actually waved me goodbye this morning when I dropped him off at nursery, lifting up his tiny hand and flapping his fingers as I left him playing with Holly. I can't imagine going through what these people have endured. To see the child they love stolen away by an addiction so cruel nobody can escape from it.

Once, Laurence watched Tom learn to crawl. Saw his first tiny wave with a chubby little fist. I can't imagine he ever thought that one day that baby would grow up and be a convicted criminal, imprisoned at the age of twenty.

What happened to these kids? Were there a series of tiny choices that led to their addictions, or were they doomed from the start. I find myself listening closer, looking for answers, hoping to avoid making the same mistakes they did.

If only I could shelter Max from harm. Wrap him up in cotton wool and chase the world away. I hate the thought he's going to experience sadness. Heartache and rejection. Perhaps that's the cruellest part of being a parent. Knowing as hard as you try, you can't protect them from everything.

"It isn't your fault," Jackie joins in. I can tell by the way she's wriggling on her seat that she's desperate to get up and give Laurence a hug. Not that he looks like the hugging type. I expect he'd endure it politely, trying desperately not to look at Jackie's more than ample bosom, but I don't think it would give him much comfort.

At this point I'm not even sure there's comfort to be had.

"We've reached the end of our hour," I say, reluctantly. It took us all a while to warm up today, and the first twenty minutes were filled with pointed silence and quiet mumbles. It's always a shame when we get only forty minutes of quality discussion time. "I'll see you here the same time next week?"

A few nods, a couple of thanks, and the loud noise of chairs scraping against the floor fill the air. I start to stack them in the corner and Laurence comes over to help me, working silently beside me as everybody else troops out.

"Thank you for today," he says quietly. "It's good to know I'm not alone out there."

Now *I'm* the one who wants to hug him. I dig my fingernails into the palms of my hands, reminding myself I'm a therapist, not a cuddler.

"I'm glad you came. I know we don't have all the answers, but we do want to listen. And everybody wants to help."

"Even Jackie," Laurence says, and the ghost of a smile crosses his lips.

"Especially Jackie."

After Laurence leaves, I take a moment to grab my phone from my bag. I've been trying to call Alex since yesterday, desperate to tell him about Max's first crawl. I left a voicemail first thing this morning, asking Stuart to get Alex to call me back, but I've heard nothing since. Of course, I haven't had a chance to try again since I got to work.

Predictably, there's a missed call and a voicemail. I press on the icon, then listen to the automated voice as she tells me I have one new message.

"Hey, I can't believe I've missed you again. The reception out here's crap. We're about to get on a bus to Chicago in five minutes, but you can try and call me when you get the message. Or I'll call you when we get to the hotel some time tonight. Love you, babe."

Frustrated, I delete the message and try the number again, but all I hear is Stuart's recorded voice. I leave a low-key message, telling Alex I'll try him again later, wishing him luck in tomorrow's concert. Then I go back to my office, ready for my final counselling session of the day, hoping at some point this week, I'll actually get a chance to talk to my husband.

\* \* \*

Max goes to sleep quickly this evening. It's as if he knows I've had a hard day and wants to make my life easy. I stand and watch him for a while, as his bow-lips pucker in his sleep, looking like his daddy when he sings softly into a microphone.

Pouring myself a cup of tea, I call Beth, needing to hear a friendly voice. If I'm brutally honest, as nice as it is to get some peace and quiet, I can't help but feel lonely on nights like this. There's an Alex-shaped hole in the flat, his absence making everything seem a bit less vibrant.

"Hello, stranger." As soon as I hear her voice it makes me smile. "How's things?"

I can't tell you how good it is to hear her voice. All the frustrations of the day seem to quieten inside me. Beth has a way of bringing inner peace.

"Different day, same problems," I say. "It's been a long week."

"It's only Monday." Her laugh is soft. "What's up?"

Where do I start? Taking a sip of my lukewarm tea, I lean back in my chair, letting my eyes fall shut. "Ugh, I don't know. I've been playing voicemail tennis with Alex for days, and he missed Max's first crawl yesterday. I haven't even had a chance to tell him."

"Aww, he'll be gutted to have missed it. Maybe you can video it for him or something?"

"I suppose so. But I want him to see it for himself, not on a stupid phone screen. I feel like a single parent. It's not fair." I know I sound spoiled, but I also know Beth understands me. I need to vent, to let it out.

It's either that or stew all night.

"It's not for long. He'll be back before you know it. Leaving the toilet seat up. Filling up the laundry basket. You'll ache for these days, believe me."

"I miss him so much." I wrinkle my nose. "More than I thought I would."

"Of course you miss him. I miss Niall when he goes away, too. But the reunions kind of make up for it."

Beth makes it sound so easy. I know Niall often has to travel for his work. Being an artist, he has exhibitions and commissions across the world. But the two of them—and Allegra, Beth's adopted daughter—make it work somehow.

That's another thing that worries me. We were already having problems before Alex left on tour, add that to his absence and it's a recipe for misery. It feels as if we're climbing a mountain wearing an iron shawl. An uphill struggle.

"It all seems so hard, you know?" I rub my face wearily. "The lack of sleep. The lack of husband. I don't know how single mums survive."

"They survive because they have to," she says gently. "And you will, too. You're stronger than you know." She pauses and I take another mouthful of tea. "How are you feeling, anyway? What does the doctor say about the post natal depression?"

I shrug, even though she can't see me. "He says I should keep going to the PND group. He wants to keep an eye on me, but he doesn't think I need medication."

"That's good, right? And we have this weekend to look forward to. Allegra's so excited you and Max are coming to stay."

Her enthusiasm makes me smile. I'm so excited about this weekend, too. Max and I are taking the train to Brighton on Friday night and spending the whole weekend with Beth and Niall. To say I can't wait would be an understatement.

"Oh God, I'm like a kid counting down to Christmas. I'm looking forward to seeing you all."

"So am I. I'm keeping my fingers crossed for the weather. And on Saturday night Niall's offered to babysit while we hit the town."

"Really?" I sound incredulous. As much as I love Niall, I can't picture him being excited about that. "He doesn't have to do that."

"Yes, he bloody does. You deserve a break and so do I. Anyway, we don't have to go out for long. We can put the kids to bed first then sneak out for a couple of drinks. And don't say no, I've been looking forward to this so much."

She sounds as desperate as I am for some child-free entertainment. I love Max to death, but I also miss the times when I could go out and paint the town red. "I won't say no."

"Good. Because I've bought a dress and everything. And I've booked the taxi."

"In that case, how can I refuse?"

"You can't," she says happily. "A couple of drinks, a bit of a boogie and you'll forget all about your worries."

"I hope so," I sigh.

Even if I don't forget about my worries, at least I'll be able to spend some time with my best friend, something almost as rare as a conversation with my husband. When we finish our call and I hang up, there's a small smile on my face.

Friday can't come quick enough.

\* \* \*

I'm lying in bed, scrolling through the updates on my phone when I remember my conversation with Amy at the picnic. Pressing on the touch-screen, I open up Facebook, and type in the search box. The *Fear of Flying* fan page is first in the results, and I'm kicking myself for not checking it before. It looks like Stuart and Alfie are keeping it updated regularly, with news of their progress, and posts about each gig they've performed.

There are photos, too. Excited, I scroll through them. Smiling when I see the ones of Alex mid-set, his slicked-back hair shining beneath the stage lights, his eyes dark and intense in the hazy atmosphere.

There are ones of the band sitting on their tour bus, laughing, Alex clutching a guitar, a pen tucked behind his ear as he strums.

Seeing him makes my chest feel tight. The sense of loss I felt earlier intensifies, growing into a black hole that fills my body. I spend long minutes staring at his face, taking in the way his brow furrows and his lips purse as he listens to something Stuart is telling him.

Later on in the album, I find photos of last night's gig in Austin, and scroll through them greedily, excited that I've nearly caught up to him. I follow the progress of their day; the sound check, an early dinner, the four of them holding bottles of beer as they toast that night's gig.

Then there are the ones of Alex performing. Like in the earlier pictures he looks glorious. Strutting sexily across the stage, leaning forward as he sings into the microphone, a smirk on his face as fans in the front row try to touch him.

God, he looks so natural. A star in waiting.

Finally, we get to the after-party. Some dingy bar with threadbare seats. They are surrounded by fans. There are photos of Stuart signing a pair of boobs, and Alfie rolling his eyes at the sight.

And then... and then...

My heart stops.

Alex is sitting down, a pretty blonde perched on his lap. Her arm is looped around his neck, while his is casually slung around her waist.

He's laughing.

Staring into her eyes and laughing.

There's something so intimate about it I feel as though I'm intruding. As if I'm the interloper, staring at him and a girlfriend.

Opening my mouth, I take a ragged breath. It catches in my throat, my chest too tight to let it in. And for a moment it feels as though I'm drowning in oxygen.

Last night, my husband let a pretty girl sit on his lap. He let her put her arms around him. While I slept in our bed, and our baby slept in his cot, Alex wrapped his own arm around her waist.

I don't care if she's a fan, or a friend. I don't care if there's nothing in it, or it's simply an awkward snapshot of a passing moment. At one point last night, that girl sat on his lap and made him laugh.

The tightness in my chest starts to burn. Though I turn off my phone, the image lingers in my mind. I can't ignore the nasty thoughts lingering there no matter how hard I try. Even if it was nothing more than a passing embrace, the bitter taste it leaves in my mouth makes me feel nauseous, angry. And I want to hit out at something.

I don't know what to do. Should I call him, demand answers? Laugh it off like I would have done previously? Seeing that picture has mixed up everything, making it hard for me to think straight.

It makes it impossible for me to sleep, too. In spite of my exhaustion, I toss and turn all night. Feeling angry, jealous, and lonely. When Max wakes up at four in the morning, crying softly for some milk, I'm feeling as miserable as he sounds.

# 17

It's been a long week. Long and hard, but not in a good way. Though I've spoken with Alex twice, both times he was surrounded by people, and I couldn't find the right way to phrase my questions. Instead, I left them unsaid, letting my mind work overtime, imagining this girl as a sex-hungry groupie following them from gig to gig, waiting for the moment she can sit on his lap again.

I torture myself with images of them. Sitting. Holding. Kissing.

By the time I get to Beth's on Friday night, I've managed to build it up into something cataclysmic. We settle Max in his travel cot and walk downstairs into her pretty cottage kitchen. Beth pours us both a generous glass of wine and I gulp it greedily, needing the numbness it creates in my body.

"So I'll admit it looks pretty bad," Beth says, staring at the screen of my phone. "But you know Alex would never do that to you."

"She's sitting on his lap." I stare off into the distance. A black mark on the far wall of their kitchen catches my eye. It's small, hand-shaped; made by Allegra, no doubt. "They're not exactly having a casual conversation."

As soon as I finish one glass, Beth tops it up. Wine sloshes over the side, dripping onto the wooden table. I suspect she's trying to take my mind off things, but even alcohol can't erase that image from my brain.

"It's a snapshot in time. Maybe she only sat there for a second." Her face softens. "The two of you were meant for each other, you know that. And now you have Max, as well. Don't let some stupid picture ruin everything."

When Niall arrives home twenty minutes later, she shoves the picture in his face, wanting a man's opinion. He stares at it for a moment, expression implacable. Then he gives me back my phone, his hand squeezing mine as I take it from him.

"He's a stupid git, but he's not a cheater." Alex and Niall have been friends for a while now, ever since Niall started working at the clinic. As soon as I introduced them they hit it off, talking music and art while making their way through a six pack. "He loves you, Lara. Any idiot can see that."

I smile, but it doesn't reach my eyes. "You would say that. Bros before Hos and all that."

Niall opens the fridge and takes out a can of beer. When he pulls the key there's a hiss, followed by froth bubbling over the edge. He lifts it to his lips and takes a long mouthful.

"Does that make you the ho?" He smirks, wiping his mouth with the back of his hand.

I narrow my eyes. "There's no need for that. If there's a ho in this situation it isn't me."

Beth reaches out and whacks him on the arm. "Don't be rude to our guest."

He turns to me. "Speaking of guests, where's the little guy? Is he asleep already?"

"For now. Give him a few hours and he'll be wide awake." I wince at the thought of a 3:00 a.m. wake up call. Maybe I should stop drinking now; I'll pay for it in the morning.

"I'll get my cuddles later, then." Niall winks, and I have to admit there's something pretty sexy about it. No wonder Beth goes all swoony whenever he's near. With his Mr Rochester looks and easy-going temperament, he's a dangerous combination of bad boy and good. When he turns his intense blue eyes on you, it's hard to do anything but stare right back. He's hypnotising.

"I'm sure Max will like that." I don't tell him he hasn't had a cuddle from a man in a while. With Alex gone, and David snowed under with work, I've been surrounded by women for the past few weeks.

"Not as much as Niall," Beth says drily, as her boyfriend leaves the room, mumbling about leaving us girls to it. Leaning forward, she whispers into my ear. "He's gone baby mad. Keeps asking me when we're going to try."

My eyes widen. "Really?" I don't know why I'm surprised. Beth's almost thirty and Niall's two years older. "I thought you said Allegra was enough for now."

Beth sighs. "She is. What with my degree and looking after her I'm not sure where I'd fit in a baby. But Niall's adamant he wants one soon. He's even said he'll stay home and do the child care. Reckons he could fit his painting around it."

I try not to laugh. I can remember thinking how easy it would be to have a newborn. That I'd get loads done while I was on maternity leave. As it turned out I was a slave to Max's needs, either feeding, burping, or changing him.

"What do you think?" I ask.

She makes a face. "I think I can barely keep things afloat as it is. As much as I want to make Niall happy, he might have to wait a couple of years. It's not as if I'm running out of time or anything, is it?"

"Wise words." I reach across and rub her arm. "Having a baby is hard work, it has to be something you're both ready for." I wince as I say it, remembering Alex's accusation. That I wanted Max more than he did. For the first time I wonder if he's deliberately trying to sabotage things between us; smoking, touring, having pretty girls sitting on his lap, while I have a baby sitting on mine.

If that's what he's doing, then he's making a good job of it.

* * *

We spend Saturday at the beach. The sun beats down, the September haziness almost pushed back by a cool, easterly wind. Allegra runs around collecting stones while Max shuffles himself across the picnic blanket, making mad lunges for shells that he promptly tries to stuff in his mouth. Every time I prise them out of his hands he protests with a squeal, turning his lips down in angry protest.

When we get back to the cottage that night, we're all feeling a little tender, our faces chapped from the wind, with hair thick and matted from the spray that carried in the breeze. After a day of gossiping, I feel on an even keel, able to laugh off mentions of Alex's antics, giving them both as I get when they tease me about my rock star husband.

After a tea of egg and chips, Beth disappears to help Allegra bathe, while Max and I snuggle up on the sofa. He slurps hungrily from the warm bottle of milk, his lips forming a vacuum on the teat. I'm staring at his downy head when a movement in the corner of the room catches my eye. I turn my head to investigate.

Niall is perched on the arm of the chair, his pencil flying across a blank page of his sketch pad.

"What are you doing?" I whisper, not wanting to disturb Max. His body has relaxed. His face taken on a sleepy glow.

"Sketching." He tilts his head to the side, cross hatching in a shadow.

"Let me see."

He chuckles and looks down at his pad. "You're as bad as Beth. She used to hound me when we were at university."

I raise my eyebrows. He rarely mentions that time, neither of them do. They met at university during Beth's first year, but then their close friend died from an overdose and they both ended up getting expelled. By the time they saw each other again—nine years later—Beth was married to somebody else. I remember back to last year, when Beth's marriage was falling apart, and how hard she fell for Niall.

If the two of them could overcome that, surely Alex and I can work through our problems.

"Does she still hound you?" I like the way he talks about her. He's a man in love and not afraid to show it.

"About everything." His lips twitch, as if he's remembering something funny. "Between her and Allegra I rarely get a moment's peace."

"Is that a problem for you?"

This time he looks up and catches my eye. "Not at all. I love every minute of it. They're my girls."

The way he says it, so naturally, makes me want to sigh. "I wish Alex felt that way."

Niall frowns. "Of course he does. He loves you. Both of you." He puts his pad to the side. "Is that photo still bothering you?"

I shrug. "I guess so. I know he wouldn't cheat on me. He isn't like that. But it's the fact he looks so casual, that it isn't a big deal. It makes me wonder if he really knows me at all."

Beth chooses that moment to walk in. "Everything okay?"

"She's still worried about that picture," Niall tells her.

"I'm not worried. It niggles, you know? I know he's still smoking weed and didn't even remember to sort his phone out. All these things that show me he doesn't really care what I think."

"You're reading too much into it." Beth shakes her head. "He's not doing it deliberately. Maybe he's going through a midlife crisis a bit early. Most guys get a sports car or a motorbike, Alex decides to become a rock star."

"I could live with a car," I mutter, rolling my eyes for effect. "It would beat lugging Max onto public transport."

I shut up when Allegra walks in, her hair damp and her face scrubbed clean. She's wearing a pair of pink striped pyjamas. "Can I try feeding him tomorrow?" she asks, reaching out to tickle Max under his chin. Without waiting for an answer she runs over to Niall, sticking a thumb in her mouth as she stares at his drawing.

"That's good," she says. "It looks like them."

Then she throws herself into his arms, hugging him tight. Niall holds her close, his eyes closed, his lips curled up into a contented smile.

A pang of jealousy jabs at my stomach. I can't help wishing Alex would hold Max that way.

\* \* \*

We travel home on Sunday evening, arriving back at the flat as the sun slips her anchor, sliding down to the horizon in a trail of orange fire. My skin is still pink from our day on the beach, making my face feel tender and tight. Max has fallen asleep in his buggy, his head lolling to the side, occasionally falling forward as we hit a dip in the pavement. Exhausted by the Brighton air, he's been sleeping for most of the afternoon.

Like mine, his nose is pink and sensitive, but from another cold rather than sunburn. He developed a sniffle last night, fretting and spluttering for most of the evening, causing Beth and I to return early from our girl's night out.

I knock on David's door as we pass it, planning to let him know we're home safely. When he finally pulls it open, I notice the shadows beneath his eyes, the way his face looks sallow and pale.

"You're back. Did you have a good time?" Leaning against the door jamb, hands stuffed in his pocket, he doesn't invite me in.

"Yeah, it was good." I haven't told him about Alex's photo. As sweet as he's been I don't want to air my dirty linen in public. At the moment, it's only Niall, Beth and me in the know. "I got a bit burnt, though." A car horn blasts through the evening air, making Max jump, though it doesn't wake him. "How are you? Still busy?"

He shrugs. "Snowed under." He looks down, pulling at the nail on his left thumb. "D'you want to come in for a cup of tea?"

I hesitate for a moment. It's already seven o'clock, I really should put Max to bed and get ready for the week ahead. But there's something about the expression on David's face that makes me agree.

I park Max in the corner of his living room as David makes the tea, and accept the steaming mug when he finally hands it to me. We sit for a minute, sipping quietly, until he breaks the silence.

"My mum saw Claire last week."

No wonder he looks so haunted. His ex-girlfriend is a tender subject for David. Not to mention the fact she won't let him see his daughter.

"She did? Was Mathilda with her?"

"Nah, it was at some reception thing. The only reason my mum mentioned it was because Claire was with someone."

"With someone?" I echo.

"A guy. Some businessman, according to Mum. She phoned in a panic, worried he was going to adopt Mathilda. Apparently he's a minor celebrity in town."

"Rich?"

"Stinking with it." David shrugs, but I can tell by the way he holds his shoulders that he's not cool with it. I reach out and grab his hand.

"How about your lawyer, has he managed to make any headway?"

"Nothing worth reporting."

I sit up, swinging my legs around until they're curled beneath me. Then I look at David. "Have you ever considered going there and seeing Mathilda anyway?"

I look over at Max, sleeping quietly in the corner. If Alex stopped me from seeing him I don't know what I'd do.

"I've done more than consider it." He looks down at his mug, as if he's avoiding my gaze. "I took her for a week, went down to my dad's cabin without telling anyone. That's... um... why I ended up with an injunction against me."

"You took her?" I don't know how to feel about that. The part of me that's David's friend wants to support him. But the mother in me is appalled.

A pinched expression moulds his face. "This is why I don't tell anybody. Yes, it was stupid and yes, I was a knob, but I was in a bad place. She's my daughter, too."

I blink at the shortness of his voice. "I'm sorry." Who am I to judge? I've not exactly been stable recently.

David shakes his head. "Nah, you're all right. It was a dick move. Stupid, too, because it gave Claire enough ammo to shoot me down."

I'm still trying not to think about someone taking Max away. A whole week? As much as I dislike the sound of Claire, she must have gone through hell.

"Everybody deserves a second chance," I say with a small voice. "We all make mistakes."

"Claire doesn't see it that way." He stares at the ground. "Nor does the judge. I'm too much of an abduction risk, apparently."

"But you wouldn't take her again, would you? Not after everything that's happened?"

"Of course not. But every day I don't see her, she's growing up. I'm scared she's not gonna know me, not going to *want* to know me. Claire will find someone else and then Mathilda won't even need me anymore. She'll have a new dad."

"You'll always be her dad," I reassure him. "No matter what happens, nobody can change that."

"What's the use in a title if I can't spend any time with her?" he asks. "She's gonna forget I even exist. I've lost her, Lara, I know I have."

His face crumples, and I close the space between us, reaching out to hug him tight. For ten long minutes he cries into my shoulder, sobbing for a child he's lost, one he so desperately misses. Though my eyes water, I don't join in. I try to comfort him as best I can, trying so hard not to think about another absent dad, touring over in the States. One who would rather spend time with nameless blondes than call his wife and check up on his baby.

\* \* \*

The next time I attend the PND support group I actually feel able to speak in front of everybody. We've taken the babies swimming, and after drying ourselves off and getting our clothes back on, we congregate in a small restaurant at the back of the sports complex. I've noticed that we all feel more comfortable with our hands occupied—whether it's holding a coffee or rocking a baby, and though often we don't make eye contact, there's still a feeling of being heard.

The swimming has worn Max out for once. He's slumped in his buggy, his head lolling to one side, fingers stuffed in his mouth like a soother. I tuck the blanket around his legs before lifting my coffee from the table, and look at the others who are doing the same.

"How has your week been, Lara?" Diane, the group leader asks. I take a mouthful of coffee before speaking, letting the liquid warm my throat.

"I saw a photograph of my husband with another woman."

There's a gasp from the others, as they whip their heads up to look at me. Their shock lessens as I try to explain the situation, finding myself making excuses for Alex, but the sympathy in their eyes remains.

"Have you been sleeping?" Diane asks.

"Not much," I admit. I look down, smoothing the wrinkles from my jeans. "Even when Max is asleep I can't drift off. I keep seeing it in my mind."

"Do you think there's anything in it?" Debbie, one of the other mums, leans forward. "You seem remarkably calm."

"I don't know... I don't think so. We've been together for seven years and he's never ever strayed, even when he's had opportunity to." I look up, catching her eye. "He's had a lot of opportunity, as you can imagine."

"Have you asked him about it?"

I shake my head. "Remember I told you about his phone? I can't bring myself to ask him over somebody else's connection. What if we end up talking for hours? What if he hangs up and I can't get hold of him? This is something I need to do face to face."

"That sounds sensible," Diane says. "From what you've told us, you've both in a volatile position right now. And this is a conversation you really should have in person."

She's right, I know that. Because I need to see his eyes when I ask him, to see his expression when he tries to explain the situation. More than that, I need him to see me, the way his actions are affecting me, the way I sometimes feel like I'm falling apart.

The only problem is, there's still another six weeks until he comes home.

# 18

Two days later Max has developed a hacking cough that a sixty-a-day smoker would be proud of. Loud dog-like barks wrack his tiny body, making him cry with the shock of it all. In spite of the heat, I wrap him up and take him to the doctor's surgery, only to be told that colds are to be expected and I should keep him cool and hydrated, and that I shouldn't take him swimming again until his breathing is better.

Though the doctor didn't say it, I got the sense he thinks I'm being neurotic. He only has to see my notes to know I've been diagnosed as having PND. Though I've heard from the others at the PND group that they have the same problems with their own GPs, this is the first time I start to wonder if it really is me.

Maybe I *am* being neurotic.

Alex has called twice since the weekend. Even over a dodgy connection he could hear Max's wheezing, and he sounded sweetly concerned, telling me to try the doctor again, offering to call his mum for advice. I have to admit I tried to play down my worries.

And, yeah, I didn't ask him about the picture, in fact it didn't even cross my mind until we'd finished talking. Maybe it was his concern that won me over, or my need to hear another human voice. All I do know is I have to ignore the nagging in my head that tells me I'm stirring up heartache, that I should get everything out in the open where it belongs.

On Thursday night, Max can't sleep at all. His nose is stuffed, his lungs full of mucus, and I have to keep him upright to help him breathe. In my sleep-deprived, slightly panicked state, I finally call Alex's mum, desperate for another opinion. Having been effectively laughed out of the doctor's office, I'm finding it hard to judge the situation. To see the line between concern and anxiety.

"Have you tried Oil of Olbas?" Tina suggests. "Fill a bowl with hot water and put a few drops in. Make him breathe in the steam."

I don't bother to point out the dangers of hot water near a baby. If I dangled Max anywhere near a bowl of boiling water, he's bound to lunge at it. The scald risk is too great.

"I don't have any," I lie. Alex has some stashed in our bathroom cabinet. He swears by it, like his mum.

Max wheezes loudly. The air he inhales mixes with the fluid in his airways, whistling as he tries to take it in. He wriggles in my arms, his sad eyes staring up at me. It's as if he's begging me for help.

That only makes me feel more useless. I hold him tight, whispering everything will be okay, and his soft cheek feels hot against my own. His chest moves rapidly with his shallow breaths, the skin beneath his ribcage looking hollow and tight.

"I'm going to try to get him to sleep," I tell Tina. "I'll let you know how he is in the morning."

"Call me first thing, I'll pop over with some stuff for him. Give you a bit of a break."

Max refuses to settle, which isn't a surprise. For the past twelve hours he's hardly taken in any liquids, turning his head away every time I offer him a bottle. His lips are red and cracked, eyes haunted and sunken. And as the night progresses, his cries become weaker.

I don't know what to do. By this time his temperature is sky high, skin red and tight. It's like holding a hot water bottle in my arms. I try to reduce his fever with a cool flannel, but he pushes it away weakly, whimpering.

In desperation, I try to call Alex. Though I'm trying to be strong for Max's sake, tears fill my eyes, my lip wobbling as I dial the number. And of course I get Stuart's voicemail. But this time I leave a shaky message, asking Alex to call me back, hoping he can hear how much I need him.

By 3:00 a.m. Max is quiet. His body has stopped wriggling, and he lies limply in my arms. At first I think he's asleep, but when I look down I'm shocked to see his eyes are still open. Unfocused and hazy.

Something is very, very wrong.

I'm not imagining this, am I? His sickness isn't a figment of my neurotic depression. His chest flutters beneath his white vest, his dry lips trembling as he tries to get enough air in. All the time he's staring at something that isn't there.

By the time I call for an ambulance I'm practically incoherent. The operator tries to calm me down, asking questions with a calm, patient voice. I answer them hysterically, noticing the skin around his mouth and nose is turning blue, crying hard as I realise he's barely breathing.

"The paramedics will be with you in five minutes. Can you make sure the front door is open for them?" she asks calmly.

"Yes, I'm going down now," I manage to answer. Holding Max in one arm and my phone in the other, I clamber down the stairs, wrenching the front door open.

"Lara?" A sleepy David opens his door. He's only wearing pyjama bottoms. His chest is bare. "Is something wrong?"

Tears trail down my cheeks. Sobbing, I try to explain. "Max isn't breathing properly. The ambulance is on its way." I look down at him. He wheezes loudly.

"Shit. Let me grab a top." David disappears, returning less than a minute later, wearing jeans and a crumpled t-shirt. Gently, he touches Max's face. Wincing as he brushes his skin. "How long did they say the ambulance would be?" He steps through the front door, craning his head to look down the street. A few minutes later, the white van arrives. Though the blue lights fixed to the top are flashing, the sirens are silent. I'm not sure if this is a good thing or not.

The next moments are a blur. The paramedics gently take Max from my arms, laying him on the hall floor as they carry out an assessment. They attach an oxygen mask to his face, then turn to me, explaining that he needs to go to hospital, where he'll get the appropriate treatment. Then they carry him into the ambulance, placing his tiny body on the gurney, one paramedic holding the oxygen mask while the other closes the ambulance doors, getting into the driver's seat.

It takes ten minutes to get to hospital. This time the sirens are loud, wailing through the night air like a lamentation. They echo my own cries as I watch the paramedic helping Max to breathe. His body is still limp and unresponsive. I keep checking my watch, shocked to see only a few seconds have passed, each moment feeling like a long, drawn out torture.

"Nearly there, love," the paramedic says. "I told your husband to meet us at A&E. The roads are pretty clear tonight."

My husband? My first thought is, how the hell did they call Alex? It's only then that I realise he's talking about David.

I hate the way the disappointment tastes bitter in my mouth.

God, I need him. I start sobbing again, so scared that Max is dying. Though I can't see his face beneath all the plastic tubes, I try to hold things together as they wheel him into the hospital, covering my mouth to muffle the sobs as I follow the gurney.

They take Max straight to an examination room, while a friendly-faced junior nurse leads me to the waiting room, explaining that someone will be in to talk to me soon. When I protest, wanting to stay with Max, she rubs my arm softly.

"I know you want to be with him but there isn't enough room," she explains. "You're his mum, he needs you to be strong. Let the doctors do their job, and as soon as he's ready, I promise you'll see him."

I draw in a ragged breath. "Will they look after him?"

"They're the best." She says it with a serious face. "He couldn't be in more caring hands. Now sit here and I'll ask one of the receptionists to bring you some forms to fill in. Is there anybody you can call?"

How sad I must look, crying on my own in the middle of an empty waiting room. I nod, showing her my phone. "I can't use this here, can I?"

"In here is fine," she reassures. "Just not near the equipment.

David arrives a few minutes later, rushing into the waiting room and looking wildly around. As soon as he spots me, he runs over, scooping me into his arms. I sob into his shoulder as he strokes my hair, my face. "Where is he?" His voice is raspy and low.

"Being examined. They said they'll come and talk to me soon."

"Is he okay?"

I shake my head. "I don't know. The paramedics said something about an infection, but it all went so fast. I couldn't concentrate."

David holds me tighter still. "Of course you couldn't."

Half an hour later, Tina and Amy have joined us, their faces pale, lips pinched. Andrea is apparently on her way, too, and Beth has already texted to say she'll catch the first morning train to London. So I sit, surrounded by a makeshift family, feeling desperately lonely without my two lovely boys.

Sensing my fear, David folds my hand in his, squeezing tight. I notice Tina glancing our way, staring pointedly at our hands, but I can't bring myself to care. Instead, I look at the clock fixed high on the wall, willing the minutes to pass quickly, wondering what is taking so long.

Is my baby able to breathe? What if he isn't? What if they're putting off coming to tell me bad news?

I bite my mouth closed, swallowing my sob. My arms feel achy and empty. Having held Max all night, I'm bereft without him.

"I'll try Alex again." Tina presses some buttons on her phone, putting it to her ear. I can tell by her expression it goes straight to voicemail. She leaves a short message, explaining the situation, asking him to call back. I'm trying to work out the time difference between here and Chicago, when a pale-looking young man walks out into the waiting room, his light green scrubs denoting his job.

"Mrs Cartwright?"

Of course, Tina and I both stand up. Despite being long divorced, she's still kept the name of her only husband.

"I think he means me," I say gently.

The doctor walks forward and offers me his hand. "I'm Doctor Logan. I've been assisting Doctor Kulkarni with your son."

"How is he?" I'm aware of how desperate I sound.

"I'm afraid he's a very poorly boy." The doctor offers me a seat, pulling his chair up beside me. The others huddle in, as anxious as I am for news. "We believe he has a condition called Bronchiolitis, which is a chest infection caused by a virus called RSV. Basically all the tiny airways in his chest have swollen, making it hard for Max to breathe."

I'm finding it hard to breathe, too. "How serious is it?"

"His oxygen levels are low, in the mid-eighties, and he's very dehydrated. We need to attach him to some tubes to help him out." He smiles reassuringly. "In most cases there's a full recovery, but the next two days are crucial. We need to increase his oxygen levels enough to kick start his system."

"Is he going to live?" Tina asks, leaning forward.

"There are no guarantees, but I can tell you that ninety percent of babies go on to make a full recovery."

My voice is small. "What about the other ten percent?"

Of course, there's no answer to that.

The doctor shifts his feet. "Would you like to come and see him, Mrs Cartwright?"

I nod, standing up. The others stand too, David grabbing my hand again, Tina pushing to the front.

"I'm sorry, only Mrs Cartwright at the moment. We're moving Max to a ward and all the other children are asleep. You'll be able to see him tomorrow."

I sense, rather than see, Tina's disappointment.

Following the doctor, I walk through the dimly lit corridors and up two flights of stairs. The children's ward is at the top of the sixties-built block, secured by electronically locked doors. When he presses the code and ushers me in I notice the brightly painted murals adorning the walls. Ariel, Belle and Cinderella on one side, Buzz, Woody and Monsters Inc. on the other.

They've put Max in a room to the left of the nurses' station. The doctor explains that until the tests come back tomorrow, letting them know the type of virus he's contracted, his isolation is a temporary measure.

Nothing can prepare you for the sight of your child lying in a hospital cot. Even through the window I can see him there, naked save for his nappy. There are tubes fixed to his tiny nose, and a drip is attached to his arm. Though he's still, his tiny chest flutters rapidly, the tight skin below his rib cage concave as he breathes.

I don't think I've ever felt so helpless.

"You can go in," the doctor says, opening the door. A young nurse looks up at the sound, gifting me a reassuring smile.

"Look Max, your mummy is here."

I choke, covering my mouth with my hand, trying to swallow the sobs back down. It's hard to recognize the scrappy little thing lying in the plastic cot. I've never seen Max so still.

"You can come and sit with him." The nurse stands back, offering me her seat. "He'll be reassured to hear your voice. He's doing so well, fighting so hard."

The doctor follows me to Max's cot, pointing out each tube and explaining what they do. He talks of oxygen percentages and prognoses, telling me we can expect Max to get worse before he starts to recover. A dip is normal, expected. They're ready for it.

"Can I touch him?" My face is wet with tears. Max's hand is curled up on his chest. Above it, on his wrist, is a tiny band with his name on, as if he's going to a festival.

"Of course, but try not to touch the tubes. When he needs a nappy change we'll show you how to do it without pulling them out." Her voice is reassuring.

Reaching out, I run the pad of my finger down the back of Max's hand. His skin feels warm but not hot. The indentation from my finger lingers long after I've touched him.

"That's the dehydration," the nurse explains. "His skin will plump up soon."

Eventually the two of them leave, showing me the call button before closing the door softly behind them. Sitting down, I keep my hand on Max's, watching as he finally sleeps. The room is silent except for the sound of his breathing, and I notice how the hospital has a timbre of its own. Hollow and damp, punctuated by the occasional cry from the ward, or a muted conversation between the nurses outside.

Though I can't think of anything to say, I sing softly to Max, a song that once meant something to Alex and me. It was on the stereo the first night we made love. The first dance at our wedding. And though I don't remember all the words, I know enough to remember how much Alex and I used to love The

Temper Trap. He used to mouth the lyrics to me, promising he wouldn't stop until it was over. I can almost see him doing it now.

That images is all it takes to break the dam. I sob the words silently as tears roll down my face, and I'm praying that Alex has picked up the message.

I don't care about that picture. I don't care about the band. All I want is for Max to get better and for Alex to come home.

We both need him.

# 19

The children's ward comes to life a little before seven in the morning. The night-time hush gives way to the bustle of morning rounds, as nurses come in and out of the room, reading Max's monitors and writing on his chart. The squeaky wheels of a loaded trolley heralds the arrival of breakfast, and a hum of chatter and cries fill the rooms around us.

Stretching, I try to relieve the knots in my neck that have formed from an uncomfortable night sitting on a wooden chair. Max is still quiet, his eyes closed, his dry lips parted. His nose looks sore where the tubes go in.

"His temperature has stabilized," the nurse tells me as she removes the ear thermometer. She's in her early thirties with a fiery mane of hair. Her name is Claire or Clara, I can't remember which; I was too busy staring at Max to listen.

"Is that a good sign?" I have to know.

She flashes me a quick smile. "It means he'll be more comfortable."

"What time does the doctor make his rounds?" Though my knowledge of the inner workings of hospitals mostly comes from movies, I know for sure that rounds happen daily. And that's when I'm likely to find out the most information.

"In about half an hour. Maybe you'd like to pop into the waiting room in the meantime, I think your family would like to see you."

Walking into the sterile-smelling room, I notice the crowd has multiplied. As well as Tina, Amy, and David, Andrea

arrived sometime in the night, and Beth has made it, too. It feels as though there's only one person missing.
That, and a corner of my heart.
"Has Alex called?" I immediately home in on Tina. A moment later she's hugging me, asking me about Max, her eyes streaming with tears.
"How is he? Did he sleep? I tried calling Alex twice, but there was no answer. I left a message, though."
It feels as if there's a lead weight at the base of my stomach. Pulling at the lining, and tearing it through. "Maybe they're on the road again," I croak.
"They finished a gig in Toronto last night," Amy points out. "They updated their Facebook page. I'll send them a message, see if they pick it up."
She doesn't offer to show me and I don't ask to look. There's too much going on. Jealousy isn't something I have room for at the moment, fear has put everything else on mute.
"I'll try him again." It's around 3:00 a.m. in Toronto, but that doesn't mean anything, post-gig celebrations can stretch out until morning for the band. Without a baby or a steady job to worry about, sleeping it off isn't a problem.
Predictably, the call rings straight through to voicemail again. This time I'm not so laid back about it. Frustrated, I leave a terse message, telling him to call me back right away, suggesting he grow up a bit, reminding Alex that the world doesn't revolve around him. When I hang up, the waiting room is silent. Tina is staring at me with wide eyes, Amy is smirking, and Beth looks sympathetic. David walks over and gives me a big hug.
"He'll call back," he mutters into my hair. "Max is his kid, of course he'll call back."
"You're judging him by your standards," I point out, keeping my voice low. The last thing I need is a row with Tina.

"Just because you'd move mountains to be with your kid, doesn't mean that Alex will."

"He loves you, he loves Max. *He'll call you back.*"

I don't know why David sounds so much more certain than I feel. Maybe he has some kind of guy-empathy I'm not feeling. The fact we've been calling Alex for five hours with no response doesn't give me much confidence at all.

Do we really mean so little to him?

The door opens and we all look over to see who it is. When I see a man wearing a suit, my heart clenches, thinking it's a doctor—one with bad news. But then I look up and see white-grey hair and a sun-beaten face, and my dad shuffles in uncertainly, as if he's not sure he should be here.

Since my mum died, he's only been to London once. Dad finds it hard to cope with the noise and the bustle, and too overwhelming to sit on a tube train for long. Yet he's here, walking up to me, his lined eyes kind and concerned, and I'm so shocked I don't know what to say.

He clears his throat. "I got your message. How's the baby?" The next moment he's pulling me into his arms, and I'm eight again, crying about an injustice at school, a broken friendship or a skinned knee. While I sob into his suited shoulder, he pats my back, his words soft and quiet as if he's reassuring a child.

"The doctor's with him now," I mutter into his jacket. "He's got a virus in his chest." Finally, I look up at him. Gently, he brushes away the hair that's sticking to my wet cheeks.

"Can they treat it?"

"Not the virus." I shake my head. "Antibiotics won't work. But he's on a drip with fluids and oxygen and they reckon that should help. The next two days are the most important."

"Have you seen him?"

"I spent the night with him. They're going to let us back in once the rounds are over." I give him a watery smile. "He'll be happy to see his granddad."

Dad's voice is uncharacteristically gruff. "I'll be happy to see him, too."

Another thing about my father: he's a stoic. Though he cried when my mum died, I don't think he has done since. But either I'm seeing things or there's a tear rolling down his cheek, and that both frightens me and comforts me.

"Is Alex on his way?" Dad asks. Silence greets his question. From the corner of my eye I notice Tina shifting uncomfortably.

"We can't get hold of him," I admit. Dad's brow furrows as he takes in my words.

"It's the middle of the night over there, he's probably fast asleep," Tina says. "He'll get the message as soon as he gets up, I bet. Be here by tomorrow morning."

"I'm sure he will," Dad replies. I'm not sure who he is trying to convince. Maybe all of us. For a moment I close my eyes, picturing Alex's face, relaxed in sleep, and I pray that dad is right.

*Please, God, let him pick up that message.*

\* \* \*

I spend the rest of the morning by Max's side. Though he's still listless, and his breathing remains ragged, the doctor tells me he is stabilising, and that we should see some small improvement by tomorrow. His oxygen levels are up to 90%, but he isn't well enough for the tube to come out.

Visitors trail in and out. Tina comes first, her face crumpling when she sees Max, and her concern touches me. She whispers softly to him, telling him he's loved, that he needs to fight. That his daddy will see him soon.

My father's visit is less emotional. Any feelings he showed earlier have been firmly locked away. He stands over the cot, his hands hanging loosely by his side, and I can tell he doesn't know what on earth to do with himself.

When Amy and Andrea come in around twelve, I walk with Beth to the café, leaving Dad and Tina in the waiting room. David has gone home to do some work.

"I'm going to try Alex again." I wave my phone at Beth. My battery has almost gone, and I realize it's not going to last through the voicemail message. I jot Stuart's number down on a scrap of paper I find in the bottom of my handbag, and borrow Beth's phone.

She brushes off my suggestions that I'll pay her back. "Don't be silly, it's only money. You can keep the phone until we get your charger." Another reason David's gone back. I've given him a list of things I need along with my set of keys. He's promised to be at the hospital by tea time.

I step through the automatic glass doors, into the outside air. After the artificial lighting of the hospital, the sunlight makes me blink rapidly.

The entrance is surrounded by anxious smokers, so I step to the side, past the ambulance bay, finding an empty corner where I can hear myself think. With the scrap of paper in one hand, I hastily press the numbers into Beth's phone. Lifting it to my ear, I wait for the now-familiar sound of Stuart's voicemail message.

Instead, I'm rewarded with a ringtone. The long beeps remind me they're in another country, a stark contrast to the jaunty ringtones in the UK. After three repeats I hear Stuart's voice, but not a recorded version.

This one is live.

"Hello?"

"Stuart? It's Lara." I'm so shocked to hear his voice, I don't know what to say. I'm momentarily dumb.

"Lara? Whose phone are you using?" Is that suspicion in his voice? I shake it off, remembering why I'm calling.

"Is Alex there? I need to talk to him."

"Nah, I'm afraid not. He's stepped out for a bit."

"Did he get my messages?" I ask. "Does he know Max is sick?"

Stuart clears his throat. "Oh yeah, how is the little guy?" He makes it sound as if Max has a small cold. Not that his life is in danger.

"He's in hospital," I explain quickly, feeling frustrated. "I need to talk to Alex. Does he know about Max?"

"Of course," Stuart sounds affronted. "He's worried sick. Make sure you keep us updated with how he's doing."

*Keep us updated?*

"What do you mean?" My stomach lurches. I wasn't prepared for this. "He's coming home, isn't he?"

A pause follows. I hear Stuart's breaths, the beating of my heart, and the sound of a car horn from streets away.

"He wants to, Lara, but we're on tour. He can't simply abandon his commitments." For the first time, he sounds uncertain. "I mean, it's not like it's life or death, is it?" Stuart gives a little chuckle, and I want to strangle him.

"Max stopped breathing." I manage to get it out, anger laced through my voice. "His oxygen levels were dangerously low and he was severely dehydrated. He could have died." I breathe loudly through my nose. "And he's still very sickly. I want to talk to Alex."

"I'm sorry, Lara, but he doesn't want to talk to you. We've got another show tonight and you know how he gets."

"He doesn't want to talk to me?"

"He'll be home in a couple of weeks. He'll see Max then. Remember what we talked about? You don't want to upset him, do you?"

"Let me speak to my husband, Stuart." I feel like throwing the phone on the floor.

"Alex!" Stuart's shout reverberates down the phone. "It's Lara." There's a muffled conversation I can't hear. I stand there, outside the hospital where our son is being treated, waiting to hear my husband's voice.

Except I don't. Instead, Stuart speaks again, sounding slightly bored with the whole thing. "Sorry, Lara, he's tied up at the moment. I'll get him to call you later."

*Tied up?*

*Call me later?*

I can't answer for a moment. I try to swallow down the bile that's collected in my throat. I think about all those arguments, about the drugs, the band, the fact I wanted Max more than he did. He's making his feelings painfully obvious, choosing his music over his wife and son. Choking up, I realise I'm all alone in this now. The man I thought I could rely on turns out to be no man at all.

I finally reply, my voice thick. "Don't bother. I don't want to talk to him."

\* \* \*

When I walk back inside I can't bring myself to look at Tina. Can't tell her that her son is refusing to come home. Instead I stick to Max like glue, avoiding her suggestions I try calling Alex again. Something stops me from telling her the truth. A misplaced sense of loyalty, perhaps, or the knowledge she's finding it hard to cope. Either way, I keep my fury to myself.

My father leaves at five o'clock, hugging me tight before he goes. He isn't used to spending a night away from home, and though he offers to stay, I gently refuse. As the night creeps in, one by one they take their leave. Amy goes first, muttering something about meeting Luke, while Andrea needs to go home and feed her cat.

Tina stays a little longer, coming in to squeeze Max's hand a final time.

"Alex will be here tomorrow." She sounds so sure, I don't have the energy to steal any hope from her. It's a rare commodity around here.

"I hope so." It isn't a lie. He needs to be close enough for me to kick his butt.

She hugs me close, still smelling of flowery perfume. I pat her back in the same way my dad did to me earlier.

Finally, only Beth and I are left. She sits on the chair while I help the nurse clean Max up. For the first time, his eyes focus enough to catch mine.

"Hello, baby," I whisper. "How are you doing?"

He stares silently.

"We miss you. Everybody wants you to get better." I pat his red skin with the cool flannel. He blinks twice, still looking up. When I brush his hand he tries to grab my finger.

"Feisty little thing, isn't he?" The night shift nurse finishes fastening his nappy. "The doctor's pleased with his progress."

It's like being told your child is a genius. That he's won a Nobel Prize. When he curls his fingers around mine a little smile pulls at my lips; I can tell he knows I'm here.

Later still, Beth and I talk quietly, while Max sleeps. There's a glow from my phone as it charges, and I've changed into the fresh clothes that David brought.

"He didn't mean it." She sounds so sure. "I bet he doesn't realise how poorly Max has been."

I sip from the plastic cup of water the nurse brought for me. "I didn't leave him in any doubt. In my messages, my conversation with Stuart, I made certain he knew." Max coughs and we all hold our breath. Then he calms and I feel my heart slow. "Not to mention the hysterical voicemails his mum left. He knows exactly what the situation is, he doesn't want to come back."

She slips her hand inside mine. "Don't make any rash assumptions. You need to talk this through with him."

When did Beth become the wise one? Out of the two of us, I've always been the stronger. The one to lean on, the counsellor. Yet I cling to her words, wishing they were true.

"Max is in hospital, fighting for his life. He can't possibly have an excuse. What reason can there be?" I ask these questions, as I'm lost for the answers. "What possible thing can keep a man from his sick child?"

"All I'm saying is wait and see. I've learned that making assumptions only leads to heartache." Beth knows what she's talking about. After a whirlwind romance, it took her nine years to get together with Niall. I know she regrets the time they lost. "Promise me you'll hear him out."

I lean back heavily on my chair. It's an impossible promise to make. Not only because I'm not sure I can ever forgive him for not being here when I begged him to, but also because he was too much of a coward, hiding behind his band mate like a frightened child.

I don't believe there's any way to forgive him for what happened. For putting the band before his son's health. And though Max is beautifully unaware right now, one day he's going to know.

A missed school play, a broken promise, a million tiny heart aches. They line the road in front of us, all the ways my son's life can be broken.

Like a lioness, I swear I'm going to protect him. No matter the cost.

## 20

Three days later, Max has not only stabilised, but his condition has improved enough for his tubes to be removed. He's started feeding from a bottle, finding enough strength to suck from a teat, his cheeks hollowing out as he tries to take in more milk.

When the doctor makes the rounds that morning, he offers me a smile, listening to Max's chest before pulling the stethoscope away from his ears.

"There's still some congestion but it's much clearer. He's making an amazing recovery."

I'm surprised at how invested all the staff have become in Max's health. It's a wonderful thing to see. Their dedication to his well-being is something I don't think I'll ever forget, and I'm more than thankful.

"He actually cried last night," I tell him. "I think it's the first time I've been happy to be woken up by his sobs."

The doctor grins at my enthusiasm. "He should be ready for discharge tomorrow. I expect you'll be glad to get him back home."

If I'm truly honest, I'm not sure I will. Memories of that night when Max struggled for breath assault me. My inability to help, the panic. The all-consuming fear.

The thought of not having the doctors and nurses around to help, should he suffer a relapse, is like an icy hand curling around my heart.

"I haven't been home for days. We don't have any food, any milk..." I trail off.

His smile is gentle, he must be used to dealing with neurotic parents. "Why don't you go home for a few hours and get things ready? Maybe one of the family can sit with Max while you're gone."

When Tina arrives an hour later, I tell her about the doctor's suggestion, explaining they plan to discharge Max tomorrow as long as his oxygen levels remain steady.

She shuffles her chair closer to his cot. "Of course I'll look after him, you deserve a break. Have a nap, too. And a shower."

I wrinkle my nose. "Do I smell?" I've been washing myself thoroughly every morning, frightened to introduce any more germs into Max's tiny body. But the antibacterial liquid soap isn't exactly Jo Malone. I smell functional at best.

"Don't be silly." Tina laughs. "I thought you'd like a few home comforts. Anyway, I expect Alex will be here soon. He can help you out then."

I'd call her delusional, but the fact is I still haven't been able to tell her about that phone call. I'm finding it hard to process myself, let alone watch her go through the same thing. I know I have to do it eventually, and I will.

As soon as Max is out of hospital.

"Maybe." I smile, but it's forced. "In the meantime, thank you for helping. I appreciate it."

Yes she can be nosy, and occasionally interfering, but Tina's heart is in the right place. She's been here for her grandson, sitting with him every day. You can't buy that kind of love.

Stepping out of the hospital, I feel like a prisoner getting an early release. Turning my head, I glance back at the grey concrete of the building now behind me, unwilling to leave. I'm scared, too.

The sensible part of my brain tells me Max is out of the woods. His oxygen levels have improved and he's started to feed. He can go back to being a normal baby. It's me who feels different. As if my heart has been scarred by the experience. Beneath the tough outer-membrane the fear that something could happen to him is all too raw.

I catch a bus back to Shoreditch, standing with my hand wrapped around the cool, metal pole, watching as people get on and off. A baby cries and I immediately whip my head around, my stomach lurching when I realise it isn't Max. Being away from him, even for a couple of hours, is harder than I expected.

When the bus finally reaches my stop, the air brakes sounding like a deep, agonising sigh, I find myself reluctant to get off. It isn't often I step off a bus without having Max's buggy to push, and my hands feel strangely empty. Even walking along the pavement feels weird, as if the world is ever so slightly mad, and I go to grab a buggy handle for balance, my fingers curling into a fist when I realise it isn't there.

*He's okay,* I tell myself.

I decide to text Tina on the off chance. **Everything all right?**

She shoots me back a reply straight away. **He's absolutely fine. Now stop worrying.**

But it's almost impossible to stop fretting. I don't think I ever will. Now that the membrane of my blind optimism is breached, I can't help think about all the roadblocks that line our future. The viruses, the bacteria, the cars that drive too fast. The kids who call names, the daddies who don't come home. They're all there, waiting for us. Goading us on.

I'm still stewing on it all when I let myself into the front door. From old habit, more than anything else, I tap lightly on David's door to let him know I'm here.

There's no response. Strange; it's early afternoon, he's usually working.

Shrugging, I make my way to our upstairs flat, slipping the key in our door for the first time in days.

There's a staleness to the air which I notice as soon as I step inside. As if it's stood still for too long, become bored and lazy. The first thing I do is open all the windows, watching the breeze lift the ends of the curtains. Though it's cloudy, the sun is strong enough to push through the hazy layer, casting a pale yellow glow on our wooden floor. It pools at my feet, turning my toes golden, highlighting the horrendous chips that have decimated the polish there. With my mangled feet, bitten down nails and general aroma of hospital, I'm a walking mess.

The shower sorts some of that out. It washes away the aroma of anti-bacterial wash, replacing it with the familiar floral scent of my shower gel. It soothes my body, too; the hot spray hammering on my muscles like a thousand tiny fingers. I stay in there a bit too long. Enough for the skin on my fingers to wrinkle up. When I finally emerge, I'm shocked to see nearly two hours have passed since I was at the hospital.

Hurrying, I dry my hair and wind it into a messy bun, pulling on a fresh pair of jeans and a T-shirt. Then I pack some fresh clothes for Max, ready for his journey home. The shelves of the fridge have already been stocked with essentials—thanks to David, no doubt—so by quarter past five I'm ready to go back to the hospital.

This time—laden down with bags and a car seat—I take a cab. It isn't much faster than the bus, especially as it's the middle of rush hour, but it's altogether quieter, allowing me to rest my head on the door and stare out of the window.

We pass the familiar landmarks: shops, the station, the pub on the corner where Alex used to play. I remember a hundred different nights spent in there with him. The way he would grab my bottom as we left, his guitar slung over his shoulder, hair messy after a night of hard rocking.

It makes me feel wistful. Though I thought I'd washed my melancholy down the shower drain along with the dirt that clung to my skin, it's come back with full force. Perhaps it's the post-natal depression, perhaps it's knowing Alex chose his band, his career over us. Or maybe it's the knowledge I came so close to losing my baby that makes my heart feel as if it's been slashed in two.

When we pull up at the hospital, I count out the money and hand it to the driver, telling him to keep the change. Then I climb out, slamming the door behind me, and walk back into the hospital with arms full of baby stuff.

Taking the lift, rather than the stairs, I press the button for the top floor. A couple of people get in after me, before the doors slide closed. By the time I get into the Neptune ward, I'm glad to put down my bounty, and I have to shake my arms to return the feeling to my fingers.

Things haven't changed in the time I've been gone. The beds are still full of children, some sleeping, others surrounded by family. The walls retain the vibrancy of the murals, the smiling Disney faces adding a cheer to the ward. In the past few days I've become accustomed to the sounds and smells of the hospital. It feels familiar. Comforting. And as I walk into the room beside the nurses' station the smile on my face is genuine.

Genuine, but fleeting.

Max is awake, being held while he sucks at a half-full bottle of milk. His hand grasps the plastic, as if he's trying to feed himself. Even after two hours he looks brighter. Healthier. His cheeks are pink and supple.

But it's not Max I'm staring at, it's the man holding him. The man with the sinewy biceps and colourful tattoos that cover his arms. The man who is looking at me, a smile breaking out on his lips.

*Alex.*

\* \* \*

Back when I worked in an investment bank, Saturdays were reserved for all the crap I couldn't get done in the week. Trips to the hairdressers, dumping laundry at the dry cleaners. Stocking up on essentials at the local Tesco Metro. What they weren't reserved for was bringing strange singers back to my flat in the early hours of the morning. Yet that's what I found myself doing the first night I met Alex.

I lived in one of those impossibly anonymous apartment blocks that surrounded London's Docklands. Red brick, and warehouse-like, they lined the waterways, their blandness reflected back in the rivers they loomed over. Even with the morning sun rising up behind them, they failed to look anything else than what they were; holding pens for City workers.

"You live here?" Alex asked, looking around the lobby as we walked towards the bank of three elevators. "Seriously?"

I glanced behind me, wondering what he found so funny. The desk was manned by a security guard, his face half-hidden by the huge vase of fresh flowers resting on the walnut countertop. The floors were marble, veined with pale blues and pinks. I couldn't see anything amusing about them.

"Yeah, why?" I wrinkled my nose.

"I dunno. It doesn't seem very you."

"What does that mean?" I couldn't work out if it was a compliment or a criticism.

We stepped through the open lift doors. "It's too boring. No life to it."

I pressed the button for my floor and watched as he leaned against the mirrored wall. A dozen Alexes reflected right back at me. "It's close to work," I protested. I didn't know why his dislike of my place annoyed me, but it did. I felt as though he was judging me.

"What do you do again?"

"I work in hedge funds." Normally people tuned out as soon as I started talking about my job. All they ever wanted to know was what I earned, and what shares they should invest in. Anything over and above that and they were falling asleep.

"Do you like it?"

He stared at me and I felt that pull again, as though an invisible cord was wrapped around my waist.

"It's a great job," I said. "It's challenging and difficult but it's brilliant experience. I get given a lot of responsibility, more than other firms would."

He raised a single eyebrow, making his ring glint in the glare of the light. "But *do you like it?*"

My head started to ache as I thought of the downsides. The times we lost millions, the way all the partners shouted at us constantly. How I always felt I wasn't good enough.

"It's a job."

I didn't like the way he looked at me. As if I was something to be pitied.

I preferred his hot stares, and when we walked out of the lift, I found myself swaying my hips in an exaggerated way, hoping to get that back.

"Anyway," I said, putting my key in the lock. "It pays for all this." I pushed open the door and we stepped inside. I hadn't been home since the previous morning, and even then I was too bleary eyed to do much more than shower and slap on some make-up. So I was relieved to see it was pretty neat—especially for me. Not a pair of dirty knickers to be seen.

When I turned to offer him a cup of tea, that hot look was back again. His eyes were dark and narrowed, his jaw tense. It knocked the breath out of me, especially when he took a step forward and traced the thin skin across my collar bone. Even though his touch was light, it still made me shiver.

"Lara," he said. "Such a pretty name. The sort of name I could write songs about." His finger dragged lower, reaching the swell of my breasts. I wanted to look down, to watch what he was going to do, but I was too entranced by his eyes.

"I bet you say that to all the girls."

"Not to ones called Ethel." He smirked and it made me giggle. Then he leaned forward and brushed his lips against my neck, and it was all I could do to breathe.

"You taste of coconuts," he whispered into my skin. "I want to cover you in chocolate and eat you like a Bounty."

I laughed again. He was funny *and* hot. "Plain or milk?"

His lips trailed lower. He pushed my collar aside, fingers dipping inside my bra, and the next moment I felt his thumb graze my nipple.

"There's nothing plain about you."

He could talk the talk so well, I liked it. The way he couldn't give a shit about my job or my rent-as-expensive-as-a-small-car flat was refreshing. Alex was the no-bullshit type. Said what he thought and took what he wanted. It was insanely sexy.

"Did I tell you I have a really nice bedroom?" I ask him. "Views of the river. King size bed. I might even have made it yesterday." I wasn't sure about that last bit.

"Do you look at the view a lot?" he asked.

"It's pretty."

"When you have sex?" He unbuttoned my dress, brushing the thin silk off my shoulders. It slid down my arms and fluttered to the floor.

"All the time." I didn't want to admit I couldn't remember the last time I had sex.

"Mmm." He pushed my bra down, freeing my breasts. Sighing softly, he scooped them into his palms, his thumbs stroking my flesh. "This is pretty."

"Yeah?" My voice was soft.

"Yeah."

By the time we made it into my bedroom I was naked except for my knickers. Still dressed, Alex spun me around, his hands gripping my waist, fingers digging into my hips. Stepping forward, he pressed me against the glass window overlooking the Thames. I could feel his erection on my behind.

"I want you to take a good look at that view," he whispered into my ear. His breath tickled and caressed.

"Why?" By that point I was all sensation. My front was cold as it pressed into the glass, my back hot with his presence. His fingers slipped inside my knickers.

"Because you won't be looking at it again for a while. I'm not one of your city boy hook-ups. I don't do sweet, I don't do respectable. When I'm finished with you, Lara, you won't be able to open your eyes, let alone appreciate the fucking vista."

*Oh God.*

I wracked my brain for a snarky reply but the impulse died as he spun me back around, my heated back now pressed to the cold glass. Then he dipped his head until his mouth was hard on mine, his demanding kisses leaving me in no doubt that his fucking would be equally as aggressive. Then he pulled my knickers down, dragging his fingers, the tips brushing the part that made my knees buckle.

"Take your clothes off," I growled, pulling at his T-shirt He stepped back, grinning, and lifted it over his head. I stared at him, open-mouthed, following the lines of his muscles, the patterns of his ink. Admiring him as if he was a work of art.

Then he pulled off his jeans, standing only in his boxers. A hard ridge was obvious at the front. I trailed my finger down him, watching him twitch, then curled my hand until I was cupping his erection.

When I sunk to my knees, I heard him mutter a low *"fuck,"* his oaths getting louder as I took him out of his boxers. My hand encircled his girth, pulling him down, enough for my lips to graze against his tip.

He gave a sharp intake of breath.

I wrapped my mouth around him. Trailed my tongue around the head. When he sighed louder, his hands tangling in my hair, I couldn't help but hum with satisfaction.

I'd finally found a way to shut up the dirty boy.

# 21

"What are you doing here?" It comes out harsher than I intend, but I'm totally blindsided. I wasn't prepared for a confrontation, not until his tour ended.

Not to mention the fact that Max is practically giggling in his dad's lap.

The same lap that had a girl squirming about in it a little over a week ago.

Alex's brows knit together. "I got the first plane I could. Things were crazy."

"Bullshi—" My retort is cut short by the arrival of Tina. She bustles in, a big smile on her face. "Oh, there you are, Lara. All better? Did you have a nice rest?"

She makes it sound as though I've popped home to freshen up. Doesn't mention the fact I've been here four days straight without a break, or that I was starting to smell like a piece of the hospital furniture.

"I got things done."

I can feel Alex staring at me, and I know he's still frowning, but I can't even bring myself to look at him again. Max grunts as he finishes his bottle and I hear Alex say something to him, but in my fury and frustration I can't make out what it is.

"How's he doing?" One of the nurses walks into the room, immediately making a beeline for Max and Alex. "Would you like me to take him for you?" I swear I can hear her batting her eyelashes.

"It's okay, I can do it."

*Of course you bloody can*, I think. *You haven't had to lift a finger for over a month.* There's a part of me—one I'm not proud of—that feels aggrieved he's waltzed back in and taken over. Everybody's smiling at him, bar me.

Even Max, the little traitor.

"Alex flew through the night," Tina feels the need to tell me. She picks up some of Max's muslin cloths, folding them neatly. "He didn't even stop to go home. He was so worried, he came straight here."

Give the man a medal. He's only four days late.

"How are you doing, babe?" He turns his eyes on me. "I'm so sorry I wasn't here."

"I'm fine." The tone in my voice lets him know I'm anything but. "We coped without you."

"Is everything all right?" He sounds confused.

Of course Tina has something to add. "She's been doing so well. But the depression is very hard on her."

It's as if I'm in a parallel universe. A few hours ago I knew where I was. My baby was getting better, my friends were taking care of me, and my husband was halfway around the world doing God knows what, with God knows who. But now... it's as though I'm upside down on a roller coaster, desperately trying to work out which way is up.

"I'm doing fine." It's the second time I've said it, but this time I enunciate each word with purpose. Alex is aware that *fine* is international woman code for 'you're in deep trouble'. Maybe that's why he busies himself by chatting with the nurse.

"Is there anything we need to do when we get home?"

The nurse launches into an explanation about bronchioles and oxygen saturation, while Alex nods with interest. Digging my nails into my palm, I try to keep myself calm. Stable. Sane.

Because *what the hell?*

The feeling that I'm in some kind of weird dream still hasn't dissipated. There's this man sitting in the corner holding my son, and I'm not sure if I even know him. I'm so confused I'm not sure what I should do next. But the anger that's been brewing in my stomach for days shows no sign of leaving.

"We can do that, can't we?" Alex says to me.

"What?"

"Keep an eye on him when we take him home. Make sure his breathing stays normal."

"You're coming back home?"

"Of course." He gives a little laugh. "Where did you think I was going?"

"Back on tour?"

"Seriously? You think I'd leave when Max has been this bad? What kind of guy do you think I am?"

It's a good question, but not one he necessarily wants to hear the answer to. At least not in front of all these people. So I bite my lip, trying to remind myself where I am.

"Can I have a word?" I ask. "Outside."

For the first time since I walked in, he looks shifty, a child waiting outside the headmaster's office. There's a part of me that wants to start shouting right now, tell him everything we've been through without him. That while he was lording it up with some blonde on his knee, I was watching our son struggling to breathe.

Okay, so maybe not at exactly the same time. But close enough.

We end up walking down the corridor and to the tiny waiting room at the other end of the ward. Thankfully, it's empty. I sit down on one of the under-stuffed chairs, feeling the springs give way as my bottom presses into the cushions as Alex takes the sofa opposite, wisely placing a table between us.

When I look at him, I wonder how we got to this. How that girl and boy who fell in love ended up sitting here, their child lying sick in a hospital bed, with absolutely nothing to say.

No, that's not right. There's plenty to say, I simply don't know how to say it. My anger feels as if it's been packaged up neatly and stuffed to the bottom of my chest, something to be dealt with at a later date. If I unwrap it now, as I think I'm going to do, I'm not sure I can contain it. I feel sick, not only from the thought of confrontation, but the knowledge that we're coming perilously close to hurting one another.

I don't want to lose him, but we can't go on like this.

While the thoughts rage in my head, Alex looks at me, his eyes dark and soft. The way he stares reminds me so much of those first few days we spent together, and it's messing with my mind even more.

"Are you angry at me?" He finally breaks the silence. "For being away when Max got ill?"

Quickly I shake my head. "That's not why I'm angry."

"So you are angry?"

"Yes." I take a deep breath. I can't let myself explode, not anymore. If I want to be heard I need to say it, not shout it.

"Why?"

I start to count the ways, and I have to close my eyes, to block out that dark stare. The way he's looking at me is unnerving.

"Because it took you so long to come home. Because you didn't return my calls. Because I felt like a single parent, watching my child dying without the one person I thought I could rely on." I bit my lip, trying to stop it from wobbling. "I watched our son turn blue in my arms. He couldn't breathe. I thought he was dead."

The small room seems thick with recriminations. For a moment, Alex remains seated. But when my breath hitches, he jumps up and crosses the room, wrapping his arms around me.

I freeze.

"Christ, Lara, I'm sorry. I got here as soon as I could. If they still flew Concorde I would have got on that. Fucking eight hour flights."

"You got here four days late." I try to shrug him off. Having his arms around me feels wrong, I can't stand it. "I left you so many messages."

"There weren't that many."

"And I spoke to Stuart…"

I feel him stiffen. When I pull my head back to look at him he says nothing. His face is blank. I wait for him to say something. To tell me how wrong he was. All I get is silence.

"Why didn't you call me?" I ask.

His voice is quiet, a whisper. "I only got the message yesterday."

"You're lying." I think of all the voicemails I left. The anguished wait for a call. The long hours of nothingness. "I called you four days ago."

"Lara, I swear to you I only found out yesterday. I got the first plane home as soon as I heard. I left a message on your phone to tell you I was coming."

I think of my phone lying at the bottom of my bag, uncharged for the past day. I suppose I could charge it, listen to that call, and let him prove he's telling the truth. But I'm not sure what the point is. Either way, I was on my own.

I have been for a long time.

"I talked to Stuart. He said you didn't want to come home, that you didn't want to talk to me."

"That's bullshit!" For the first time, Alex looks furious. "I never said that. He's a fucking liar."

My voice is strangely calm. "It doesn't matter. Not anymore. It's all symptomatic of the same thing. You weren't ready to be a father, you told me that yourself. I should have listened to you."

Alex is kneeling next to me, one hand on the arm of the chair, the other balled into a fist by his side. "That's not true. I love Max. When I heard... Christ, Lara, I couldn't think straight. All those hours on the plane, wondering if he was okay. If you were okay..." His voice breaks. "Babe, I'm so sorry."

I close my eyes, trying to block out the words. All my tears have dried up, and I'm a piece of fruit left out in the sun too long.

"It doesn't matter."

"It fucking does." A tear forms in the corner of his eye. It's too painful to watch. I have to look away, staring instead at a wall full of medical posters.

"Alex, I'm tired, exhausted, as if I haven't slept for weeks. I want to take Max home and cocoon myself away from the world. Forget any of this happened." I think of my bed. Of fresh sheets. Of escaping from everything.

"We can do that."

That's when I look at him, and I realise he doesn't have a clue how unhappy I am. How hurt I am, or how angry I am. I've coped with everything else, but I can't cope with this, with him. Not now.

"I don't want you to come home with us." I say it while looking at my knees. "It's all too much. I need some space to work out how I feel."

"What do you mean?" His brow knits into a frown.

After all these days of waiting, it's ironic how much I need some space. The thought of Alex coming home, of us being cooped up in the flat together, makes me feel jittery. With the emotional roller coaster of the last few days, I think I might implode.

"Can you stay at your mum's?" I beg. I hate the way his face crumples when I say it.

"You're breaking up with me?"

"No! Of course not." To be honest, I'm not sure what I'm doing. I can barely believe it myself. "I need some time to think things through. You've been away so long, and with everything that happened…"

"Then what, Lara? What do you want me to do? To get on my fucking knees and beg? I will if that's what it takes. I love you. Don't fucking do this."

"I love you, too," I tell him quietly. He looks up at me through thick, dark eyelashes. His eyes glint beneath the light.

"Then why?"

Though it kills me, I keep my gaze firmly locked on his. There's a lump the size of a rock in my throat. Making my voice husky. Low. "Because I can't go on like this."

"Tell me what to do. I'll do anything." He reaches out, takes my hand. "Please, tell me."

I'm finding it hard to breathe. Even when I take a mouthful of air, it fights against me, catching in my throat, refusing to reach my lungs. "Just give me some space."

\* \* \*

A week later, Max is home and we're living a strange kind of half-life. I've taken unpaid leave from the clinic, promising to return next week, though the thought of it claws at my heart like a hungry animal. I spend my days watching Max improve, smiling when he starts crawling again, clapping the first time he pulls himself up to standing. He holds on to the coffee table, his eyes wide and his plump legs wobbling. The expression on his face is hilarious, as if he can't believe he's finally done it.

The next moment, he falls unceremoniously to the floor. Whimpering, he reaches up for me.

"Come here, you clever boy," I say in a sing-song voice. "That didn't hurt."

The second time he does it I have my camera ready. I send the video to Alex, my fingers trembling as I bring up his contact details. Every time I think about him I feel sick. I know there's talking to do, decisions to make, though I don't know where to start.

*Can I come and see him tonight?*

Alex's text makes me feel desperately sad. Should he even have to ask?

*Of course. Any time.*

I mean it. No matter what happens between Alex and me, Max comes first. He deserves to have both parents doting on him.

I spend the rest of the morning cleaning feverishly, in a way I never did when Alex and I were both staying here. I bathe Max after his tea, dressing him in a fresh onesie, then I brush my hair and fix my make-up.

There's no denying this feels weird. It's a dance millions of ex-wives do every weekend; the passing over of a child, the keeping up of appearances. The desire to show the other person what they're missing.

Except I *know* Alex is missing us. He texts me all the time, calls me every day. Last night, as I was drifting off to sleep, my phone lit up, showing his name, and I practically snatched it off the bedside table.

*"Hey."*

*"Lara."*

*I've always loved the way he says my name. It sounds like he's smiling. As if I do that to him.*

*Checking my watch, I climbed out of bed, not wanting to wake Max. He was curled up on his side, three fingers in his mouth. Thankfully the slurping noises had died down.*

"You okay?" I sat on the armchair, tucking my legs beneath my bum. "What are you doing up so late?"

"Thinking about you." His voice was soft; an aural caress. "Missing my family."

"We miss you, too," I whispered. It was so dark in the room it was like having my eyes closed. I could picture Alex, lying in his childhood bed, unable to sleep. It made me feel like the worst person in the world. Refusing to let him come home, denying him time with his son. At moments like those, it was hard to remember why he wasn't here.

Then I remembered the tour. The drugs and the photos. There was so much for me to work through—for us to talk about—and having him living here would confuse everything. I was mixed up enough as it was.

"How's Max feeling?" I heard a rustle. Like he was turning over in bed. "Are you managing to get any sleep?"

"Max is fine. The doctor says his lungs are clear." Apparently miraculous recoveries are the norm when it comes to babies and bronchiolitis. Looking at him now, you'd never believe he was in hospital last week.

I didn't tell Alex I was hardly sleeping at all. Twisting and turning in bed, listening for the sounds of Max's breathing. Second guessing myself over my decisions. I was drowning in a sea of recriminations. "How are you?" I whispered.

Silence. I heard the sound of his breathing, low and long. Could picture his face. Brow drawn down, lips thin. Thinking of a response.

"I'm not good," he said eventually. "I just..." His voice broke then. I felt it inside, stabbing me like a knife. Tearing me apart. "I want you back. I want Max back. I know you hate me right now—"

"I don't hate you," I interrupted. I couldn't have him thinking that. "I'm so mixed up I don't know what to do. And I need to concentrate on Max."

"I know." He sounded so sad. "But I'm not giving up on us and I won't let you, either. I thought about you and Max every day when I was in the States, I was miserable without you. Even before I heard about his illness I wanted to come home. There has to be a way to make this work."

*Squeezing my eyes shut, I tried to banish the tears. "I hope so."*
*"There is," he said, firmly. "I want my family back."*

* * *

When the door buzzes at six that evening, I sweep Max into my arms and run to open it. Alex is leaning on the door jamb, holding a bunch of flowers in one hand, a teddy in the other. Except this isn't an ordinary teddy; it's wearing a punk outfit, holding a tiny microphone in its paw.

I laugh out loud. "What the hell is that?"

He shrugs, a smile threatening at the corner of his lips. "A present for Max."

"A fetish teddy. He'll be delighted." I smile, taking the flowers when he offers them to me. In return he takes Max, swinging him against his chest.

Max lunges for the teddy. "Da da da," he babbles.

Alex smiles, his whole face lighting up. "Did he say 'Dad'?"

For some reason, I don't want to tell him it's only a babble. That he's been doing it for days. There's something about Alex's reaction that makes my heart stutter. So I look at him, and he stares right back, and the tension between us brings goose bumps out on my arms.

It takes Max grabbing the teddy and stuffing the microphone in his mouth to dispel it. Shakily, I laugh, trying to calm my racing heartbeat.

"A microphone eater like his daddy. I'm so proud."

We go inside and I put the kettle in, unable to shake off how surreal it is to be treating Alex like a guest in his own home. When I carry our coffees back in, he's on the floor, Max climbing over him, big grins splitting both their faces. When Alex pulls him in for a kiss, Max opens his mouth and slobbers on his cheek. He hasn't quite got the hang of closing his mouth yet.

It's one of those moments when you want everything to stop, to freeze time so you can appreciate it. Watching them makes my chest hurt, it's so full. Why can't it always be like this?

Max makes a grab for Alex's hair, curling his tiny fist around a chunk, yanking hard enough to make Alex laugh. Gently, he releases Max's hold, kissing his knuckles as if to show him he isn't angry.

It's too painful to watch them. So I sit down and look out of the window, trying to regulate my breath.

"I thought maybe you could have Max for the day on Sunday," I say, to cut the tension as much as anything else. "I'm sure your mum would like to see him." Tina popped around two nights ago, but I pretended to be exhausted. She was asking way too many questions about Alex and me.

Alex sits up, cradling Max to his chest. "You're not coming for lunch?" He looks hurt.

I have to remind myself to breathe. "I can't." I practically choke on my words.

"Why not?" He frowns. "Everybody wants to see you."

"Because I can't pretend that everything's okay." There's no way I can go back into our old routine.

"Then tell me what's wrong. Tell me what to do to make it better. This is killing me."

Lowering my head into my hands, I can feel my voice shaking. "It's everything. The way you put the band above everything else. The way you lied about smoking. The fact you forgot to sort out your phone before you went. How we hardly talked when you did get around to calling." I blow out a big breath and my voice lowers. "I waited for you to call me for four days when Max was ill. You didn't even bother."

I can't bring myself to tell him about the photo, even though I know I should. It still makes me feel sick to think about. I don't want to hear his explanations, his excuses; I'm not ready for them.

"Stuart didn't tell me," he explains quietly. "I spoke to him yesterday. They knew I'd leave as soon as I heard so they didn't say anything. It's only when I listened to your message that I found out."

My stomach churns harder. "What?" I drop my hands, looking up at him with red rimmed eyes. "He didn't tell you I called? He didn't tell you about Max?"

Slowly, he shakes his head.

"But I talked to him, he said you weren't coming back. He said you didn't want to talk to me."

This time, his eyes narrow. "You believed him? You really thought I wouldn't come home?"

His question shocks me. Did I really think so little of Alex that I believed Stuart's lies? That sounds awful. From the way he's staring at me, I can tell he agrees.

"Why did he lie?"

"He wanted us to finish the tour. He was going to tell me when we made it to New York."

I laugh bitterly. "That was good of him."

"I said the same thing, but with a lot more swearing." Alex kisses the top of Max's head. "If something had happened to Max..."

My heart hammers in my chest. I hate that I doubted him. "It didn't," I say, thickly. "Thank God."

Max is starting to get tired; I can tell from the way he keeps shuffling on Alex's lap. He's fighting it, but the exhaustion is winning. Alex settles him on his legs, letting him snuggle in close. "Are we ever going to get back to what we were?"

It's the big question, and I wish I knew the answer to it. Instead, I take a shaky breath and try to summon up some courage. "I hope so."

## 22

The next day I wheel Max into the doctor's surgery, taking a seat on one of the orange plastic chairs in the waiting room. Max is holding a cardboard book, eating it more than reading it, and I pull it away from his mouth, panicking about all the germs he could catch here. Ten minutes pass before we're called in, though it seems like longer, and Max becomes bored, kicking at his chair, wailing to be let out.

I carry him into the doctor's office. Doctor Jensen glances up at me when I walk in, his pale grey eyes taking us both in, and he nods at the chair next to his desk.

"How's Max doing?"

"His breathing seems much better, and he's eating well," I tell him. "If we could just get him to sleep through the night my life would be complete." I smile at him, letting him know what a relief it is to know that Max can thrive again. After the fear of the past few days, it's a welcome respite.

"Bring him over to the couch and I'll examine him."

Max, of course, has other ideas. I have to hold him down while the doctor listens to his chest with a stethoscope, then attempts to look inside his airways to see if everything's okay. Max protests at being held still, his arms flailing, his legs kicking, and he manages to hit the doctor right on the groin.

"Yep, he's definitely feeling better," the doctor groans, his eyes bulging out as he steps away from the examination couch. "I think he's going to be a footballer when he gets older."

The second part of the appointment is about me. Dr Jensen asks me about the PND group, and I confirm that until last week I'd been attending regularly, and I'm planning to go back next week. He asks me to retake the Edinburgh test, and as I tick the boxes I realise that I really am able to see humour in life again, and that happiness doesn't seem like an abstract concept.

"Your score's in the normal range," he tells me, after he looks at my answers. "That doesn't mean everything's magically okay, but it means you're making some progress. I have to say that's a pretty good result considering everything you've been through recently."

I think it is too. "Does that mean I'm discharged?" I ask.

He smiles. "I'd like to see you in a month, just to make sure everything is on track. Keep going to the group, and keep an eye on your feelings, but I think you've got things under control right now."

Max squirms in my arms, making an attempt for freedom, and I have to pull him back. He's getting stronger, enough for it to hurt sometimes when he's wriggling, but after everything that's happened, I love his hardiness.

As soon as we leave the doctor's surgery, I call Alex with the good news. His warm, happy voice is enough to make my heart thump against my chest, and I realise that this newfound control I have doesn't quite extend to my reactions to him.

* * *

Alex picks Max up at nine on Sunday. I stand behind the curtain, watching him out of the window as he pushes the buggy down the street. Though it's almost autumn, the weather is still warm, and he's wearing a thin shirt that does nothing to hide his muscles. I have to grab hold of the wall to steady myself, trying not to let the need for him sweep me under.

*Are we ever going to get back to what we were?*

His question echoes in my ears. I hate that I don't know the answer. He's my best friend, the love of my life, the man I wanted to grow old with.

And I'm watching him walk away.

The flat seems empty and hollow without the boys. Though I try to keep my mind occupied by cleaning madly, my efforts fall far short. Eventually, I tire of folding tiny clothes and dusting painted surfaces, and grab my jacket, shrugging it on as I leave the flat.

Autumn is my favourite time of year. Though the Indian summer is trying to cling on desperately, there's no hiding the leaves as they turn golden, and the pale blue of the sky as it readies itself for winter. When a gust of wind lifts up the tendrils of my hair I feel the chill against my neck, bringing goose bumps out on my skin.

I walk for a while, ending up at a small café in Hoxton Square. The whole place is heaving, full of people trying to get their fill of fresh air before the winter makes hermits of us all. I sit alone at a tiny table overlooking the fenced-in green. The trees sway softly in the breeze, dry leaves rustling. A small girl darts between the rugged trunks, chased by her dad, and I find myself wondering what Max and Alex are doing right now.

It's as if somebody is squeezing my stomach when I think of them. We should be here together, enjoying the last of the sun. Sharing a picnic as we watch Max trying to stand up.

Is this how it's going to be? Stilted conversations as I hand over our son. Lonely Saturdays spent thinking about what could have been. Sundays stuck in the flat, surrounded by silence and memories. A life none of us ever wanted.

Alex once told me I was everything to him. Held me close and whispered that nothing else mattered. I take another sip of coffee, feeling the bitter liquid burn at my throat, wondering if there's anything I can do to get my old life back.

"Lara?"

I crane my head to see Laurence Baines from group therapy standing over me. His tall frame blocks out the sun, casting a shadow across my table. I order my expression into a smile, seeing how awkward he looks, shifting from foot to foot as if he's fifteen, not fifty.

"Laurence, how are you?" Hastily, I stand up.

"I'm good." Even his smile is awkward. "Am I supposed to talk to you? Outside of the clinic, I mean?"

"Of course. As long as you're happy to say hello, I am too." It's something I've encountered before. Clients never know how to treat me outside of the confines of the clinic. I've always let them take the lead. If they want to acknowledge me, I'm happy to respond, and if they'd rather pretend I don't exist, that's fine too. Looking at Laurence, I notice that in spite of his reticence there's a need in his eyes. To talk. To share. To be heard.

"Would you like to join me?" I ask. There's something about him that makes me want to speak formally. Perhaps the fact he's a head teacher.

"Only if I'm not disturbing you."

"Company would be nice."

Immediately, his shoulders relax. I watch as he pulls a chair over from a half-empty table and orders an Americano. In spite of the fact it's a weekend he's still perfectly turned out. Dark blue slacks and a white button down shirt.

"What's new with you?" I ask, after his drink finally arrives.

Laurence pours a packet of sugar into his coffee, stirring it slowly as the brown granules slowly sink into the liquid. "Same old, same old. We saw Tom again on Friday. He had a black eye. Won't tell us how he got it."

Tom is only twenty years old. He's been in prison for nine months now. It's been less than a year since Laurence's world was torn apart.

"How did you feel?" Old habits die hard. Seeing this proud man tremble before me, I can't help but feel sympathy piercing my heart.

"Like I've failed him. Completely and utterly. Didn't manage to teach him right from wrong. Can't protect him from the thugs that slam their fists in his face. I'm in charge of a generation of children at my school and I can't even bring my son up right." Laurence stares down at his feet. "And to top it all, Julie's talking about separating. We don't talk anymore. I used to think I had everything. The best job, a perfect family. Turns out it was all an illusion."

Horrified, I watch as a single tear falls onto the plastic table top. The urge to take him in my arms and hug him is huge. He's a shadow of a man, confused and stumbling. Not able to understand how it all went so wrong.

"Why don't you talk anymore?"

He rubs his face with the heel of his hands. "I don't know. Maybe she blames me for everything. God knows I blame myself."

"Do you really think you're to blame?"

Looking at me through red-rimmed eyes, Laurence shrugs. "I'm not sure of anything anymore. I used to be so certain, thought I knew right from wrong. But if you offered me a way to get Tom out of prison I'd do it. Even if it meant breaking the law."

I reach out, covering his hand with my own. "Of course you would."

"But I can't change any of it. I just want to go back in time. Make sure I listened to him, spent time with him."

"You can still do that, when he's released." I try to find the words to reassure him. But there's no reassurance when his world is crumbling around him. Laurence slides his hand from beneath mine, running it through his silver hair.

"It might be too late. I'll have lost everything by then. My son, my wife, my family." A flock of birds choose that moment to swoop down, landing on the concrete around us, pecking at the crumbs left behind by a multitude of diners. "You have a son, don't you?"

I nod. "He's a baby."

"Where is he?"

His question takes me by surprise. It's a Sunday morning, of course I should be with Max.

"He's with his father."

"Make sure you appreciate your time with him. Tell him you love him. Don't make the mistakes I did."

Long after our coffees cups are empty, and Laurence has headed back to his silent house, I'm still contemplating his words. Remembering the lost expression on his face as he talked about Tom and Julie. It makes me think about Max, and about all the trials we have ahead of us. The cut knees, and the broken hearts and the rivers of tears before bedtime. We came so close to losing him, and somehow we *did* manage to lose ourselves. That special spark that tied us together. The certainty that it was us against the world.

I want it back. All of it. The sleepless nights and the too-early mornings. The tears and the giggles and the warm feeling of Alex's body wrapped around mine. I want his voice to wake me up and his hands to hold me when I drift off to sleep.

I want my family back.

I just have no idea how to make it happen.

\* \* \*

My first month with Alex was filled with frantic kisses and stolen moments. With hot, sweaty sex and middle of the night conversations that seemed to take on a rhythm of their own. With his shift work and gigs, along with my crazy hours in the City, Alex turning up at 2:00 a.m. and pushing me against the wall as I desperately tore at his clothes wasn't an uncommon occurrence.

It was enticing, it was sexy; I had no idea where it was going.

One night, about five weeks after that first gig, I was lying on my side, staring at him as he slept. Dawn was trying to force her way through the cracks in the blind, casting little shafts of light that illuminated the ink etched across his body.

I was captivated by his tattoos. It was one of our main topics of conversation at the time. I traced them with my fingers, asking him what each one meant. When he got them, why he got them. Was he planning on having any more?

In return, he questioned me about my job, my family and the private girls' school I attended until I was eighteen. Wanted to know if I wore a short skirt and tight shirt. Was I as beautiful then as I was now?

I basked in the warmth of his attraction. Loved the way he would look at me from the corner of his eye. He'd stare at me for long minutes, the smallest smile on his lips, and it made my stomach lurch every time.

Between the desperate sex and the questions, and the stupid hours we both worked, there didn't seem time to talk about us. Where this was going. Was it going anywhere? Were we in a relationship or messing around?

Alex rolled in his sleep, breathing softly. I traced the line of his jaw with my eyes. It was razor sharp, darkened by stubble. I wanted to trace it with my tongue.

I was about to do just that when the shrill ring of the phone cut through the early morning silence. Groaning, I rolled over, feeling the bed dip as he did the same.

"Hello?"

"Lara? It's Dad."

My father never called me. *Never.* We would talk on the phone very occasionally, but only after my mum had called first.

"Dad?"

Alex sat up, the sheet falling to his waist, and ran a hand through his messy hair. When he looked at me, there was a question in his eyes.

"I'm at the hospital. Mum's had a funny turn. The doctor said I should call you."

"What kind of funny turn?" I reached up to wipe the sleep dust from my eyes. "What's happening?" They'd only recently come back from holiday. Mum hadn't even called to tell me about it yet. "Is she okay?"

My dad sobbed, and it made me queasy. He never cried. Not my career-focused, go-getting father. Shouted, yes. Ranted, all the time. Cried? Never.

"Dad, you're scaring me."

"She woke up in the middle of the night and couldn't breathe. She was coughing up blood. They said it could be an embolism. I'm waiting for someone to tell me what's going on."

"But she's going to be okay, right?" I asked. "I mean, she's in the hospital now. She's going to get better?"

Silence. I glanced to my left to see Alex staring at me. He reached out to take my free hand, squeezing it tight. The look of compassion on his face took my breath away.

Then my dad finally broke the silence. "She wasn't breathing by the time we got here."

I started to cry; big sobs that wracked my chest and echoed in my throat. I could hear my dad doing the same down the phone line, and that frightened me more than anything.

Gently, so carefully, Alex took me in his arms, stroking my hair and whispering comforting words. Then he took the phone from my hand, lifting it to his ear. Clearing his throat before speaking.

"Mr Stanford? My name's Alex Cartwright. Can you tell me what hospital your wife is in?"

I didn't hear the rest of the conversation. The next few hours were a blur. Somehow we got dressed, left the flat and climbed into my car. Then Alex drove us to Dorset, one hand on the steering wheel, the other holding my hand securely in his as I fretted and cried. Every now and then he'd glance across at me, his face soft, and his eyes gentle.

Though I didn't realise it then, I was starting to fall in love with Alex Cartwright. Not because of his sexy body, or the hot tattoos. But because when it came to a crisis, he was there for me.

He held tightly to my hand when we walked into the hospital. He stroked my hair when I sobbed as they lowered my mother's coffin into her freshly-dug grave. Three months later, when I left my high-paying, high-flying job, he pulled my body to his and told me everything was going to be okay, that I'd made the right decision, and life was too short to stay in a job that made you miserable.

He was a keeper, he was everything.

I miss him like crazy.

# 23

When I was a child, Sunday evenings meant *Antiques Roadshow*. The aroma of roast beef would waft through the house as I bent my head over the geography homework I should have finished a week earlier. That night had a taste of its own, the sweetness of the weekend turned bitter by the promise of Monday morning. It was as sharp as a lemon.

Now, Sunday nights mean ironing and packing Max's bag for nursery and mine for work. Folding tiny sleep suits and pint-sized nappies for somebody else to dress him with.

I'm counting vests when the door buzzes, and I abandon the pale blue cotton clothing on the bed. A sense of anticipation nestles in my stomach, making itself cosy. A cat in front of a fire.

"Hello."

"Hey." Alex looks tired but happy. Max is in his arms, head nestled in his shoulder, fast asleep. His thumb hangs loosely in his mouth, a lock of hair has fallen over his eyes. I haven't seen him look so peaceful in a long time.

"Come in." I speak softly. "Where's the buggy?"

"At the bottom of the stairs. I'll go get it when I've put Max down." His eyes catch mine. "Is it okay to take him through?"

It's on the tip of my tongue to tell him this is his flat, to make himself at home. But I don't want to send out mixed signals. This situation is confusing enough.

"Of course. Excuse the mess, I was getting things ready for tomorrow." I can't shake off this sense of weirdness.

After Alex has placed Max in his cot and brought up the buggy, things only get stranger. I busy myself in the kitchen, putting away pots that have been bone dry on the draining board for the past few days. Leaning on the counter, Alex watches me, looking as awkward as I feel.

"How was lunch?" I ask, switching the kettle on to break the silence.

Alex shrugs. "It was fine. Mum fawned over Max. I ended up chopping down a tree. Andie's got a promotion at work." He looks up at me through thick lashes. "It wasn't the same without you."

I ignore his sweet words. "Was Amy there?"

He stares at me for a moment, as if he's trying to read my thoughts. Finally, he speaks. "Yeah. And Luke, the knob." It's no secret he doesn't like Amy's boyfriend. "I don't get why she stays with him. He treats her like shit. Ended up leaving halfway through lunch to meet up with a mate. Didn't even finish his dinner."

"I bet Tina was pleased."

"You can imagine." He rolls his eyes. "Not clearing his plate was worse than committing a crime. Amy won't hear the end of it."

"It's not her fault."

"She puts up with it. She should give him the elbow."

I pour hot water into our mugs. Swirl around two tea bags. I still have my back to him when I speak again. "Maybe she loves him."

"Doesn't mean she should let him treat her like shit."

Turning around, I offer him one of the mugs. "I know." This time I stare right back at him. I wonder if he can read my thoughts now. I'm remembering all the arguments we had, the way he never answered the phone on tour.

That girl sitting on his lap.

Tearing my eyes away, I take a sip of my tea. Then Alex steps forward, gently taking the mug from my hands. Places it onto the counter. He puts his hand up to mine, palm against palm, fingers against fingers. It sends a jolt of electricity down my spine.

"I love you," he says, out of nowhere.

I can't deny the way his words affect me, every syllable warms my skin. But they can't obliterate the memories, not matter how hard I try.

"They're only words." I pull my hand away, unsure who I'm trying to convince.

Alex steps back as if I've slapped him. The pain in his face is clear and it makes me feel like a bitch. But I'm scared to open up, to let him in. So afraid this time he could actually slay me.

"I know it's going to take time." His fingers grip the edge of the counter. "I hurt you, and I'm so sorry for that."

My lip trembles, but I say nothing. I can't look at him.

The next moment he drops his bombshell. "I've left the band."

"What?" This time he has my attention. Alex has been with the band since he was a kid. Long before he met me. They're his second family.

"I told Stuart I was leaving." He runs a hand through his hair. His expression twists. "After everything he did, I can't stay. I won't let it tear us apart."

"But it's all you've ever wanted," I breathe out. "You're letting go of your dreams."

Alex glances down at his trainers. There are lines on his face where there used to be smooth skin, thin as thread but they're there. I want to reach out, to smooth them, and make them disappear. The last few months have taken their toll on both of us.

Finally, he looks up. "It was never my dream. Stuart's maybe, but not mine." Taking a step towards me, he grabs my hand again and wraps it in his palm. "You're my dream. You and Max. I won't be giving up on that one."

* * *

Life goes on. Max settles back in nursery, I go to work, and I try not to flinch every time he coughs. I don't want to be one of those suffocating mothers who squeal when they see a graze or a scratch. I see them everywhere, fussing and cooing, wrapping their kids in layer after layer, even while the autumn sun still warms the air. I want him to be strong, be free. Grow up to be a man.

It's hard, though. I still jump when my phone rings at work, and shudder when I hear his cries of pain. He's started to pull himself up on everything, and I know it won't be long before he's cruising between furniture.

He's growing up. I love it and I hate it.

One night a couple weeks later, Alex calls me before midnight. I'm wrapped in that cosy blanket between sleep and wakefulness, my voice low and drugged when I answer the phone.

"Hi." I'm breathy and deep. So relaxed I'm not thinking about the way I come across.

"Babe." His voice is lower; gravelled and thick. He's winter walks in the wood and smoky bonfires. "Did I wake you?"

"No." A smile curls into my voice. "I wasn't asleep yet."

"You in bed, baby?" He sounds like pure seduction. I'm too comfortable to do anything but absorb it.

"Yeah. Under the covers. Nice and snug."

"Wish I was there with you."

"I wish you were, too." I say the first thing that comes to mind, and it's so damn true. I wish a lot of things.

"I want to come home. Look after you."

I open my eyes. "Alex..."

"I love you, gorgeous. I love our son. Let me come back." There's the merest of hint of a slur to his voice. The product of no more than a couple of drinks. I can almost smell the beer on his breath, warm and musky. "What's it gonna take?"

It's a fair question. One I've asked myself. Weeks of introspection and I'm still not sure of the answer. I'm the stubborn one, clamming up every time we talk. I know I have to tell him eventually.

"Just give me some time." It's my familiar refrain. Time and space.

"I will, if you give me a chance."

A fair exchange? Quite possibly. I can't keep stringing things along, not when there's more than us at stake. It isn't fair on Max to have this indecision over his head. And yet when I squeeze my eyes closed all I can see is that photo. The way his fingers rested on her stomach. Holding her.

Touching her—another woman.

It's like a brick wall between us. One he doesn't even know is there. He's made it clear he wants to be with me, that he wants us back, yet I can't bring myself to wipe the image from my mind. If I was counselling myself I'd look deeper, try to work out the reasons behind my obsession with it. But I'm too tied up with fear, scared to hear the answer. Instead I let it fester like an infected wound.

The more I avoid asking him, the bigger it looms between us. And he doesn't even know.

"I should get some sleep. Good night, Alex."

"Sleep tight, babe." I hear the hurt laced in his voice. It makes me want to tell him I'll give him a chance. To offer him a hint of hope. But instead I stay silent, ending the call with a slide of my finger.

Sleep is elusive that night.

\* \* \*

The following day, there's an emergency at work. A girl holes herself up in the bathroom, threatening to slash her wrists unless social services give her baby back. I spend three hours, leaning against the red-painted door, trying to talk her down.

I fail.

She ends up being blue-lighted to the accident and emergency room, while we all put on protective equipment to clean up the blood. All I can think about is her baby girl.

It doesn't matter how many times this happens, each occasion makes me want to scream. We're supposed to be here to help people, and yet there's still a girl fighting for her life tonight.

By the time Max and I return home to our empty flat I realise there's only one person I want to talk to, and not about the suicide, either. He's been honest enough with me, it's time to lay my cards on the table. To tell him what I'm really thinking.

Putting the kettle on, I warm up Max's dinner—an elegant concoction of mashed carrot and potato—then I grab my phone and text Alex.

*Can you come over tonight?*

His reply is as fast as lightning. *What time?*

*If you get here before seven you can put Max to bed.*

He arrives at quarter to. While he finishes off the bedtime routine, I clear up the kitchen and pull a bottle of wine out of the fridge, filling two glasses and putting them on the counter. I need some liquid courage for the conversation we need to have. Perhaps Alex does, too.

When he strolls out of the bedroom, carrying a now-empty bottle of milk, I can see contentment softening his features. It's the same expression I know I have after seeing Max sleeping cosily. The knowledge he's safe and happy. *Protected.*

"Everything okay?" I ask, handing a glass to Alex. He raises his eyebrows at the gesture but doesn't comment on it.

"He's fast asleep. They must really wear him out at nursery."

"Thank God," I laugh out, lightly. "I'm still recovering from the last string of sleepless nights."

Alex leans on the counter, his arms stretched out in front of him. The tendons in his forearms flex. "How are you doing?"

I take a long, deep sip of cool white wine. "It was a bad day at work. But I'll be fine." For now I need to concentrate on Alex. On Max. On finally getting everything out there. Over the past few days I've realised that hiding the one thing that's still niggling at me isn't only unfair, it's counterproductive. It's been weighing on my mind for too long.

"Anything you want to talk about?"

I know he's referring to work, but I nod anyway. "There's something I need to show you."

I already have the laptop out. I'm logged in to Facebook, and am on the group's fan page. It looks as though it hasn't been updated since Alex left the tour.

"What's this?" Alex leans forward, eyes squinting he looks at the screen. "I haven't seen this before."

I guess that explains why he didn't tell me about it.

"Amy found it. She's been following you all on there." I click on the photographs. "There're lots of these."

Alex doesn't reply. Simply clicks through the pictures. There's a smile on his mouth as he looks at them silently, as if he's reliving the memories. "God, we look a right state," he finally says, seeing a photo of them all half-asleep, eating breakfast at some diner in the middle of nowhere.

He clicks through a few more, following the progress of the tour in the same way I did weeks ago. With each image he sees, I feel the nervousness build, my stomach churning.

Finally, he comes to the night in Austin, shaking his head when he sees the photographs of him on stage. He's never really liked seeing pictures of himself, and he scrolls through them furiously, missing the ones of the after-party.

"Go back," I say, my heart hammering in my chest. He looks at me curiously, but does it anyway, slowly pressing the button on the laptop, until we're back at the gig. And because the tension is killing me, I lean forward and scroll to the pictures at the bar, starting with the one of Stuart signing a groupie's tits.

"Typical Stuart," Alex mutters. "Why the hell did he post that one?"

I click again, and there's Alex and the girl. This time I can't bring myself to look at it. I know it intimately, anyway, as I've seen it a million times in my head. I could close my eyes and describe the exact position of his hands. The curl to his lip as he grins at her, the way she clings on to his neck.

"You saw this one?" he asks softly.

"Yes." I can't look at him. Instead I grab my wine glass and drain it in one gulp.

"It's not what it looks like."

"That's what all the guys say."

There's a clink as he puts down his wineglass. Then his hands are on my wrists, pulling me towards him. "It isn't, Lara. I promise you. I don't even remember it being taken."

"Do you remember her sitting on your lap?" My voice is hoarse. I pull away, not wanting to feel him touching me. It's making it hard for me to breathe.

"No."

I take a deep breath, finally looking up at him. "Who is she?"

"I've no fucking idea. Listen, Lara, I promise you this is only a shitty picture. I haven't done anything wrong." He takes hold of my chin, lifting my face up so I'm looking at him. But I can't stand it, and twist my head away, closing my eyes.

"You let some random woman sit on your lap."

"It must have been for a millisecond. No more than that. I'd never do something to hurt you."

"But you did. You did hurt me."

Agitated, he starts to pace. "Listen, you can blame me for the smoking, you can blame me for not sorting out my fucking phone. Hell, you can blame me for not getting to the hospital fast enough. But not this. I'd never cheat on you, you know that."

It's true. I nod my head. "I do."

"Then why won't you look at me?"

"Because it's the straw that broke the camel's back," I tell him. "After everything else, I had to see that. And it doesn't make me feel any better when you tell me you don't even remember it, because it just about broke my heart."

"But I didn't do anything." He sounds hurt. When I finally bring myself to look at him, Alex is standing in front of me, staring down. "You're not being fair."

By this point, I'm not even sure what is fair anymore. Even though I hoped this would make me feel better, showing him the picture has only inflamed the situation.

"You were so trashed you can't even remember a girl sitting on your lap." I lean back against the counter, putting space between us. "That sort of makes it worse. How do I know I can trust you?"

"Because I've been in love with you for the past seven years and I'd never do anything to endanger that." His voice is firm, almost angry. "To suggest otherwise is pretty fucking insulting."

"But if you don't remember what you did..." My voice trails off.

"I could be comatose and I wouldn't do that. Jesus, Lara."

"But how do you know?" I persist. Because I need to hear this. I need to know that nothing happened.

He's glaring at me, and I'm glaring right back. Neither of us moves; the only sound in the room is our heavy breath and the ticking of the kitchen clock. I curl my fingers around the edge of the counter, trying to ground myself, to cling on. My heart beats in time to the second hand and I wait, wondering what's next.

"You really think I'd cheat on you?" he finally asks. The hurt expression hasn't left his face.

"No." My reply is as soft as his. "But I do think it shows you weren't thinking of me at all. How would you feel if the tables were turned?"

His eyes flash with anger. "Murderous."

"Then you know how I feel. It's another symptom, like the weed and the phone."

He swallows, his Adam's apple bobbing up and down. "I can't argue that one. But I can tell you I'm trying to make up for it."

I know he is—he's been trying to make up for it for weeks. I've let him, allowing him to call me, send me flowers. Giving him hope we'll regain what we've lost. But this one's all on me, and I know it. I need to get over it, to stop dwelling on that bloody picture. To stop thinking about it all the time. I need to stop closing my eyes and seeing it etched in the blackness. My worst fears in photograph form.

I need to do a lot of things. I just don't know how.

## 24

"Look, you know I'm not his biggest fan, but I do think you need to cut the guy a break."

I'm walking with David through Hoxton market a few days later, buying big brown bags of fruit and vegetables to make up some meals for Max.

"You're right, I know you are." I hand over my money to the stall owner, waiting for my change. "It's easier said than done, though."

"What is it about the picture that upsets you?" David asks. It's the first time I've told him about the photo, and I've deleted Facebook from my phone so I can't even show him. Even if I could I'm not sure I know the answer myself.

"I don't know, but it gets me in the gut."

I've been analysing my reaction for weeks. From a purely professional point of view, I know I'm overreacting. I believe Alex when he says that nothing happened. It's like when a doctor hits your knee with a hammer. Even if you don't want to kick out, you do anyway. A purely instinctive reaction.

"What would you say to me if I was in your position?"

"As a friend or a counsellor?" I ask.

He laughs. "Either."

Putting the brown bag into the basket below Max's buggy, I ponder on his question.

"I'd tell you to get over yourself."

David smirks. "Good answer."

"Ugh." I rub my face with my hands, allowing David to take over the buggy-pushing. "I know this, I do."

I'm being stupid and immature, and I know it's a symbol of everything that's gone wrong. I'm homing in on the picture, but there's so much history behind it. So much angst.

We carry on down the road, passing vans selling falafels and Jamaican street food. The spices linger in the air, drifting towards us, their meaty aroma making my stomach rumble. I stop at a stall selling jewellery, sifting through the beads and bracelets, wanting something bright and joyful.

"How are things with you, anyway?" I ask, wanting to move the subject off myself. In the past few weeks I've hardly seen anything of David. He's been holed up in his flat, rarely surfacing. Blaming workload, tiredness, anything he can. It took a lot of cajoling to get him out today, and I swear when he emerged from his flat and into the sunlight he was blinking hard, like a mole breaking the surface of the earth.

He shrugs, his eyes trained ahead as we push our way out of the market. "Fine."

"What have you been doing? I've hardly seen you for weeks."

"I've heard from my lawyer."

Oh. I reach out to hold his arm, trying to slow him down. His muscles are taut, tense. Like iron against my palm. "What did he have to say?"

"Claire's agreed to mediation."

I can't understand why he's being so calm about it. Emotionless. "That's good, isn't it?" I want to sound more enthusiastic, but I'm not sure how he'll take it.

We stop outside a house, leaning on the gable wall. "I have to fly back in two weeks."

My stomach drops. "So soon?"

"They've offered us a slot at the end of the month. I need to fly back as soon as I can. I should be able to wrap things up within a couple of weeks."

"You're coming back, though?" I let my voice trail off. What a stupid question. If things go well then clearly he won't be returning. And the alternative... I don't think either of us want to contemplate that.

"I hope not." His thoughts must echo my own. "We'll keep in touch, though, Lara. I promise."

"Yeah, of course." I try not to let him see my miserable expression. I should be pleased for him—and I am—but it's come as a shock. Everything's changing, slipping out of my grasp. First Beth moves away, and then Alex is at his mum's. Now I'm losing David, as well. I push myself off the bricks, rearranging my face into a smile. "Hey, you could be seeing Mathilda again within a month."

For the first time, he smiles. "Yeah, I know." Though his voice is still low I detect a little wonder inside it.

"Then why the long face?"

He looks at me through baby blue eyes. When he blinks his eyelashes sweep down his cheeks, sandy and thick. "She's not going to know me at all. It doesn't matter that I've been thinking about her, or that she has my genes and my blood. She hasn't seen me for months, she won't even recognise me."

I glance down at Max from the corner of my eye. Mathilda is older than him by a few months. She must be walking, saying her first words. Maybe 'Mama' and 'Dada'. Words that should be meant for David. "She'll get used to you. It won't take long. She'll only have to look at you to know how much you love her. Kids are resilient like that."

When I glance at him, David doesn't catch my eye. Instead he stares at his feet, kicking the toes into the dusty concrete slabs. "There's something else, too." His voice takes on the tone of a confession, low and pleading. I reach out and take his hand, sensing this need for connection.

"What is it?"

"I've... met someone."

"As in a girl?"

His expression is pained. "Yeah."

I guess that explains a lot. The reason why I've hardly seen him for the past few weeks. I don't doubt he's had a lot of work on, but that's obviously not the only thing that's kept him busy. I remember the early days of love enough to know how it feels. That opaque fog that surrounds you, the need to be with the other person constantly. The feeling that the world has stopped and the only thing moving is you.

"She lives in London?"

He seems agitated. Stepping back, he wrings his hands together. It's not until he speaks again I realise the reason why. "It's Andie."

I blink, momentarily silenced. It takes a couple of moments for me to process his words. "Andie? As in my sister-in-law Andie? Andrea Cartwright? How the hell did that happen?"

I run through my memories, trying to place them together. I can only remember them being together once, at the festival.

Oh, and the hospital, too. I guess somewhere along the line his librarian fantasies really did come true. My stomach aches for my kind sister-in-law; the one who's always calm and supportive.

"I haven't told her about the mediation yet. I'd rather you didn't say anything."

"But you're going to tell her, right?"

David starts walking again, pushing Max's buggy in front of him. I follow behind awkwardly, my mind full of questions that don't want to be voiced.

"I'm going to tell her." He's back to the monotone. "I just haven't worked out how."

"You should talk to her soon," I say. "Keeping secrets isn't going to help your relationship."

"You should know I'm rolling my eyes now," David replies. And though all I can see is his back, I know he's telling the truth. "I'm not going to take relationship advice from you."

"How rude."

He cough-laughs. "Have I upset you?"

"Nope. I'm practically uninsultable. It's like water off a duck's back."

"I think you made up a word."

"Duck?"

"Uninsultable."

"Oh, it's a word," I insist. "Look it up in the dictionary."

"Yeah, of course, I'll do that. I'm pretty sure it's right next to gullible."

Just like that we're laughing again. Trading minor insults and the occasional mock-punch. As we walk back to our flats, the afternoon sun casting a pale, fuzzy glow on the concrete pavements, I realise how much I'm going to miss this. *Miss him.* David only moved in a couple of months ago yet we've become firm friends. He's been there when I needed him.

So I reach out my hand and squeeze his shoulder, knowing I'll try to be there for him, too.

* * *

The rest of the afternoon is spent with my head buried in paper, staring at bank accounts and bills, trying to make them all add up. When I try to pay the electricity, the balance is showing as zero, and I scroll through the payments to work out what's going on. I'm usually pretty good with money—things are so tight I have to be—and this unexpected credit is worrying me, making me think I've done something wrong. When I call up the helpline, it all becomes clearer.

"The balance was paid two days ago, Mrs Cartwright." The operator sounds too damn chipper for a Sunday afternoon. I wonder what they put in the drinking water.

"But I haven't paid it since last month," I reply patiently, even though it's the third time I've told her this. "There must be some kind of mistake. Can you see if it's the right account?"

"It is, Mrs Cartwright. The balance is fully paid up. Is there anything else I can help you with?"

I sigh. It sounds stupid, but I hate surprises like this, because I know in a few days' time I'm going to get an angry letter telling me I still owe £250 and there was some kind of mistake when I called up last time. I'm never this lucky.

"Can you tell me who paid the bill?" I ask, fully prepared for her to tell me she can't release that sort of information. Instead, she shocks me with a jaunty 'no problem' and I hear her tap away on her computer.

"The balance was cleared by a Mr Alexander Cartwright."

My throat tightens. "Alex?"

"That's correct."

There's a fluttering in my stomach. I say goodbye, not really hearing the reply. Then I go through every bill I have on the table, calling the helplines to double check the balance, and each one of them has been paid off. I'm not sure whether to laugh or cry, because I've always been the one who sorts out the finances. There's something about him doing this, without being asked—without expecting thanks—that makes me feel a little giddy and high. The two hours I have to wait until he brings Max home pass unbearably slowly, long seconds stretching into interminable minutes, until I'm fidgety and anxious. I want to see him, to touch him, to let him know I'm thankful.

Damn it, I want him here.

Alex arrives, knocking on the door with a brief rap of knuckles, tapping out a rhythm that matches my heartbeat. I push myself up from the sofa, leaving behind a Lara-shaped dip, and walk to the door with my pulse rushing through my ears.

"Hi." I'm breathless when I open the door, and a little bit wary. I don't trust myself not to crumble in front of him. As soon as I see him, I know I'm pretty much dust.

He's had his hair cut; razor sharp at the edges, longer and messy on top. His black T-shirt clings to his chest, ink scrolling up from the neckline as if it's trying to escape. Alex gives me a melted-chocolate look, his lips curled up, eyes crinkled at the edges.

I dig my fingernails into my hands.

"Mam mam mam," Max immediately breaks the tension. When I look at him in his buggy he gives me a just-like-daddy grin, kicking his bare feet out with delight.

I attempt to compose myself

"No socks?" I ask. My smile matches Alex's. I lick my dry lips and he follows me with his eyes.

"He kept throwing them on the pavement. Eventually I gave up trying." Alex pulls a ball of fluff from his pocket. Grey socks rolled into each other. "He's clearly a hippy."

"Barefoot and happy." I reach down and tickle one of Max's tiny feet. He squeals and curls it up, kicking out at me. Then he starts to wriggle, trying to escape the straps that are fastened around his little body, keeping him safely in his pushchair.

"How was your day?" I lift Max out and up into my arms. Surreptitiously I glance at Alex from the sides of my eyes. It feels silly, but I can't help it. There's just something about him.

"We had a good time. There was a barbecue at the park, Max managed to flirt with nearly every woman there."

"He's a dirty dog." When I look up, Alex is still looking at me. I meet him stare for stare. "Just like his daddy."

Alex smirks. "You like me that way."

My reply is light, full of air. "I do."

There's a delicious feeling in my stomach, and it uncurls like a contented cat. My heart beats a little faster than normal. I can't remember the last time we flirted—something as natural to us both as taking in oxygen—but God, it feels good.

"And how was your day?" Alex folds up the buggy and stashes it by the door. "Did you manage to entertain yourself?"

"I went for a walk with David." I look for the flash behind his eyes. When they narrow, satisfaction warms me from head to toe.

"Oh yeah?"

"Mm-hmm." I put Max in his bouncy chair and walk over to the kitchen. I've deliberately chosen a tight-fitting pair of jeans, taking advantage of the fact that stress has brought me back to my pre-baby shape. Alex has always been an arse-man, and I can feel the heat of his gaze as he watches me. I feel in control, sexual, and the power invigorates me. It lasts for about five seconds, right up until I go to fill up the kettle with some water.

I manage to pull the tap clean off from the spout.

Water gushes upward in a geyser Yosemite would be proud of, drenching my hair, my face, and my clothes. I jump backwards, screaming, trying to reach out and block up the gaping hole, and only managing to cover the whole kitchen with spray.

When I turn around Alex is doubled over with silent laughter, clutching at his stomach as he looks at me. His grin is so wide it's splitting his face.

I think about helping it along.

"Fuck, bugger, fuck!" I jump about, reaching for a tea towel to cover up the spray. It's next to useless, becoming soaked in moments, and my resulting curse does nothing to dampen Alex's humour.

"Language, the baby's listening."

I whip round and mouth "fuck off," in response, and he starts to laugh even harder.

"Fat lot of good you are," I shout at him. "Aren't you supposed to be the handyman around here?"

"You want my help?" He's a walking smirk. Sexy and hot, yet completely frustrating. He takes a step towards me, his feet squeaking on the wet tiles, and I flick the now-sodden tea towel at him.

"Hey!" He grabs my wrist when I try to whip him with it. "Lay off with the violence."

I'm soaked from head to toe. Water gushes out, pouring over the surfaces and the floor, sloshing around my feet. Yet I'm grinning at him, joining in his laughter, feeling my heart flutter when I catch his eye.

He looks good—too good. His hair is perfectly messy, his clothes bone dry. So I grab his arms and pull him towards me, twisting him until his body is firmly in the firing line.

Then we're both soaked, our clothes clinging to our skin. Giggling and laughing, we wrestle with each other, trying to push each other beneath the spray.

His arms circle my waist, pulling me to him. My T-shirt sticks to his, and the laughter that was bubbling in my throat only a moment before turns into air, sticking and catching before it dies away completely.

"Fuck, you're beautiful." He wipes a wet lock of hair from my forehead. My chest tightens as I stare at him, his hair inky black with water, droplets pouring down his face.

"So are you."

He presses his lips to mine, hot and needy. I feel their movement in my stomach, between my thighs, and I'm kissing him back, breathless and demanding, closing my eyes when I feel his hands pushing underneath. His palms slide against my wet skin, warm and firm, and I loop my arms around his neck, pulling him closer.

We kiss, hard and fast, as if there's no other way. As if we have no choice. I can feel him hard against my thighs, right where I ache for him. The sensation shoots pleasure to the tips of my toes.

"Lara," he breathes against my lips. I answer him with a moan, low and long. Then he's kissing me harder than ever, his tongue sliding against mine, and I'm nothing but a mess of desire.

"Baby, I need to sort out the tap." He pulls back, his lips still touching mine. "As much as I want to keep kissing you."

When he moves away, my body throbs with disappointment. I step back, leaning against the counter, trying to catch my breath. I'm still silent as he grabs his tool box from the cupboard and turns off the water at the mains.

When Max calls out, I'm almost relieved. I leave Alex in the kitchen, messing about with a wrench, and walk out, dripping onto the carpet. Max stares up with wide eyes, as if he's trying to work out why the heck I'm so wet.

While I'm trying to work out what the hell just happened.

# 25

"So he left without mentioning it again?" Beth asks down the phone. She sounds as confused as I am.

"Yeah, he mended the tap and put Max to bed then left, wet clothes and all." I frown. "And then he called me last night and was all flirty again."

I try not to remember how sexy he sounded. The dirty words, the small laughs. The way my body clenched at his voice.

"Sounds like he's doing something right." Beth laughs.

"What do you mean?"

"Well, if he's trying to win you back it sounds as though he's succeeding."

I can't deny the fact he's making me fall in love with him all over again. When I got to work this morning, the café down the street delivered a huge mug of coffee and a box full of pastries, a small white card inside.

*Thanks for the wet T-shirt competition. You looked beautiful.*

He's a sweet, dirty boy. Just like the first time, he's seducing me with a mixture of sexiness and cheekiness. Filthy words said with a taunting smile. He knows how to hit every one of my buttons, likes to squeeze them until I submit.

"I can't remember why I was so angry with him," I confess. A car slams on its horn as a bike pulls out from a side road and I wince at the sound.

"Ah, the soundtrack of the city," Beth sighs. "Sometimes I miss it."

"So what should I do about Alex?" I reach the entrance to the tube station, lingering by the stairwell, not wanting to say goodbye.

"What do you want to do?"

"I don't know," I wail. If she'd have asked me yesterday, when I was staring at Alex as he leaned over the sink, his jeans clinging to his muscled thighs, I'd have told her I wanted him back. But now, out in the cool London air, I'm more reticent. Afraid.

"You're scared." Beth knows me too well. "That's normal."

"What if we try again and it goes wrong?" I ask. "I don't know if I could take it."

She's silent for a moment. I take a deep breath, watching as a gust of wind scatters a pile of abandoned leaflets across the pavement. They lift and dance in the breeze, before slowly drifting back down to the concrete, ready to be stamped on by a crowd of commuters.

"I know it's easy to say, but love is always a risk. When it's good it's amazing, and when it's bad..." She trails off. I wonder if she's thinking about her own relationships. Her own heartbreak. "I guess you have to decide if Alex is worth the gamble. If you could actually live without him."

I squeeze my eyes shut at her words. It's impossible to imagine a life without Alex in it. He's been my rock for too long. And yes, the past few months have been hard as hell, but neither of us have been angels.

We're human. We make mistakes. Isn't that what life is all about? Tripping over, dragging ourselves back up. Learning to step over the cracks in the pavement.

\* \* \*

Unlike some of the court-mandated counselling I offer, attending group therapy at the clinic is entirely voluntary. So it's no surprise a few days later when I walk in and see half the chairs empty. People drift in and out depending on what's going on in their lives, and in those of the ones they love.

It's only when everybody's sitting down I realise Laurence isn't here. I look at his empty chair for a moment, my brows knitting into a frown. I was so sure he'd make it after our talk last week.

Jackie walks in a few minutes late, blustering through the door like a whirlwind. She's the one mainstay of the group, never misses a session, though timekeeping isn't her strong point.

"Sorry I'm late." She sounds breathless. "What did I miss?"

"Nothing yet. We were about to get started." I've learned to wait until she arrives. "Has anybody heard from Laurence?"

The room quietens for a moment and Jackie shuffles nervously. Then she pulls a folded up newspaper out of her oversized bag, unrolling it and passing it to me. "Haven't you seen this?"

I cast my eye across the newsprint. It's a local paper, printed cheaply, and the ink has smudged where Jackie has been reading it. But there's no hiding the photograph of Laurence, or the headline beneath it that cuts me to the core.

*Local Headmaster's Son Dies in Prison Fight.*

My hand tightens around the newspaper as I read the details. About the stab wounds that caused Tom to bleed to death. The cut across his jugular, the panicked race to hospital. Squeezing my eyes shut, I remember Laurence's pained expression as we discussed his problems on Sunday. The way his hand shook as he held his coffee cup. The tears in his eyes as he talked about his wife.

"I didn't know." I hand the paper back to Jackie. When she takes it, she squeezes my hand, and for a moment, I feel as though she's the counsellor, not me.

"I only found out yesterday," she says. "I tried to call him but there's no answer. Understandable, I suppose."

The rest of the group is looking at us with interest. When I turn to explain to them what's happened, they go silent, their eyes wide. Staring.

For them, it isn't only the shock that turns them mute, it's the knowledge that this tragedy could have been theirs. They all have addicted children and they're all treading the line between compassion and anger, and sometimes veering off wildly. The rest of the session is muted, with quiet voices and considered conversation. Minds that are far away, thinking about our own children, wondering if that could be us.

When we finish, we're all a little stunned. As I leave the clinic, making my way to the nursery, I decide I'm going to hold Max a little closer tonight.

\* \* \*

Alex calls me later when we're both in bed. For long moments we say nothing, simply listening to each other breathe. I lay on cotton-soft pillows, my pyjamas tangled around my legs, and find myself dreaming of ink-etched skin. We talk about nothing, our voices drifting, my eyes fluttering. My body tingles with the need to have him close.

"I miss you." There a soft cadence to his voice. "I miss feeling you, touching you. I want to wrap myself around you, have your skin next to mine. Run my fingers down your stomach."

Closing my eyes, I can almost sense him next to me. His breath warm on my neck, strong fingers digging into my hips. He used to wake me up with soft kisses and hard licks, making me gasp with a waking breath.

"Do you remember that time in Rhyl?" he asks. "When we took a blanket down to the beach."

"I remember." He peeled off my clothes, inch by inch, lips and fingers stirring me until I couldn't stop shaking. "That's where we made Max."

"That first time I felt him move, I thought I was going to cry. In the middle of a field, surrounded by our mates, and I was a blubbering fucking mess."

We'd been at a festival, lying on blankets, listening to bands. I grabbed his palm and pressed it to my stomach, watching his face shine with amazement as the baby fluttered against his palm.

"That night..." I close my eyes, my breathing ragged. He couldn't stop touching me, even as I slept. Woke me up twice to make love, his movements gentle, and his breath slow. It was uncharacteristically tender, as if he was holding himself back. But it felt right. So right.

"You were beautiful. Soft pink skin, perfect little bump. And your tits, God your tits. Fucking sublime."

My nipples tighten at his words.

"I used to daydream about them. Imagine them pressed against me. Your soft skin against my hard on."

The bed feels too big, too empty. I reach out to the spot where Alex used to lay, feeling the coolness of the sheets. "I wish you were here."

"So do I, baby." His voice is pure seduction. "I want to feel your body against mine, your sweet little arse pressing into me. Want to touch you until you're chanting my name."

I run my palms down my stomach. "Alex..."

"Say it again."

A breath, a plea. "Alex."

"Yes, baby?"

"I need... I want..." My skin tingles as if it's covered with tiny bubbles, crackling and popping as I shiver. My thighs clench as he speaks, warm and trembling.

"What do you want?"

"You."

"I fucking want you, too. So much, baby. Wanna push my fingers inside you, until you tighten around them. Want to slip inside you from behind and listen to you moan. Can you feel me? My chest against your back? My hand sliding down until I make you sigh?"

God, yes. I can feel him. His warm skin, his hard muscles. The strength of his chest, the way his taut abdomen leads down to harder, tighter places. I want him; all of him. The dirty words and the sexy grin. The sweet touches and the caring glances. As we whisper and moan, our bodies throbbing in a rhythm we can never control, I'm finding it hard to remember why he isn't with me right now.

## 26

I wrap a cream and black scarf around my neck, standing back to look at myself in the mirror. My hair is up, my skin is pale, and a slash of nude lip gloss brightens up my otherwise-drawn face. Though I try to breathe, it's as if the oxygen doesn't want to slip down my airways. It sticks in my throat as my stomach contracts with panic.

Funerals; I'm not good with them. Not that anybody is, though I've noticed the older people get, the more stoic they become. Talking about the passing of friends as if they're characters in a soap opera. An interesting occurrence in a normally humdrum life.

But for me, funerals mean life taken too early. My mother, lying in a coffin at the age of sixty-seven. Clients who try to kick the habit only to be drawn back in, the bony fingers of death helping them plunge in a needle, lay a tablet on their tongue. Leaving a trail of grief behind them.

Tom Baines's life was taken by the sharp tip of a knife pushed deep inside his neck, but it was crack that wrote the script. The drug led to his arrest, landed him in jail, led to an argument with a gang that wanted to assert their authority. And now Laurence's son is being laid to rest, his young life little more than a footnote in the history of life.

The air has cooled since the weekend. The clouds hanging low in the sky carry a tinge of winter, their greyness reflecting the morbidity of the day. I shrug on a jacket, black like my dress, and try to ignore the nagging pain in my chest.

The funeral is taking place at the Baines's local church. A sixties-built edifice, the roof is pale green copper, falling down from a central cross into a shallow hexagon, joining six white-brick walls that circle around it. People hang around the garden, next to autumn primroses that do little to brighten up the dull brown earth, their low-level flowers a reminder that summer is over.

That's where I see *him*, leaning against a waist-height wall, wearing a trim black suit with a skinny black tie. Though his arms are covered up, a small hint of ink curls out from his cuffs, licking at the base of his hands. Alex notices me and pushes himself up to standing, and his wedding ring glints as it catches a ray of pale sun. The expression on his face is sombre, but his presence already soothes me, a balm to the anxiety I've found hard to kick away.

"You okay?" He comes to a stop in front of me, reaches out, then pulls back. Though his hand falls back to his side, I can still feel the sensation of his finger brushing against my face.

We talked about the funeral last night. I'd told him how much I was dreading it, that I found them so hard. I can't help but remember another funeral when he was there, holding me up as my mother was lowered into the ground.

He always stops me from falling.

"I don't know... I..." From the corner of my eye I see the funeral procession arriving. Though we're in the East End of London, there are no horse-drawn black carriages or professional mourners. Instead, two black cars draw up, and I watch as Laurence and his family climb out of the back one. The men congregate around the hearse, waiting to play their role.

"Shall we go in?" Alex cups his hand around my elbow. Not too soft, but not tight either. Enough to steer me around, to lead me in, to stop me from screaming. We slide into a wooden pew, beside strangers who give me only a cursory glance, their eyes drawn to Alex's neck, to his ink.

When I look at him, my heart clenches, and I have to bite down on my lip to stop it from trembling. Noticing my discomfort, he grabs my hand, wrapping it in his own, then places his other on top, until I'm totally enclosed.

The organ starts up, and the family walk in. I watch as Laurence comes first, his shoulders stooped as he half-carries his wife in. Her hair is bright-white and hardly brushed, curling out from her scalp in a hundred different ways. She looks about thirty years older than her husband. It's painful to watch as he helps her to sit down in the front pew, and they both turn around to stare down the aisle as the coffin comes in, carried on the shoulders of family and friends, dark mahogany encasing the body of their beloved son.

When the vicar stands up, I tune him out. He talks about Alpha and Omega, his voice a monotonous hum, and all I can think of is that Tom never had a chance to live his life. He was handed opportunity and twisted it into something unusable. Did things he'll never even have a chance to regret.

But it's his parents who draw my eye. I watch as Julie Baines's life disintegrates, her wails piercing through the thick atmosphere of the church. Somehow, she manages to stand up, walk over to the coffin placed on a plinth in front of the altar, and throws herself onto it.

"Tom!" Her voice is almost a scream. I feel it as a mother; her baleful pleas speaking right to my heart. Nausea rises in my stomach, as I imagine myself in her place. Mourning the death of my son so many years too soon.

When I look at Alex, his face is tight. There's a twitch in his jaw where he's clenching it too hard. Though the church is dark, lit by candles and pale lights, I can still see the glint in his eyes as he stares straight ahead.

When Laurence stands and holds his wife, gently steering her back to the front pew, talking to her softly like a child, I realise I can't do this anymore.

I can't pretend it's all okay. I don't want to be alone. It's difficult and it's harsh and it's needless. I know I'm strong enough to do it on my own—we both are—but I also know it isn't what I want.

Alex shifts next to me, and I look again, feeling his hands squeeze mine as he struggles to breathe. A few tears escape from his eyes, and though he isn't crying for Tom Baines, I know he's mourning as hard as I am.

\* \* \*

We walk back to the flat—three and a half miles. Not talking; our words are swallowed up by deep thought. But there's peace between us, understanding even, the awareness that maybe we'll finally say the things we need to. We walk away from death, trying to shrug it off, knowing there's always a part of us that feels its touch. But it's this knowledge that makes us live, makes us love, allows us to appreciate every single day for the precious gift it is.

Inside the flat I make us both a mug of steaming hot coffee. I consider adding some whisky to it, wanting to ward off the chill of Tom's funeral, but I have to pick Max up in a couple of hours and there's no way I want to be half-cut.

"Thanks." Alex's gaze flickers to mine when I hand him the mug. His eyes are dry now, but the pinkness surrounding them reminds me of his tears. Sympathy softens my thoughts, and I have to sit down, my legs wobbling beneath me.

Placing his drink on the coffee table, Alex shrugs off his jacket, loosening his tie and unfastening his top button. He leans back on the chair, long legs splayed out in front of him, and I notice concern etched across his face.

"You okay?"

I nod. "I am now. Thank you for being there, you didn't have to." I'm glad he did though. I hope he realises that.

His voice is cracked. "Where else would I be?"

"I don't know." I look down at my feet. "I don't know what you've been doing."

There's silence as he takes a sip of coffee. "I've been working," he finally admits. "They've offered me a permanent job."

"On a building site?"

His lip curls up. "Yeah. It's not something I want to do forever, but it'll do while I'm looking around for something better."

I look at him carefully. "What do you want to do?"

"Whatever it takes to make you happy." His eyes don't waver from mine. "I don't really give a shit about the job or anything else. I only want to look after you and Max. Make everything okay. Get my family back."

He's so earnest I can almost taste it. Leaning forward, his elbows on his thighs, hands clasped together. I want to believe him, I'm so close to it, I simply need to take that final leap of faith.

But I'm scared; that's what it all comes down to. The fear he'll turn around and tell me Max and I have stolen his dreams, his life; the things he always wanted. I don't want to be the one who holds him back.

He shifts in his seat and scratches his chin with his left hand. He's still wearing his wedding ring.

*For better or for worse.*

We've been through both. In the long months since Max was born, I think we've challenged the hell out of it. My depression, Alex's dreams. They all added up to a calamitous result.

"What about the band?"

"It's over." His reply is unequivocal. "I'm not going back."

"Is that your choice?"

"It was mutual. I don't want to be in the band, I have things that are more important, and Stuart understands that now." Alex glances down at his right hand. For the first time, I do, too. His knuckles are red and raw. Livid red flesh peeks out from beneath his torn skin.

"What did you do?" I breathe. "Your poor hand..."

"Stuart came over last night to apologise for not telling me about Max." For the first time, Alex looks embarrassed. "I didn't accept his apology."

"You hit him?" I don't know how to feel about that. I'm so against violence, and yet if anybody deserved a whack, it's Stuart. The bastard kept Alex away from us when we needed him most.

Alex leans closer still. "Only once. But I caught his teeth. That's how my hand ended up being so... mangled. Not that his teeth were much better."

"Did you knock them out?" I ask.

"No."

"That's a shame." I've changed my mind, I know how to feel and I'm bloody happy. It's a pity I wasn't there to see it. With his smug smile and his lying tongue, Stuart deserves to be beaten up a bit. "So it's over?"

"It's over."

I breathe in deeply, knowing I've been waiting forever to taste fresh oxygen. My chest expands, letting the air in, and all I can think is *thank God.*

Alex is still looking at me, his eyes trained on my face, unblinking. He doesn't say a word, simply watches as I take it all in.

I'm trying to work out what this all means.

"Are you okay with that?"

"Absolutely."

"You're not going to turn around one day and think you missed your chance at fame? Or start blaming me and Max?"

He tips his head to the side. "Babe, I don't know how to make it any clearer. I don't want fame. I don't want to make it big. I only want to be with you and Max, however you'll have me." He looks down, thick lashes sweeping his cheeks. "When I saw that coffin today, and how that woman threw herself at it, all I could think of was Max. How close we came to losing him. How I wasn't there to hold you when I should have been." His voice wavers on the final sentence. Enough to make my eyes water.

"It's okay, Alex." And for the first time, it really is. Because we've been lost for so long, trying on these roles that never really seemed ours. Mum, Dad. Husband, Wife. They're all characters we play until they begin to seem real. And they do seem real now, as we talk about our son. But we can't lose sight of the people we used to be, either.

"I want to come home," Alex states firmly. "I want to put Max to bed and turn on the telly and let you put your feet in my lap. I want to leave the toilet seat up to hear you moan at me. I want to wake up in the morning and feel your breath on my face, and your legs slung across my waist so I can't bloody move."

"You old romantic." I bite my lip. "Keep going with that smooth talking tongue and who knows where we'll end up."

"I could talk about watching your breasts leak," he offers. "Or the fact that your fringe sticks out to the side when you wake up, making you look like something out of *Star Wars*."

"Seducer."

"Temptress."

"Dirty talker."

"Sexy bitch."

I smirk. "Arse licker."

"Can I come home?"

I don't miss a beat. "Okay."

Before I know it I'm in his arms. Alex sweeps me up from the sofa, swinging me until my feet are only just in contact with the ground. We're laughing and crying, our cheeks pressed together, our skin plump with smiles even while damp with tears. He slides his lips along my cheek and everything in my body responds. My mouth falls open, a sigh escaping my lips, as finally he presses a kiss to them.

Soft skin, hard teeth. Tongues slowly tangling until we're short of breath. His fingers dig into my behind, pressing me against him. He's never tasted so sweet; like a treat I've been waiting a lifetime to have. Even though my heart's beating frantically against my chest, our kiss is slow and languid, as if we're taking our time to get to know each other again.

"I've missed you," he whispers into my mouth. His fingers run up my spine, cupping the back of my head. He drags his lips down my throat, pressing them against my sweet spot, and the muscles in my inner thighs start to quiver. I have to put my hands on his shoulders to steady myself. It feels strange, like coming home to find that something's different. Something I can't quite put my finger on.

"I've missed you, too. Missed this." My head tips back as he runs his lips to my collarbone, nipping at my skin. His breath is warm, tantalising, and I gasp as he dips his mouth lower.

"Babe." He reaches the swell of my breasts. "Christ I love these."

"You do?"

"Mm-hmm." His words are muffled by my skin. Slowly he pushes my top down, revealing my black lace bra. His fingers trace around the ribbon trim, and I feel my body react, my nipples harden. When he moves his mouth down, sucking me gently through the fabric of my bra, I let out a small moan. My fingers press into his scalp, my nails digging into his skin, and he groans loudly.

"I want to touch you."

"You are."

"Everywhere."

He looks up at me, his eyes dark and round. I see myself reflected back in them. And it's been so long since I felt him, felt *this*, that I'm breathless and needy.

"Can I take you to bed?" He sounds as desperate as I am. His thumb brushes my nipple, making us both sigh.

I nod quickly, letting him drag me through the living room, pushing the door to the bedroom so hard that it crashes into the wall.

I don't have a chance to check if I made the bed, or if the room is tidy, because before I know it I'm on my back, his body pressing into mine. I feel his chest on my breasts, the line of his erection against my thigh. Then we're scrambling to undress each other, our shaking fingers releasing stiff buttons, until we are skin against skin.

"Lara, Lara, Lara," he whispers my name between kisses. Cupping my breasts with rough hands, he pushes them together, lips brushing against one nipple and then the other. "Pretty girl."

I love it when he calls me that. *Pretty. Beautiful.* He dances his fingers up my thighs, softly, so softly, and it's all I can do not to cry out. Because he's gentle and sweet, with an edge of dirty. My pretty boy with the potty mouth. We touch and we stroke, hands loving and caressing, and it feels so good it makes me shout out loud.

When he finally pushes inside me, his lips pressed to my ear, his words hot against my cheek, I call out his name. It makes him groan, his hips slamming into mine, his lips stealing my tears like they're some kind of nectar.

We laugh and we weep, giving pleasure and taking it back. It feels good.
It's perfection.
It's home.

# 27

Later that evening, Alex lays Max gently in his cot, pulling the pale blue blanket over him while being careful not to disturb his slumbering body. Then we tiptoe out, softly flicking the light switch, pulling the door closed with the most feather-like of movements.

He sighs and I look at him with amused eyes.

"That was hard work," he says.

My grin widens. "I think he suspects something's up." Max did seem extra sensitive tonight; whiny and needy. It was past nine before his eyes started to flutter with sleep. When Alex tried to feed him, he spat the milk out, soiling his dad's trousers. It looks like he's had some kind of accident.

"You think he knows I've been messing about with his mum?"

"Messing about?" I raise an eyebrow.

"Yeah. And I wanna mess you up some more." He grabs me by the waist, spinning me round until we are chest to chest. Brushing the hair from my face, he kisses me, and I sigh.

Then a cry comes from the bedroom. It's loud and angry—insistent. Alex's lips curl against mine and he pulls away, his hands still clasping my waist.

"Your baby's crying," I point out helpfully.

"So's yours." He smiles at me and walks to the bedroom, as I fall onto the sofa with a sigh. It's been a long day. Full of lofty highs and dark-as-night lows. I think about Laurence Baines, sitting in his house, his son dead, his wife a broken shell, and once again I thank God for all I have.

Alex is gone for a while. Long enough for me to curl my legs up on the sofa, and for my eyelids to become heavy, as my breathing evens out. I loll my head against the armrest, letting my eyes close for a minute.

*Only a minute.*

It's eight hours before I wake up. Eight glorious hours of uninterrupted sleep. I shift in the bed, stilling when I feel a warm body next to mine.

My eyes fly open.

"Hi." He's staring at me as if he's been awake for a while. "Did you sleep well?"

"It was the best." I smile and nestle into the bedcovers. My hands are clasped together, beneath my cheek. I never want to move.

"Good." He does that sexy little smirk with the corner of his mouth. I could eat him up.

"Did Max wake up?"

Alex shakes his head. "He slept through. We must have worn him out."

"You wore *me* out."

More smirking. "We need to get a bigger flat."

"Why?"

He says nothing. Instead he grabs my hand and pulls it down, until it meets hard, hot flesh. His, of course.

"Oh."

"Yes, oh." He sighs loudly. "I'm not used to waking up in bed next to a gorgeous woman."

This time it's my turn to smile. "I bet your mum brought you in a cup of tea every morning."

He groans. "Don't talk about my mum." He's deflated, in every sense of the word. Which is a good thing, because I can hear Max stirring at the foot of our bed. It won't be long before he starts to stand up in there, demanding attention. Alex is right, we do need a bigger flat.

One with two bedrooms.

"We can't afford anything bigger in Shoreditch," I'm thinking out loud. "We might have to move out East."

He raises an eyebrow. "Plaistow?"

I make a face. "Stratford maybe. Or Romford." It's one thing to move closer to his mum, another to live right on her doorstep. As much as I love Tina, that would drive me crazy.

"I'll call some estate agents tomorrow."

Taking advantage of Max's slow return to wakefulness, I roll over and close my eyes. Alex spoons into me, his arm slung across my waist. It feels so natural, so easy. Very different to the awkwardness of the past few months. The perfect contrast to the arguing, the bitterness.

He's grown up. We both have.

"How are you feeling?" he murmurs, lips pressed against my neck. "Have you been to the PND group recently?"

"I went last week after I heard about Lawrence's son. I feel so much stronger now, I think I'm going to be okay."

His lips press against my skin. "Yeah?"

"Mm."

He runs a finger down my spine, lingering at the sensitive base. "That's a shame. I've got a really good cure for depression."

I'm smiling as he says it.

"All you have to do is swallow three times a day."

"Piss off," I say in good humour.

"Seriously. It cures everything. Depression, stomach ache, you name it. I'm a walking bloody miracle."

"You are." I reach behind and punch his side. "Now shut up, I'm trying to sleep."

"It's good for that to—" His retort's cut off by Max's cry. I watch as he clambers out of bed, boxers slung low around his hips, revealing curling vines that climb up his side. He reaches down, scooping Max into his arms, grinning at his son who smiles toothily back. "Hey, Maxie."

The baby's wails melt into babbles, and he reaches up to grab Alex's ear, tugging hard enough to bring water to his eyes. I simply sit and watch, pleased that for once I'm not the one bearing the brunt of the injuries. Then Alex carries him back to bed, putting Max between the two of us, so his pudgy soft baby skin is pressed into ours. It's warm. Smooth.

"We made this," Alex whispers, looking over Max's head and right into my eyes. "The two of us, we did this together."

His words choke me enough to fill my throat and wet my eyes. Because he's right. Max is amazing. He's everything.

"The job isn't done yet," I say. Max rolls over, grabbing hold of my pyjama top; he scrambles to his knees, ready to lunge. Before he can, Alex sweeps him up again, holding him above us, swooping him up and down like an aeroplane. Love for them both rushes through my body. It marks me, burning me, because they're *my* boys, *my* men. The two people I can't imagine being without.

I don't want to waste a single minute.

"We'll never be done. I wouldn't want to be." He pulls Max in for a kiss. Dark stubble rubs against chubby cheeks, making Max cry out. His tiny nose wrinkles and he pushes Alex away, indignant.

When Alex kisses me, there's no pushing away. No anger, no cries, only the tiniest sigh that escapes my lips, whispering across his own.

"I love you," he murmurs.

"I love you."

Max clambers over us, giggling delightedly at this climbing frame made of flesh and bone. Our eyes meet again and I see mirth buried deep beneath the brown, a wrinkle of the skin, a curl of the lips.

"Shall we stick to the one baby?" I ask.

Slowly Alex shakes his head. "In for a penny, in for a pound."

And though I know it might be years before we have another, I marvel at how far we've come. Somehow we've made it through the first months of Max's life by the skin of our teeth. Battered but not broken. It makes me proud. Lucky. Not everybody gets second chances at love, at life. But we've got it and we're taking it, letting life lead us where it wants to.

And it feels good.

It feels amazing.

It's everything.

# EPILOGUE

## *2 months later*

I hold up a chipped mug with the words 'Aussies do it better' emblazoned in red across the front. "You want to pack this?"

David grabs it from my hands. "Of course. It's my favourite mug."

"I've never seen it before. And what exactly is it that you do better?"

"Oh, surfing, sex, life." He gives me a smile that's full of happiness. He's only back for a few days, just long enough to finish packing up his flat. Then everything's being shipped back to the northern territories. To Mathilda. To home. He's finally got a custody agreement and he's chomping at the bit to start it.

"So…" I wrap glass in bubble wrap and glance across at Max. He's sound asleep on a pile of cushions. His fingers are bunched in his mouth and he's slurping rhythmically. "Have you seen Andie since you've been back?"

It's none of my business, I know that, but I'll be seeing her on Sunday and I don't know what to say. Since David left six weeks ago she's not mentioned him once. But there's been this expression on her face that makes me want to cry. She looks so sad.

"She won't talk to me."

"Have you tried?"

He looks resigned. Eyes downcast. "Yeah, I've tried calling her. Texting her. I even wrote her a letter. Nothing." His shrug does nothing to make me feel better. There's too much emotion bunched in those shoulders.

"Maybe she needs time."

His smile doesn't meet his eyes. "I'm going to be nearly ten thousand miles away. If she's not talking to me now, I can't see that helping much."

"Maybe I can talk to her?" I offer.

He smiles again, bumping his shoulder against mine. "Just because you're all loved up, doesn't mean everybody else has to be. You can't sort out everybody's lives, Lara."

I sigh. "But you were here for me when I needed you. I want to help you in return."

"It doesn't work like that."

"Well, it should."

The door opens and Alex walks in, carrying a corrugated cardboard tray of coffees. Placing it down on the bare table in the middle of the room, he pulls out a Styrofoam cup, passing it to me. As much as I want to carry on the conversation, I know I can't, because this is Alex's sister we're talking about, and Alex is blissfully unaware of her relationship with David. That sort of thing will only ruin the small entente that David and Alex have managed to build.

I may be nosy, I may be well-meaning, but I'm not an idiot.

"How's it going?" Alex asks. "Do you need any more boxes?" We have a stash of them upstairs. It's in disarray. Half our things are packed, while the other half is in piles where we've been trying to empty the drawers and cupboards. Max has been wearing the same three outfits for the past few days. I wash and dry them when he's asleep.

I don't care. I'm so excited to finally be moving into a flat with two bedrooms, I'd happily live out of boxes for years.

"Better than yours, or so I hear."

I try not to grin.

"Kids have a lot of stuff," Alex says.

"I know."

The two of them exchange a glance. It's not friendly, exactly, but it isn't full of ire either. It's interest mixed with wariness. The type of look two captains from opposing teams give each other right before a match. Shake hands then in for the kill.

I shudder at the analogy. Maybe it's better if Andie and David are over. I can't begin to imagine Alex and David as brothers-in-law.

Alex passes David a coffee and we all sit and sip, making small talk about Mathilda and about David's plans for work. He's hoping to buy a house once he's back in Darwin.

Alex is on his best behaviour, hardly sniping or remarking, and I reach my hand out to take his. He squeezes and I squeeze back.

I love the way he's become so much more chilled out since we've been back together. Both of us have managed to smooth our ups and downs into small hills and dips, rather than the mountains and ravines they were before. It feels as though we've overcome the challenge, slayed the beast. Now we get to run off with the virgin and enjoy the spoils of victory.

Or something like that.

"I reckon that's about it," David finally says. He steps back, running a hand through his over-grown sandy hair. He already looks more Australian. A few weeks back there and his skin has darkened, his hair lightened. It's as if the sun has stolen any English influence away.

"You're all done." I nod, and for some reason I want to cry. Which is stupid, because we're moving, too. It's not as if we were going to be living near him forever.

"Thanks for the help." He reaches in to hug me, then shakes Alex's hand.

"You're welcome." My reply is gruff. I don't tell him I'm going to miss him, even if I am. And I don't let him see the tears, even though they want to fall. I simply hug him again, and tell him to keep in touch, smiling when he promises he will.

When Alex takes us back to the flat, he holds me a little tighter, as if he knows I'm feeling fragile and sad. His lips are soft against mine as he pulls me through the maze of boxes that line our living room, and his words are sweet against my ear.

"I love you," he says, swinging me around until I'm pressed against the wall. "Always."

And that's enough for me.

\* \* \*

## *Two Years Later*

"We're going to need a bigger place." Alex glances around at the living room. It's stuffed to the gills with garish toys, plastic primary colours covering every surface. Max knocks down the bricks he's built, laughing loudly, begging us to "look, look!"

When we don't go immediately, he gets up and barrels towards us, throwing himself against me. I stagger back, half-laughing, half-wincing, and Alex kneels down to Max's height, looking carefully at his son.

"Max, you need to be careful with Mummy, remember?"

Max nods seriously. "Yup."

"You okay?" Alex glances up at me, reaching up to rub my bump. "Anything hurt?"

I shake my head. "I'm fine."

"Baby." Max points at me.

"That's right, Maxie." Alex nods, still looking serious. "There's a little baby in there. Your sister. You need to look after her, all right?"

Max's eyes widen. For a moment he looks so much like his daddy. I touch my stomach, wondering if this tiny life is going to be the same. Dark hair, dark eyes, serious smile.

I hope so.

"Everything okay?" Tina walks out of the kitchen, carrying a mug full of steaming coffee. "Are you two not off yet?"

I smile. "We're saying goodbye to Max."

"Goodbye, goodbye, goodbye," Max sings. I try to work out which of his many favourite programmes that song is from. All of them, maybe.

"Bye bye. Be good for Nanny." I lean down and press my lips to his head. He smells of baby shampoo. It's still one of the best smells in the world. "We'll try not to be too late."

"Take your time," Tina says, shooing us out. "I'm going to catch up with all my programmes while this little monster sleeps."

"Not little monster," Max protests. "Little boy."

"Of course you are, Maxie."

Eventually we get away. Alex holds my hand, carrying his guitar case in his other. It swings along as we walk. I get a flashback to the old days, to the way he'd tense up before a gig. Getting angry and cocky.

The way he'd smoke too much.

He's not like that at all, anymore. He hasn't been since he's been playing small venues again. Nowadays, it's only Alex, his guitar and the mic. He says he likes it better this way, prefers the connection with the audience.

I only care about his connection with me.

"You okay?" he asks again, looking down at my stomach. "I'm not walking too fast?"

His concern irritates and gratifies at the same time. I hold on to the gratification and ignore everything else.

"I'm good, honestly. I've got another three weeks yet, anything could happen."

He smiles. "We should take advantage while we can."

I raise my eyebrows. "Before we have another little kid sleeping in our bedroom for months."

"Cockblocker." He grins when he says it, even though I elbow his stomach.

"Language," I chide. The smile remains.

When we get to the pub, it's already full. He's become a minor celebrity around these parts. The man who chose art over fame, family over celebrity. A site manager by day and YouTube sensation by night.

Yeah, he still gets his fix. Although, this time the only hits he gets are on his website, and I'm okay with that.

I quite like it. It's kind of sexy.

"You want a drink?"

"Can I have a water?"

"Of course."

"Thank you." He brings it over and chats with me, while slowly sipping a pint of beer, and I feel warmth wrap around my body. The past two years haven't always been easy, but they've been worthwhile. Every time I see him sitting behind the microphone, a big smile on his face as he sings slow and deep, it makes my heart clench.

Tonight, he's trying out a new song; a slow melody accompanied by clashing chords. He closes his eyes as he breathes into the microphone, words spilling effortlessly out of his lips and carrying across the room. Though it's dark I can see the pulse in his neck, the rise of his chest as he takes in some air. And as the song comes to a stop, and he thanks the audience, I notice his eyes locked on mine.

"Okay?" he mouths.

I nod, smiling.

"Stay there."

I've seen those words before. Mouthed across a crowded room while an audience cheers and sweat pours down his face.

And though we're older, wiser, maybe slightly jaded, they still make me feel things.

*Everything.*

When he reaches me, pulling me up, against his damp chest, I'm still breathy from his performance. He kisses me with warm lips, laughing when the baby kicks him through my stomach.

"Was it all right?"

I kiss him back, this time pushing my fingers into his dark hair, while his palms press against my hips. "It was amazing," I say. "I'm a lucky girl."

He laughs. "I'm the lucky one."

The baby kicks again, hard enough to make us both jump, and he reaches down to press his hand onto my stomach.

"The luckiest guy in the world."

**The End**

# ALSO BY CARRIE ELKS

Coming Down (Love in London #1)
Fix You

## COMING SOON

Shining Through (Love in London #3)

## ABOUT THE AUTHOR

Carrie Elks lives near London, England and writes contemporary romance with a dash of intrigue. At the age of twenty-one she left college with a political degree, a healthy overdraft and a soon-to-be husband. She loves to travel and meet new people, and has lived in the USA and Switzerland as well as the UK. When she isn't reading or writing, she can usually be found baking, drinking wine or working out how to combine the two.

www.CarrieElks.com
www.facebook.com/CarrieElksAuthor
www.twitter.com/carrieelks
carrie.elks@mail.com

# Acknowledgements

Thank you to Lucia, Meire, Kate, Melanie and Claire for pre-reading this book. Your feedback is always invaluable, I hope you know how much I appreciate you.

D, your patience with me is amazing. You make editing fun. Well almost! (did you see those short, choppy sentences?)

Thanks to Emma for your fast work in proofing the document, it was a pleasure to work with you.

All my love to my online friends—writers, readers, bloggers. I love the romance community, and the way we all support each other. I also need to give a shout out to my fellow writers at the Romance Writers' Weekly blog. They helped me polish up the blurb, and I can't thank them enough.

Finally, lots of love to my family; you guys are my rock. I couldn't do this without you. I wouldn't want to.

Made in the USA
Charleston, SC
02 March 2015